Kamal Ruhayyim, born in E Cairo University. He is the auth five novels, including *Days in the Diaspora* (AUC Press, 2012) and *Menorahs and Minarets* (AUC Press, 2017). He has lived in both Cairo and Paris.

Sarah Enany has a PhD in drama and is a lecturer in the English Department of Cairo University. Her translation credits include works by Yusuf Idris, Mohamed Salmawy, and Jerzy Grotowski, and Kamal Ruhayyim's *Days in the Diaspora* and *Menorahs and Minarets*.

Diary of a Jewish Muslim

Kamal Ruhayyim

Translated by
Sarah Enany

hoopoe

AN IMPRINT OF AUC PRESS

This paperback edition published in 2018 by
Hoopoe
113 Sharia Kasr el Aini, Cairo, Egypt
420 Fifth Avenue, New York, NY 10018
www.hoopoefiction.com

Hoopoe is an imprint of the American University in Cairo Press
www.aucpress.com

Exclusive distribution outside Egypt and North America by I.B.Tauris & Co Ltd., 6
Salem Road, London, W4 2BU

Dar el Kutub No. 26098/16
ISBN 978 977 416 841 3

Dar el Kutub Cataloging-in-Publication Data

Ruhayyim, Kamal
        Diary of a Jewish Muslim / Kamal Ruhayyim.—Cairo: The American
    University in Cairo Press, 2018
        p. cm.
        ISBN 978 977 416 841 3
        1. English Fiction
        823

1 2 3 4 5   22 21 20 19 18

Designed by Adam el-Sehemy
Printed in the United States of America

To Suzanne, wife and mother, and to the companion of my childhood and youth: to the memory of my brother Lt. Mohamed Ruhayyim, lost to us in the war for liberation, the October War.

1

WE ONLY HEARD ABOUT MY father's death a month after the fact.

We heard two knocks on the window inset into the house's front door, and I tried to wriggle out of the grasp of Umm Hassan, the neighbor who had volunteered to nurse me along with her own son, Hassan, after my mother's own milk had run dry. She pushed me gently into her lap with a deft motion of her wrist. I ignored her, twisting my head backwards, eyes smiling at this newcomer, who I thought was my grandfather. It turned out, though, to be one of my mother's acquaintances, wearing a black dress and shawl. She was there to offer condolences on the death of my father, only to discover that no one in the house had heard the news.

She sat on the sofa looking from one to the other of us, wondering how we hadn't heard a thing until now; my mother stared at her, her face losing its bloom with every passing moment. She said she had only learned about it by chance herself; a distant cousin of her husband's had told her about it while visiting the day before yesterday. My father and some of his courageous fellow soldiers had been on a boat on Lake Manzala in the north of Egypt, heading for Port Said. There were quite a lot of them, double the capacity of the boat in fact, further weighted down with food, weapons, and supplies. The boat had capsized in the middle of the lake, killing my father and two others. She told my mother all that the cousin had related. He'd told of my grandfather, the village elder, of the ceremonial tent erected for the funeral, and of the vast number of people who had poured in from every direction—some on foot and some riding donkeys—of the women weeping in their homes. And all the while, my mother stared at nothing, stunned, eyes lowered. She only managed to look up and speak after a long silence. She said in a choked voice, "Whatever did he go there for? What is this war to us, anyway? What is to become of me now? Where shall I go? What shall I do?"

The visitor bent and hugged my mother, who began to cry. Umm Hassan jumped up out of her seat, with me still in her arms. She leaned close to my mother, patting her on the head. "Patience is a virtue, my dear."

"Patience? What are you talking about? Patience is for when you have hope! It's been a year with no news of him, and I've been patient, never said a word. But now what use is patience? How could you, Mahmoud? Leave me like this? Leave your son, your son whom you've never even seen!"

The guest looked toward me, saying to Umm Hassan, "Great heaven above! Is this fine little fellow Mahmoud's son?"

"Yes," my mother said. "This is Galal. What's to become of him now? What am I to do with him? The whole world conspires against me! The family, the marriage, the way we live—nothing ever goes right for me!"

The radio played loud in the kitchen, where my grandmother stood at the sink clattering and banging cups, plates, utensils, and everything she laid eyes on, occasionally letting out a sharp cough that offended my ears.

"Yvonne! Hey, Umm Isaac!" Umm Hassan yelled.

My mother gestured. "Not now, Umm Hassan. Not now."

"She has to know, Camellia."

"Listen to me. Listen to me: let it wait, now. I can't put up with her needling—not now."

Umm Hassan sat back down, murmuring, "Heaven help us." She offered me her breast, but I refused. She patted my back until I acquiesced and started to suckle on the delicious milk flowing into my mouth, deliberately not swallowing so that it dribbled out between my parted lips and flowed almost to my neck. A lugubrious silence fell, broken only by my grandmother's coughing from the kitchen; she had turned off the radio as soon as the Qur'an for the evening prayer had started at eight o'clock.

I must have sensed something, or been frightened by my mother's face buried in the chest of the woman visiting us, and her audible gasps as she drew breath; I looked up at Umm Hassan questioningly. Her eyes, too, were red, tears clinging to her eyelashes and about to fall on my brow. Her face looked unfamiliar; I had never seen her like this before. I pushed out her nipple immediately, and my body arched in fear. She took hold of my clothing for fear I should fall, but I squirmed out of her grasp and flung myself at my mother. Feeling Umm Hassan's attempts to get me back, I could only cling to my mother's neck and scream as loudly as I possibly could.

Later, when I had grown up, my mother told me that this was my usual habit. Whenever something happened at home—a sad or even a happy event—I would forget the whole world—food, toys, nursing, everything—and fling myself upon her breast. She would hold me, slipping her palm under my clothing, and rub my bare back until I calmed.

Umm Hassan held back a moment; then she slipped her breast back into her gallabiya, covering the hole up with her veil. My mother and the guest were too busy talking about my father's family to pay attention to her. I took to looking at her as she used her big toe to turn her discarded shoe right-side up, then as she tied her scarf more firmly about her head. When she leaned down to pull her other shoe from where it had slipped under the couch, I realized she was getting ready to go. At the last moment, though, my mother pressed a hand on her knee, urging her silently to stay and finish my feeding.

It was then that I stiffened, arching my back, and began to reformulate my plans.

Her hand still on Umm Hassan's shoulder, my mother introduced her to the guest as more than a neighbor, closer than a sister, and privy to all her secrets. Umm Hassan was the woman whose kindnesses could never, ever be repaid no matter what.

Umm Hassan's eyelids had sagged, without her noticing; her lips remained pursed for a moment, then she approached my mother, patting her hand and offering condolences. My mother gave her a grateful glance.

I stood erect in my mother's lap, playing with her and teasing her, pulling at her earlobe and at the collar of her gallabiya and slapping my little hands against her neck and cheeks. I remained aware, of course, of Umm Hassan's movements. I only started to whine when I saw her pushing her veil back and opening the button at her breast. Understanding what she meant to do, I bent my knees, trying to escape from under my mother's arm. Umm Hassan was quicker, though. She snatched me up, while I struggled and gasped with the force of my crying, and comforted and rocked me. Then she took me in her arms and held me close, her chest rising and falling as her breath mingled with mine.

I was more like a toy than anything else in her hands. Realizing that resistance was futile, I relaxed in her embrace, feeling her breast, and began to nurse again, never taking my eyes off my mother. When sleep overcame me, Umm Hassan laid me on the couch and left.

I do not know how much time passed after that; perhaps a minute, perhaps an hour. All I remember is waking, frightened, at the sound of my grandmother's voice.

She spoke in a nasal, fast-paced patter, incomprehensible unless you were ready for it and listening intently. It appeared that the news had reached the kitchen. She rushed in, standing with her short, squat figure and red hair, wiping her hands on the apron she wore over her housedress and gesturing at me. "So who's going to raise this little scamp, then?"

My mother didn't answer. The guest started to look embarrassed; she half-stood, making to leave, perhaps hoping to avoid being the jury in my grandmother's show trial, but was halted by my mother's grip on her arm, lowering her to the couch once more.

My grandmother waved her hand. "Is it Papa who's going to raise him, then? He repairs watches, and his income's not stable! And you know perfectly well I can't see well enough to be a seamstress any more! As for her—" she pointed to my mother, causing our guest to squirm in discomfort—"she's been out of work since her husband made her quit her job at Bank Sednaoui!" It was not really a bank; that was what they called department stores in those days. She untied her apron, flung it impatiently onto a nearby chair, and sat beside me, putting her knee right next to my head. I lay stretched out on my back. I shifted carefully until I was a few inches away from her and rolled my eyes backwards so as to still see her.

At first glance, her nose from this angle looked larger than usual, but that was of no concern to me; what drew my attention was the familiar tic at the left corner of her mouth. It always came over her when she was spoiling for a fight. I knew too well what often came next. I found my attention being inexorably drawn to her hands, which never stopped moving. My eyes moved in circles with them as they rose and fell, her fingers closing and opening until she suddenly waved her palm at me. I thought she meant to slap my face and started up; I think I fell on my face, and I would have fallen off the couch but for my mother, who leaped up and snatched me away from my spot next to my grandmother, gesturing angrily at her to calm down.

My grandmother paid her no heed. She half-turned toward our lady visitor, saying, "I told her, 'My girl, this person is not meant for us. Marry a Jew, like Susu your cousin, or Makram, our neighbor who lives at the top of the street.' But it was no use! She's hardheaded, just like her father. What on earth did you see in that Mahmoud? He's not worth a millieme to me!"

The visitor responded indignantly, "Let's not speak ill of the dead, now, Grandmother! He's a martyr, and that's no small thing to God!"

"A martyr, she says!"

"Yes, a martyr," my mother snapped back. "He was going to fight for his country, wasn't he? That makes him a martyr."

"War and martyrdom aside for a moment, what on earth did Little Miss Precious Princess see in that fellow? He wasn't one of us; he was of another religion . . ." My grandmother appeared to notice that she was embarrassing their guest and caught herself. "Heaven forgive me. Heaven forgive me. What have I said? I didn't mean it. I didn't mean a thing; I swear! I just mean that this miserable marriage was no good from the start."

Silence reigned. Finally the guest said, "Don't fret, Aunt. You know how much Camellia loved him, and how attached she was to him."

"Love! What good's love to us now? Now he's gone, and ruined the girl as well."

"Aunt, these things are fated—"

My grandmother leaned forward, wringing her hands. "Fate!" she muttered. "I tell her the girl is ruined, and what's her answer? Fate! I tell her this and that, and what's her answer? He's a martyr!"

"Mother . . ." my mother hissed. "That's enough!"

My grandmother, ignoring her completely, pulled her snuffbox out from beneath the sofa cushion, taking a pinch and tilting her head back, eyes clenched, nostrils red and slightly quivering. She immediately burst out into a violent fit of sneezing, the guest staring at her, leaning back as much as possible to avoid being hit by the spray. When she was done,

Grandmother pulled a black handkerchief out of her bra and commenced to pick her nose with it.

Then, leaning into the guest's personal space, she whispered at her usual frenzied pace, "Four years, my girl, four years of nothing but fighting! We see him for a day, then he's gone for a month! And when he came, she'd jump for joy and say, 'I'm so happy, Mom.' I'm so this and that and the other and a huge, long romance . . ." She paused for breath. "Then I'd take him aside and tell him, 'For heaven's sake, son, find an apartment for yourself and your wife instead of that garret you've got!' And he'd nod his head. 'Son, have you told your papa and mama that you have a wife, and that she's pregnant?' He'd nod his head! 'Son . . .' Always with the nodding. And I never found out whether he told or whether he didn't. 'Son, have your papa and mama drop by for a visit.' And he'd nod! 'Well, how about we go pay them a visit?' And he'd nod! Whatever I said, he'd nod! Whatever I said!"

My mother had slipped away into her room. I could hear her weeping. I tried to get off the couch and crawl to her. I cried, too.

At midnight, my grandfather arrived. My grandmother told him the news at the door. He bowed his head. "Merciful and Compassionate God, be with him!" And he opened the door to my and my mother's room, his eyes troubled.

2

THE HALL OF THE HOUSE we lived in functioned as a living room. It only had two old-fashioned armless wooden couches, placed facing one another and upholstered with cheap cretonne that sported a number of cigarette burns from falling ashes, especially where my grandfather usually sat. At the start of the passageway leading to the kitchen sat two cane chairs, partly hiding a Singer sewing machine that had remained locked for ages. A small woolen kilim rug barely covered the space between the couches. It was worked with a black circle at its center, from which multicolored lines branched out in all directions. At one of its corners were two tears that my grandmother had failed to repair, having grown too old for the job. They were very obvious.

The walls were almost colorless; my mother told me that she had never, not since she was born, seen anyone take up a brush and paint them. There were holes in the wall, holes that had once held family portraits: my uncle Isaac, who had left and of whom we had had no news at all; my uncle Shamoun, who had taken his portrait to hang in his new apartment. The two remaining photographs were of my aunt Bella standing there in her school uniform, my grandmother sitting next to her in a leather armchair, and the other of my grandfather, Zaki, in a worn golden frame, wearing a most uncharacteristic frown. His tarboosh, the traditional tall Egyptian hat sometimes called a fez, was canted to the left, and you could see one side of his navy blue jacket collar and gray tie; come winter or summer, he never wore anything else.

To the right of the hall were two rooms: one was my grandparents', the other mine and my mother's. At the door to each lay a brown sheepskin rug. No one else lived in the apartment; my uncle Shamoun lived at the top of the street with his wife, Sarah, and Aunt Bella, my mother's sister, had gotten married last year and gone off to live in Port Fouad with her husband and their daughter, Rachel, whom she'd been pregnant with before she was married. Most of the rest of my mom's family had emigrated; there was only one family who lived by the Primus stove store in Ataba and a sister of my grandmother's who lived alone on Cioccolone Street in Shubra.

My grandfather was always the first to wake in our home. I would hear his movements in the hall on his way to the bathroom. Looking at my mother and finding her asleep, I would commence my attempts to dangle off the bed and thence drop off. They were usually successful, but sometimes I would fall on a knee or twist my leg, whereupon I would break into loud shrieking, making no effort to muffle it, until a pair of arms picked me up off the floor and rocked me and kisses rained down on the source of the pain until I was satisfied.

The hands usually belonged to my grandfather, Zaki. He would rush to my side from wherever he happened to be in the apartment, even before my mother woke. After skirmishes with my mother and attempts on her part to make me go back to bed, I would crawl out of the room to find him sitting on the couch. He would smile at me, whereupon I would crawl faster until I reached his feet. Astonished by how huge they were, I would sit on my rear end in front of them, lost in contemplation of what I was to do with them! I started by pummeling them while my grandfather looked down from on high. The more satisfied he looked, the more enthusiastically I pummeled, until I was breathing hard, my hands stilled, only my chest rising and falling rapidly.

In a few seconds, I would be entranced by the black hairs growing out of his big toe and bend over them, seeking to pluck one. The hair would obediently slide through my fingers but quickly escape my grip. I would try again, once, twice, seven times, until I grew bored with it; then I would have to try the easy things, like scratching my fingernails against the arch of the foot or placing anything within my reach between the toes: a matchstick, a shoelace, or even the remains of a piece of caramel in my pocket.

My grandfather would pick me up, laughing, and adjust my clothing. When he found I had wet myself, he would search in the closet, beneath the chairs, and sometimes in the dresser drawers for clean, dry pants, all while my mother slept on.

As soon as my grandmother awoke, my mood changed. I became instantly alert as she emerged from her room, hair wild, usually clutching a hairpin between her fingertips. She would stand close to us for a few moments, tucking it into her hair. I would fall still, leaning back against the edge of the sofa, eyes on her. She would greet my grandfather, say a few words to him, and leave; she ignored my presence, and I, for my part, avoided her. If the hem of her gallabiya brushed against me on her way past, I would consider this a kind of harassment and begin to whine. My grandfather would catch me, picking me up off the floor and placing me in his lap, tossing me into the air and catching me, or grabbing all the old odds and ends in the house and heaping them up for me to play with: bottle caps, a watchband, an old whistle, a broken plate, some empties.

When the balcony called, though, I would suddenly abandon my play and head for it. Once it had called me, I would drop everything and crawl toward it, heedless of any attempts to pull me away. They would call me, but I ignored them.

11

They brought out the 'dwarf'—their name for a doll I liked—to change my mind, but it was no use. They would take hold of me by the waist and legs; I would keep crawling on just my hands. My mother would slap my behind, but I would just scream, never giving up my quest. Growing tired of me, they would allow me onto the balcony, but my grandfather, in particular, never took his eyes off me.

As soon as I was through the balcony doors, I would pause for a few moments to rest. My eyes would always go to the rail; if there was a fly or a cockroach, or if the garlic hanging in the corners was shaking in the wind, I would watch it avidly. But then, remembering the mission I was there for, I would come back to myself; first, though, I would look behind me, in case I was still being followed. I would struggle to stick my head out between the iron bars of the balcony rail. A joy, magical in its intensity, came over me. I could see the people, the boys and girls; Amm Marzouq the pie seller's shop; the spice store owned by Hagg Mahmoud, Umm Hassan's husband; Abu Agwa's bakery; Khawaga Cavores's grocery store; and Abu Auf's café.

Sometimes I would catch sight of Umm Hassan walking in the street. I could recognize her from afar, and I would gurgle to her and drool on my bib. If she looked up and saw me, she would wave, and I would laugh aloud, drumming on the balcony tiles with my feet. What fascinated me more than anything else, though, was the sugarcane juice store opposite our building. I adored the sight of it, especially when twilight came, and it was lit up with white, red, and green neon lights blinking over and over as I stared in wonder, waves of pleasure clawing at my entire body. No one, come what may, could tear me away from that sight; I would scream so loud that they would leave me to it, only later, when I fell asleep, picking me up and carrying me carefully to bed.

My mother told me many stories of those days, especially the night when my grandparents decided to celebrate their wedding anniversary on the balcony. My father bought a dozen

French pastries from a sweet shop in Midan al-Geish, biscuits with dates in the center, ghurayiba cookies, petits fours, and breadsticks with sesame, plus two bags of peanuts and sunflower seeds. And upon my grandmother's request, he brought a bottle of beer from Cavores's grocery store—the large size.

My mother poured the tea with milk and they placed everything on the table, but my grandmother was displeased by my presence and by my attempts at standing on my grandfather's lap to partake of this feast. So she swore by all that was dear to her that she would not start the revels until my mother had put me to bed and I was asleep, by force if necessary.

The sounds from the bedroom stilled, bringing a smile to my grandmother's face, but not a quarter of an hour passed before they found me crawling back to join them, pacifier dangling cheerfully from my mouth. It was my mother who had fallen asleep! My grandfather laughed loud and long, picked me up, and dandled me on his knee.

It was a miserable night for my grandmother: I would pull her plate away, I would throw the rest of my cream puff at her. As for the bags of peanuts and sunflower seeds, one swipe of my hand scattered them irretrievably about the floor. And when my grandmother started drinking the beer, I stopped breathing, staring at her in astonishment as she raised the bottle and poured some into her glass. When the liquid splashed, my pupils would grow wider, staring as the foam bubbled up with a gurgling noise, until it overflowed from the rim of the glass, whereupon I went completely insane.

My grandfather was unable to hold me back as three-quarters of my body lunged across the table, my hands grabbing for her glass, resulting in a fight. The night was not a success, with losses sustained by both sides. She pinched me in the arm, leaving a bruise that lasted a week, and I smashed her glass into fifty pieces. After that night, she swore never to let beer into the house until I had grown up. She drank wine instead.

3

Uncle Shamoun came to visit.

My mother let him in, then flew to her room. Another guest came in with him, and the two men sat side by side on the couch while my grandparents came out of the other room. My grandfather was freshly shaved, which was not his habit for a weekend. He held a fly whisk, wore a navy blue jacket over a white gallabiya, and had his tarboosh on—the same attire in which he went to synagogue on Saturday. My grandmother wore her wine-red velvet dress that she saved for special occasions. They sat on the couch facing my uncle and his guest. Only my mother stayed in her room.

I was in the hall with a goodly collection of odds and ends and in the mood for play. I punched the doll in the head several times, then pounced on him and bit him in the stomach long and hard, hoping he might cry or make some noise, but he didn't. I set him aside and blew into an empty bottle, occasionally rolling it back and forth or pounding on an old watch discarded by my grandfather.

Suddenly I was startled out of my play by an exciting spectacle: one of my grandmother's slippers, the orange one topped with a red bow. It was the very same one she would lift up high and threaten me with, making me run away in fear—the horrible one with the pointed heel for which I had a healthy respect indeed. It had come off her right foot completely and dangled from her big toe. My grandmother,

absorbed in staring at the guest, was swinging it monoto-
nously back and forth.

The sight provoked me! Without conscious thought or planning, I found myself crawling carefully toward my grandmother.
I snatched it off her foot and quickly crawled back to my original
spot, my eyes shining with triumph. As soon as I got my breath
back, I flung it with every ounce of strength I had through the
balcony doors, then went back to playing as though nothing
had happened.

Uncle Shamoun chuckled at what I had done, and the
guest smiled. My grandfather, though, could not contain himself; he burst into uproarious laughter, head and shoulders
shaking with mirth. He only stopped when my grandmother
raised her left eyebrow and gave him a look; apparently she
had poked him in the behind with some sharp, unseen object,
perhaps a needle or a pin, for I saw him suddenly leap forward, then teeter back and forth on the couch, moving away
from her, placing a hand on the site of the injury.

Because we had company, and so as not to give the guest
a bad impression of me, she did not shout at me but merely
indicated to my uncle that I should be taken inside with all
my paraphernalia. I immediately sought refuge with my
grandfather. He placed a hand on my head but did not lift
me into his lap or up to his side as usual. I divined that the
wind was not blowing my way, so I sat at his feet quietly,
hands in my lap, not moving so as not to further provoke my
grandmother's wrath.

"Mr. Labib Qattawi," Uncle Shamoun said to my grandparents by way of introducing his friend.

"Pleased to meet you," they said in unison.

"He is a cashier at Chemla Department Stores," my uncle
went on, "and his father has a pastrami factory in Faggala."
Waiting a moment, he added, "And he's asked for Camellia's
hand, too. He knew her when she worked at Sednaoui, before
she . . . ." He broke off.

My grandmother caught him, smiling at Mr. Labib and asking him if he was one of the East Abbasiya Qattawis. He said that he was not related to them, and she clarified that she did not mean Qattawi Pasha's family, but the Qattawi family who were silversmiths.

He gave no answer, sticking out his lower lip. She cleared her throat and fell silent too.

Mr. Labib had thinning hair; the front third of his head was almost completely bald, although he was still young. He was quite strikingly short, only a little taller than an older boy; his feet did not comfortably touch the floor. Only his toes reached the rug, soon lifting up to about an inch above it. Mr. Labib had to shuffle forward a little until his feet landed on the floor easily.

He looked at me and found me looking at him; he turned away, looking around at the inside of the apartment: the clock on the wall, the top of the sewing machine, and a little cockroach crawling down the curtain that hung by the passage to the kitchen, heading in his direction. But the thing that drew his eye the most was the photograph of my grandfather on the wall facing him. He peered at it, then his gaze traveled down to my actual grandfather, sitting beneath it, staring as surreptitiously as he could at him, as well. For a moment, Mr. Labib seemed to be comparing the photograph to the original; then his head drooped, and he fell so still I thought he had gone to sleep.

My grandmother got up and knocked at the door to our room, saying a few words to my mother through a crack in the door. Then she hurried into the kitchen. Before my mother closed the door, she caught sight of me, staring wide-eyed at her; she smiled, and I laughed aloud back at her. Her face was strange, not as I usually saw it; her skin was sparkling with powder and makeup, and her delicate ears bore large earrings, each in the shape of a six-pointed star.

My grandmother returned bearing a tray with a jug, two bottles of fizzy drink, and empty glasses. Mr. Labib took the red bottle, and my grandfather reached for the second. I was fond of red. I surged to my feet, taking a step toward it, then fell on my face. This was my first attempt at standing, and it was completely spontaneous. I thought nothing of the fall and didn't even think to cry. I crawled like the wind toward the guest to wrestle the bottle from his grasp.

My grandmother was furious. I only grew more intent, remaining at the man's feet, pulling on his sock for him to hand it over. He patted me on the back and let me have it. I returned to my place in front of my treasures, rolling the bottle, half of whose contents had spilled onto the rug. My uncle hurried to the kitchen and brought out a second bottle. Still standing, he removed the lid with a bottle opener. "Mr. Labib is an old acquaintance. Donkey's years! From Khedive Ismail school, when we still lived on al-Khalig Street."

Mr. Labib nodded, smiling, and took off his spectacles, breathing on them. He asked my grandfather for cigarette papers, whereupon Grandfather brought him an entire book of rolling paper. Labib pulled out a couple and used them to clean his glasses.

"You bring back such memories, Shamoun!" my grandmother said. "Those were the days! True, the building was old and on a bit of a side street, but a quarter of the neighbors were Jewish and it was comfortable living there. Not like the wretched folk in this building!"

"Here or there; what does it matter, dear?" said my grandfather, trying to smooth things over. "We all have our own lives to live after all; we're all born of Adam and Eve." He smiled at the visitor. "You're very welcome here, I'm sure, sir."

My uncle hastened to say, "Mr. Labib wanted to ask for Camellia's hand in marriage."

My grandfather stroked the ends of his mustache, saying soberly, "Does the gentleman know how it is with her, though?"

"How it is?" Labib said softly, leaning in toward my grandfather.

My mother had opened the door to the room; everybody looked up at her. She made a little gesture of greeting and sat down between my grandfather and grandmother. Immediately she said, tension filling her voice, "I know Labib, and I've met him before, not once, but ten times. And I've no objection. But what about the child? That's the main thing: the child."

Mr. Labib looked at her questioningly, as if to say, What *about* the child? His eyes gleamed as he glanced over at me. After a moment's silence, he looked at my uncle, worry plain on his face. My grandmother captured everyone's attention, though, putting a hand under the sofa cushion and pulling out her snuffbox. My grandfather elbowed her as if to say *Not now*, but she paid him no heed and made to open the box. She put it back again upon discovering Mr. Labib's eyes riveted upon her, fascinated by her actions. Scratching at her head, she said, "What about the child? He's an orphan and needs care and kindness. And if God wills it and the match is made, he can stay with us half the time, and half the time with you." Then she leaned over to Mr. Labib, adding, "Isn't that so, sir?"

He responded, bewildered, "Child? What child?"

"The child—Galal—Camellia's son—this little squirt! See what an angel's face he has!"

Labib rolled his eyes. "Ah, I see."

"Isn't that so, sir?" my grandmother repeated.

Labib's face had gone pale; he saw that unless he stood up to my grandmother and fast, he would soon be in a fine mess. His defenses, though, yielded no immediate rebuttal, so he remained silent. He nodded and grew even more alert.

My grandmother went on. "The first few months, of course, he'll be staying with me. Then his mother will take him, and I'll be happy to take him anytime at all you want to send him to us."

"Of course," my uncle said, "there's no question but that he must stay with you at first, Mother, if only for the wet

19

nurse." Swallowing, he added, not meeting Labib's eye, "He can't be apart from Umm Hassan until he's weaned."

My grandfather, who had stayed silent, looking from one to the other as they spoke, abruptly stopped waving his fly whisk and said decisively, "Look, my boy. The child is a Muslim. His father is deceased. His mother dotes on him. Does that suit you?"

Leaping up, Labib suddenly found his voice. "What? What was that?" He turned to my uncle. "I didn't think it was like that, Shamoun! Why didn't you tell me from the start? It's enough that she has a kid, and that's hard enough to swallow as it is. But a Muslim? You want me to raise a Muslim child in my own home? That really is the icing on the cake, dummy!"

My grandfather's tone began to grow sharp. "What's the matter, Labib? Why are you making such an issue of it? You know that any child born from a Jewish woman's womb is a Jew."

Silence reigned. Even I stopped playing, watching.

Evidently feeling that he had committed a faux pas, Mr. Labib sat back down while everyone watched him, waiting for what he would say next. Quietly, he said, meeting my grandfather's eyes, "My dear uncle: If your question is, 'Does this suit me?' then I say no, and a thousand times no. And to be frank, I want Camellia, just Camellia. Keep the boy yourselves. Know your limitations; that's my motto." He muttered to himself, "Good God! My mama would have had a heart attack!"

"Whoa there, Mr. Labib!" said my grandmother. "Easy, easy. This matter requires some thought. I told you from the start that the boy would stay with us, and just think how long it'll be until he's weaned!"

Labib looked at her impatiently. "Let's have no talk of nursing or weaning. Keep the boy. This is a matter of principle. It's not open for discussion or negotiation."

"Well, son, how about you think about it and give us your answer later?"

Mopping his brow, Labib said, "Think about it? I'll think about it all right. Think about it! Sure, I'll think about it!"

When he was gone, my grandmother snapped at my mother, "Did you *have* to bring up that wretch the minute you stepped out of your room?"

"That's enough, Mother! Shut up, shut up!" She burst into tears and ran into our room, and I crawled after her on all fours, crying because she was crying.

My mother's chances were ruined because of me; Mr. Labib never came back, nor any of the young Jewish suitors who came after him. No sooner would one of them set eyes on me than things changed—and not in my mother's favor.

4

WE GREW UP TOGETHER, THE kids in my apartment building and I. Hassan, whose mother had nursed me, making
us brothers; Fahmi, the son of Mr. Husni, the courthouse
clerk; the twins, Ali and Mustafa; and Nadia, the daughter of
Madame Subki. They all managed to convince their mothers
to let them go play in the street and went to my mother. They
stood, paces from the door, begging her to let me come out
and play, while she refused. None of the children would dare
set foot inside her apartment. They could only stand at her
door, and then some distance away.

Our apartment was not like any other in the building; it was
different. No sooner did the children venture near it, especially
the younger ones, they would be overcome with trepidation, as
though at the portals of an enigmatic world filled with exotic
Jewish mysteries. It was an attractive mystery, though; they were
avid to know us as we really were. What did we eat and drink?
What did we wear and do when we were alone together? What
did we keep in our house that they did not keep in theirs? They
could never contain their curiosity; their eyes would always
betray them, peeking through the crack of the door as they
spoke to us in hopes of glimpsing one of our hidden secrets.

In the end, though, the problem of me going out to play
with the neighborhood kids was resolved. My grandfather had
not yet weighed in, you see. He entered into discussion and
consultation with my mother, and she eventually acquiesced.

Our mothers chose a Friday, when the traffic was lightest, on condition that they should be watching from the windows. The list of instructions they gave us was long: we each memorized them, counting off on our fingers, and recited them back to our mothers. The first was that we should all hold hands and walk in a formation not unlike a line behind Sitt Shouq, the doorman's wife, and the last was that we were to come back immediately, no dawdling, the minute we were called.

Zero Hour was at 10 a.m. We all gathered on the landing outside Umm Hassan's second-floor apartment. When we started to move, Mustafa took hold of Sitt Shouq's gallabiya as his mother had instructed. His brother poked him, telling him that this action would make us lose prestige in the eyes of passersby, and we supported him in disapproving of his brother's childish act. We were very serious! We felt that we were already men. But that was exposed as a sham as soon as we set foot outside the building.

The open space, the comings and goings, and the loud voices bewildered us. We froze in fear, like puppies with their tails tucked between their legs. We didn't know which direction to go; and the moment we saw older children passing by, we would take several steps back spontaneously until they had moved away. We had no fear of the adults who passed by; we regarded them as not unlike our fathers and mothers. It was the older boys we feared, instinctively, at first sight.

Sitt Shouq led the way, and we followed like chicks, hands interlinked, looking at ourselves in disbelief. We lingered at store windows and bought soft pretzels, biscuits, and baked date pastries from Abu Agwa's bakery; then, like arrows, we shot toward the fizzy drinks. Some of us had Sinalco, Orango, or Spathis; others were content to suck on lollipops. When Khawaga Cavores's boy made to annoy us, Sitt Shouq took it upon herself to defend us and put him in his place.

We did not walk more than two hundred meters before coming back perforce after the doorman's wife exchanged hand signals with our mothers at the windows. We screamed and jumped up and down and pounded our feet on the stairs as we came home, returning victorious from conquest.

I asked my mother again for permission to go out with the others. She said, "Wait till tomorrow; it's your grandfather's day off, and you get to go out with him."

It was a Saturday. My grandfather sat in his usual place on the couch reading out of a black book with raised gold ornamentation. My grandmother's staccato coughing sounded from the inner room. He didn't notice when we crept in and sat facing him. I asked my mother what he was reading. She said in a hushed voice, "The Holy Book," and she held a finger to her pursed lips for silence.

When I walked in the street with my mother and grandfather, or when I stood on the balcony, I would hear the children swear by the Qur'an. I leaned in closer and asked her in a whisper if that was what he was reading. After a moment's silence, she said no and asked me to keep my mouth shut.

Apparently my grandfather had heard us. He pushed his glasses down on his nose, his brow furrowing as though something strange floated atop his face. His eyes never stopped sending coded messages in my mother's direction. She clearly understood what she was being told and made answer with her face instead of her mouth, which remained resolutely closed. They conversed for several moments like this in a language I could not understand, a language all their own. Then my grandfather closed the Holy Book, stood, and took me out of the house.

After only a few steps, he paused, me in tow, outside the sugarcane juice store. The owner, Muallim Habib, the best friend my grandfather had among all the folks on our street, came out to greet us. He was thin with an erect posture and an erect mustache. All the renowned pride and self-respect of the people of Upper Egypt was in him. The shawl he used for a turban was bright white, wrapped in an awe-inspiring curve unlike anyone else's on the street. When there was a shortage of shop attendants, he would hitch up his gallabiya around the tops of his thighs, in the manner that has become famous, and draw the hem of it up through the front opening of his traditional sayyala, or waistcoat, and go into the bowels of the shop to help out. His legs were a little lighter in hue than the rest of his complexion and visibly bowed. I never knew what happened to his turban; all awe-inspiring properties would immediately dissipate, and Muallim Habib would appear an entirely different personage than the one I saw sitting cross-legged in front of the store or behind the counter collecting money for the drinks.

He called out for seats for us and two glasses of sugarcane juice. Looking at me, he said, "Isn't that the dear girl's son?"

My grandfather nodded.

Muallim Habib frowned, saying, "Still no news of the blighter, her husband?"

My grandfather made a noncommittal motion of his head in silence, hand encircling his chin.

"What's going on, Abu Isaac?" Muallim Habib burst out. "Whenever I mention it, you look tragic and never say a word."

My grandfather raised his head and said softly, stroking my hair, "Not yet. As the proverb says, only the absent know what keeps them absent."

"What about his family, Amm Zaki? Why couldn't you ask them? Something's up, no doubt about it!" With a quick look at the shop entrance, he waved a hand. "Tradition demands it, Amm Zaki; it's only right. You have to know what's going on so you can take action accordingly! He has been away for a very long time—years. It's not like it's been a few months."

My grandfather ran a hand over my neck. "That's true. That's true; it's only right."

He looked down at the tips of his worn shoes. I closed my eyes for a moment against the sun's glare and was struck by a sudden desire to go back home and sleep.

Muallim Habib called for one of his shop boys and asked him to bring him his cup of tea, which he had forgotten on the counter. He took a sip, tapping the top of his pack of Belmonts to shake out a cigarette. "You do know his family— don't you?"

"Know them? Of course we know them. They live in a village on the outskirts of Giza."

"Yes, but have you been there? Do you know exactly where it is?"

"But of course! Naturally we do."

"Well, in that case, why haven't you asked them, Amm Zaki? Things are different now that he's been away all this time." He leaned closer, lowering his voice. "Does Galal have a, a birth certificate and so on?"

My grandfather seemed rather put out. "A birth certificate? What did you think we were, Muallim? Not only that, I have Camellia's marriage contract with Galal's father, signed by the ma'zoun, registered with the Registry Office, and signed by witnesses!" Catching his breath, Grandfather went on: "You know Hagg Mahmoud, who owns the spice store? He's witness number one, and Labib, the shoemaker at the end of our alley, is witness number two."

Muallim Habib leaned back, stroking his mustache. "You are a funny one, Amm Zaki. Well, if everything's aboveboard, why all this time and never a word out of you? You really must go to his father's house, you know, the family home, and ask after the man."

My grandfather started in shock. "I?"

"Yes, you! You or your son Shamoun. Or did you expect Umm Galal to go all by herself?"

Eagerly leaning forward, I burst out, "Do you know my father, Amm Habib?"

He patted my head. "Naturally! I know him well! Many's the glass of juice he had at my store, him and your respectable mother."

My eyes glittered. "What does he look like, Amm Habib?"

He tapped his brow with a forefinger, as though to shake loose a memory from long ago. "He looks . . . he looks . . . think, Habib, think; what does he look like? Ah! He's a fine figure of a man, tall and broad and so healthy it gladdens your heart to look at him."

He excused himself for a moment to take care of store business. My grandfather took the opportunity to leave, taking me along.

We never did take the jaunt my mother had promised. He took me home without another word from either of us.

That night, I asked my mother about my father. She said, "He went to the war and never came back."

"When is he coming back?"

After a long, drawn-out period of thrust and parry, and many questions, she snapped, "He died, Galal. He's dead."

I yanked my arm out of her grasp, flung myself onto the bed, and burst out crying. She followed, pulling my head out from where I had buried it into the pillow and pulling it into her lap. After my attack of sobbing had died down, I raised my head to find tears rolling down her cheeks. We clung to each other, and I said roughly that my grandfather didn't know he was dead, that he was going to visit my father's family and ask the reason for his absence.

I began to think about my dead father. I was young, though, and I hardly knew where to begin. There was no one to answer the questions that filled my head. Neither my mother nor my grandfather would, and I had no contact with my mother's brother and sister. All I could do was paint a picture of him in my head. Even in this, though, I was unclear: even I had attained the conviction that he had been tall and husky, as Muallim Habib had said. I would reimagine him as short or fat, now looking like my grandfather, now with features that I fabricated myself and changed from time to time.

My mother, God forgive her, had never told me much about him, nor described him to me when I asked. Umm Hassan was loath to go against my mother's instructions by talking to me about him, so whenever I asked, she would either change the subject or weigh her words carefully, rationing out information. All I could find out in those days was that my father had been a student at law school and that he had met my mother on an errand to buy some woolen fabric for his father at Sednaoui's. They fell in love and were married a month later in the garret of one of the buildings on that street.

Little by little, I took to creating my own little world where I had my own secrets. I might hear a word about my father and use it to build upon, a giant building of the imagination wherein I would lose myself. I would do this not only at bedtime, when the comings and goings in the house had quieted, but even when I was busy playing, surrounded by other people.

My mother, noticing this, sought to keep me occupied with stories: she would tell me of mighty Samson, and once of Saul, who conquered the people of Canaan and wrought havoc with them. The stories that she never tired of telling were the tale of Moses, who parted the sea with his staff, and the people who were burned with fire.

"Who are they?" I asked her.

"Our unfortunate relatives," she said.

5

MY GRANDFATHER CLOSED THE HOLY Book as soon as he saw me and my mother dressed up to go out. He stood up, tarboosh in hand. My grandmother remained bent over her book, which she had gotten from a rag-and-bone man in exchange for four empty bottles—it was a pocket book, translated into Arabic, about a murderess in the Italian countryside who had dispatched twenty souls without batting an eye. My grandfather asked her to reconsider and come with us; there was still time. She said no, never taking her eyes off the book. Next to her sat a tray heaped with onions, and next to that lay a sharp, gleaming, long-bladed knife. My grandfather cleared his throat. "Oh, do come on, Yvonne! You'll enjoy the film no end."

She looked at me. "What film? Are there fight scenes, like in the movies of Farid Shawqi and Mahmoud al-Meligi?"

"Come on, what are you saying of fight scenes? It's a nice film, romantic, full of tender feelings!"

"Then I won't enjoy it." And with that, she rolled up her sleeves and grasped her knife. We closed the door on her.

We walked out of Abbas Street, where we lived in the Daher district, traversing al-Khalig al-Masri and al-Madbah al-Ingilizi Streets. I alternated between holding my mother's and my grandfather's hand until we got to al-Geish Street. My grandfather paused before a bicycle cart with a large box where the front should be. A large picture of Mickey Mouse

31

covered one side, and another, smaller picture decorated the other. The mouse was sneaking up on a large cat with its eyes closed and tying its back legs together with a rope he held in his hand. The owner of the bicycle was an elderly man who never stopped looking about him. No sooner did he see children passing near or far than he shouted, "Ice-cold ice cream! Ice-cold!"

As I looked at him, he noticed me and called aloud again in a tone that delighted me, "Get your ice-cold ice cream here!"

My grandfather bought me a cone for 6 milliemes. Unsatisfied, I handed it back to the man, saying, "This one's too small." He smiled and gave me another, larger one and refused to charge my grandfather for the difference. Even so, I said, "And another lick." I said it in imitation of the older boys who said the same thing to the ice-cream man who passed sometimes through our alley.

My grandfather laughed out loud, bending to kiss my head. "Yes, indeed! That's my boy and no mistake! That's how to wangle it, Gel-gel!"

We stopped again outside a store that sold roasted sunflower seeds and nuts and bought two paper cones, one filled with seeds, the other with peanuts. Then my grandfather got ready to cross the street. I hung onto his hand tight, for the tram, with its loud, clangorous bell, was approaching from afar. I had a healthy respect for it and had always looked at it with fear and awe since I once glimpsed it crushing a bicycle a careless owner had left touching the rails. The tram had pushed it along like a ball.

We stood outside the door of the cinema—Cinema Misr—at ten o'clock sharp, and people were readying themselves to get in. On the outside of the theater, a wooden billboard bore the image of the lady who was probably the star of today's film, Leila Murad. In the remaining space appeared the image of the great comedian Naguib al-Rihani, wearing a tarboosh, and young star Anwar Wagdi, handsome and dashing in a pilot's uniform. To the left of that, a slightly smaller billboard displayed a photo of rugged men from the land of Uncle Sam, in cowboy hats and jeans and bearing guns, fighting over a half-naked woman while one of them lay in the background, bleeding.

My grandfather only paid for two tickets; he managed to convince the ticket collectors at the door that I was too young to understand movies anyway, and that we usually only watched one picture of the double feature and then left our seats to the management to do with what they would. In any case, the matinee was sparsely attended, leaving about half the seats empty, so they let it go. One of them even joked that he knew us and that my grandfather always said the same thing and never bought more than two tickets no matter how many people accompanied him!

We sat in the theater watching the *Speaking Newspaper*. It was all about the Revolution and the men of the Revolution and the achievements of the Revolution. Whenever President Gamal Abd al-Nasser appeared on screen, people would break into applause, and there was one person who always whistled loudly and said, "Hang in there, Our Leader!" and someone else would take up the call: "That's it, Abu Khaled; show 'em what it is to be strong!"

I too fell in love with the president, finding myself bursting into applause with the rest of them and elbowing my mother to do the same. She looked surprised, whispering to my grandfather. When the movie *Ghazal al-Banat* began, silence fell over the cinema. Every eye was on Leila Murad. My grandfather was affected by Naguib al-Rihani's performance. He leaned into my mother and whispered, "Poor fellow; he died suddenly. He was killed by an overdose of medicine to cure an attack of typhoid, and left others to reap fame and fortune." And then he started to talk about Jewish singing superstar Leila Murad. He said that she came from a family of actors; her brother was Munir

Murad, the leading man; and her father was Zaki Murad, and what a voice *he* had! He sighed. "And if you could only hear the song 'Why So Confused,' by the composer Dawoud Husni!"

She said she had never heard of the song before, nor of the famous Egyptian Jewish composer Dawoud Husni.

He shook his head in derision. "When we get home, I'll tell you just who Dawoud Husni is."

The people behind us muttered in complaint at the disturbance my grandfather was causing. "Silence in the theater!" said someone, while another said, "Keep your voice down, venerable sir! We're here to watch the movie, not to chat! And what's more, take that tarboosh off your head! I've been angling left and right to try and see past it till I'm cross-eyed!"

My grandfather turned very slightly back, then took his tarboosh off and placed it in his lap. There wasn't another peep out of him until the movie was over.

When the house lights came up for the intermission before the foreign film, he begged off on the pretext of a headache and left, to my mother's reproaches.

Another, later, Saturday, my grandmother accompanied us to the cinema, and we watched *Love and Revenge*, starring Anwar Wagdi and prima donna Asmahan. As soon as the foreign movie started, my grandfather went back to his old tricks, this time claiming that his glasses would not allow him to read the subtitles. We left, my grandmother fighting with him all the while for having deprived her of one of her beloved action movies.

The Saturday before that, though, he and I had gone out by ourselves. We took the bus from al-Geish Street to Sabil al-Khazindar Street, where our synagogue was, the Karaite Synagogue. A small crowd stood at the door as older Jewish gentlemen alighted from big American cars—Fords, Cadillacs, and Chevrolets—wearing mohair coats. The ladies wore dresses, and the men wore navy and gray suits and French neckties. They held by the hand little children with blow-dried hair and in clothing that qualified them to grace the front pages of fashion magazines. They walked into synagogue with their heads held high, not sparing a glance for anyone else; the rest were simple folk, like us, who bought their clothes from Moski and Clot Bey Street, or even from the alleyways where secondhand clothing was sold. Two or three elderly ladies still wore the Star of David around their necks.

As soon as the service started, my grandfather handed me over to an acquaintance of his, one of the synagogue cleaners. The man placed me among a group of children who sat silently while an attendant read Exodus to them. When he was done, they all started reciting the Psalms of David from memory with a distinctive rhythm. I felt out of place at the start, but I gradually started to copy them, moving my lips and nodding my head like them.

On our way back, my grandfather asked, "Did you have fun, Gel-gel?"

"It was all right," I said offhandedly. "But I'd have preferred the movies."

He patted me on the shoulder. "Next Saturday we'll all go. Even Mama. If she won't go, we'll tie her up with a big rope and bundle her up, and off she'll go with us."

I burst out laughing. "And if she falls asleep in the theater, like she did last time, let's leave her in her seat and go off home."

"Yes, we must. That'll teach her."

Startling me, he asked, "Did you learn any of the Psalms of David?"

"Who's David, Grandfather?"

"Sayyidna David? Heavens above, Galal, is there anyone alive who doesn't know of King David? He is one of our kings."

"A king?"

"Not a king like today's kings! Something much greater.

35

Like . . . something like a prophet." He went on, "And Zechariah is a prophet too, and Jacob and Isaac and Moses. All those and many more." He looked at me and said with gentle reproach, "You should really know these things, Galal!"

I asked him, "And is Sayyidna Mohamed a prophet like them, too?"

He crouched to me and whispered, "Who did you say? Mohamed?"

"Yes. You see, I hear the kids in the street saying Sayyidna Mohamed this and Sayyidna Mohamed that, and they think the world of him, and they swear by him, too."

He raised his head slightly, scratching at his mustache, and looked at me. "Have it your way, Mr. Gel-gel. Mohamed is a prophet, too."

6

I WAS A LITTLE OLDER; it was now my job to buy the cooked beans for breakfast, instead of the doorman's wife. My mother would sing out my name: "Galal! Oh Galal! Gel-gel!" She would keep calling until I opened my eyes to the sunlight streaking in through the closed shutters on the window, laid out in lines on the wall facing me. Remembering the beans, I would jump out of bed at once. A second in the bathroom, then my mother would be putting on my slippers and rolling up my pajama pants at least three times; sometimes she would roll them up several times by the waist elastic, or pull them up completely from the center until they reached the top of my chest. My grandfather had a special policy with regard to buying my clothes: he would always buy them several sizes larger, so that they would last me from three to four years, never mind that I looked like an idiot in them.

My mother would hand me the deep dish and the piaster and remind me to always stay on the sidewalk, and not talk to anyone, and as soon as Amm Mohamed had ladled out the beans, to ask him for an extra ladleful. At first, she had pulled me by the ear as she made me memorize these instructions; she had stopped after I proved myself worthy of the task.

In truth, it was hard at first. The first day I had gone out, bearing the dish, I found a huge crowd outside the foul store: a horseshoe-shaped circle of boys and girls, and people in smarter gallabiyas and pajamas, and women, and doormen, and mechanics, and people of every stripe and color. Everyone stood thronged around the marble counter of the store: behavior ranged from gentle nudges, to mild insults, to outright elbowing.

Naturally, I did not dare to approach. I stood there like a lost boy for a long time; indeed, I thought of turning tail and going home. I don't know where I got the courage, but suddenly I barged into the throng. I pushed through bodily, using the dish as a helmet. It was a mercy that the area where I had slipped in was further away from the fights and shouldering and elbowing. Making a virtue of slightness and shortness, I opened up a gap between people's thighs and knees, through which I arrived at Amm Mohamed. My endeavor was crowned with success when I stood on tiptoe and rested my chin on the edge of the marble counter, finding myself face to face with a pair of awe-inspiring pots of beans. I shrieked out, face stunned, voice shrill, "A pennyworth, Uncle!"

He took a look at me and said with the voice of one at the end of his patience, "Put the dish on the counter and the piaster beside it!" I did so, and he added impatiently, "Plain or with oil? And the oil, do you want corn oil or flaxseed oil? Or do you want it with ghee?"

This had not been in the instructions; I found myself in a fix. As was usual in these situations, I found myself unable to breathe or say a word. I simply stared like an idiot into Amm Mohamed's face, until my eyes found his mustache and rested there. It was a funny mustache, to tell the truth; well might it attract the gaze of a child like me. It had been freshly burned and was sticking out in all directions, with a goodly portion of it missing, utterly hairless. The entire mustache was not the same uniform black; the tips, especially, were more of a dark gold. Perhaps the problems of this mustache had their source in the relentless heat of the furnace, or the merciless burns of the taamiya oil. He yelled at me, spittle flying, "Whose kid are you, boy?"

Nobody had ever asked me this question; I grew even more flustered, especially as I had no ready response in mind, and I didn't even know the rest of my father's name. I swallowed, never taking my eyes off the mustache, which had become my only port in the storm. He fixed me with a fiery glare and kept urging me with motions of his head to speak up, already. To be honest, he scared me so much that I felt a drop of urine dampen my pants. Who knew if he would throw the ladle at me, by way of a projectile, and if he did not, I would surely be insulted by the people seething with impatience at this delay. He shouted hotly, "Go away, then, boy. Go on and let other people have their turn."

I had to do something, so I stammered, "I'm the son of Khawaga Zaki al-Arza'."

He stared full at me. "Is that so? You'll be Madam Camellia's boy, then. Are you Galal?"

I nodded, and he smiled, "Right, so; plain, then." And he ladled out the beans.

After he had done so, I said, brimming with confidence, "And another ladleful?"

He burst out laughing and added two.

I became his youngest and most beloved customer; he greeted me all smiles, and before I asked for the extra, would say, "And here's the extra ladleful, Gel-gel, and my best to Amm Zaki."

It became automatic for me to come and go every day with the dish of beans, walking on the sidewalk and never deviating an inch from my mother's preordained path, until I discovered that the matter did not merit so many precautions, after all; and gradually, my fear of the street diminished. I grew to know the people: Amm Husni the clerk, who seemed always in a rush; he would run out of the building and his wife would call to him from the balcony. He would look up at her impatiently, looking at his watch. She would ask him where he had left her the house money or toss down his handkerchief, or his fly whisk, or his cigarettes. His face would be immediately wreathed in smiles and he would say to his wife, "It's true what they say: haste makes waste." And he would look around to see me, carrying the plate, and playfully pull my ear. "That's it, Gel-gel, little manikin." Not waiting for a reply, he would keep walking fast, his wife standing above, looking after him, until he disappeared into the street.

There was the shop boy at Hagg Mahmoud's spice store, who would pull up a chair from the store next door where they sold sunflower seeds and nuts and sit there until they brought him the key; Amm Tolba, the street sweeper, with his tattered government-issue uniform, bearing a broom with a handle as high as his shoulder, sweeping for a minute in between ten-minute breaks. At the first corner, I would turn into the next street, the empty dish in my hand, or on my head like a hat, and look at the shop windows: the grocer's, the haberdasher's, the cigarette kiosk, or even the bakery. When I arrived at the flower shop with its window down, where water flowed like tears, I would stand mesmerized.

I started noticing the sounds coming out of the radio at Abu Auf's Café and enjoying the songs that were broadcast in the early morning. Umm Kalthoum sang, "How lovely you are, son of Egypt, at the tiller!" Or she held her head high and sang, "Egypt, on my mind and on my lips, I love Egypt with all my blood and all my soul!" Mohamed Qandil, with his flirtatious voice, sang *Dark and Lovely*, or lovingly crooned, "Three times hello, I've missed you for three days; I greet you with my hands, my eyes, and my heart." And there was the music! The music of the song, "God is greater than the plotting of the enemy!" And Mohamed Abd al-Wahhab, mourning Palestine, singing:

My brother, the unjust ones have gone beyond the pale.

Take up the sword, for words are of no avail.
To sacrifice is but our right,
Our privilege, our due to fight.
The glory of Arabia shall not be lost,
Defend her honor and sovereignty we must.
Our voices never shall be heard
Unless the pen cedes to the sword.

At that time, I had no understanding of what he meant. My heart recognized the song, though, amidst the others.

What enchanted me then, what still rings in my ears today, was the voice of Sheikh Damanhouri. I had no idea then that what he was reciting was the Qur'an; I was drawn to it without any comprehension of what he was saying. He mesmerized me, and I couldn't shake the impression that the owner of this voice was a good man, who cared for me as I cared for him. I lingered outside the café until he was done with his recitation; indeed, I started to paint a picture of him in my imagination: a white beard; a round face; a turban bigger than Muallim Habib's; a stick to lean upon as he walked.

I was still confused; the world was all blurry and indistinct. I asked my mother what Sheikh Damanhouri was saying. She made no answer, and when I became more insistent, she said carelessly, "Damanhouri? Who might this Damanhouri be?"

"I hear him on the radio at Abu Auf's Café."

"And why might you be dawdling around cafés? That's why it takes you an hour every time I send you out for beans."

"What am I supposed to do? The café's on my way."

She prodded me in the back with a finger. "Right. Go on then, child; we want breakfast." Before I was out of her sight, she added severely, "And don't you dare dawdle around again. I'll be standing on the balcony watching from now on."

My grandmother sat on the couch, frowning at us, digging with a matchstick into her decayed molars.

7

WE WERE ON OUR WAY back from buying the beans: me and Hassan, whose mother had nursed me. I was swimming in my too-large pajamas, the deep dish balanced on my hands, leaning right and left, never spilling a single bean. I was yelling proudly, "Make way, make way! Make way for Gel-gel, the Valiant! Gel-gel the Brave!"

Hassan looked at me oddly; I dared him to do as I did. The poor fellow tried, but the dish shook in his hands, and the juice from the beans started spilling over. He stopped and looked at me in annoyance. I couldn't really blame him! I had three whole months of experience with getting the beans and practicing this trick, but he was still a rookie, just two days out into the street. I remembered my conversation with my mother about Sheikh Damanhouri, so I stopped playing around and asked Hassan what he had been singing.

"Don't you know him?" Hassan asked, surprised.

"No."

"It's God's word, silly! It's the Qur'an! Is there a Muslim who doesn't know the Qur'an?"

"A Muslim?"

"Yes, a Muslim."

Seeing me staring at him, he added, astonished, "You idiot; don't you know you're a Muslim? You're every inch a Muslim. Your mother and her family, Heaven protect us, they're the ones who're Jews."

"Jews?"

"Yes, Jews. And Lord, what'll happen to them on Judgment Day! Straight to Hell!"

I sagged back against the wall of our building as he kept talking. "And you have to pray, and fast, and learn the Qur'an by heart, or you'll go to Hell, too." Seeing me stunned at his words, he went on, "You'll sure go to Hell! And not just that—before you go to Hell, the angels will lay into you with an iron bar."

"Me?"

"What did you think? And each iron bar as big as a lamp post, and flaming fire!"

I asked him about my family.

"Family? What family, man? They'll be first into the flames!"

"Mommy too?" I whispered in terror.

"Of course."

"And my grandfather? My grandfather, going to Hell too?"

Decisively, he said, "Your grandfather? Your grandfather's a special case! The angels are waiting for him! They're sitting there, just hoping for the day he's going to die! As soon as Judgment Day comes, they're going to run and catch him by the scruff of the neck! And beat him! And when their hands get tired, they're going to grab him by the wrists and ankles and fling him into the fire!"

"Liar!" I screamed at him. "It's your parents who're going to Hell!"

"So you don't believe me?"

"No, I don't, dirty liar!"

"Silly, you're not going to Hell! You're a Muslim and you're going to Heaven, same as us."

"How do you know?" I whispered.

"Know? It's not just me who knows. Everybody knows. Ask anyone on our street. They'll tell you."

I staggered up the stairs, leaving him to argue with the doorman's wife. He caught up to me on the second landing, tugging at me by the shirt, panting, "Let's set the dishes aside and race on the stairs, like yesterday." I didn't answer. "We can see who's first to the roof!" I took another step up, ignoring him. "Come on, come on; don't be a stick-in-the-mud!"

He stood there, looking at me in bewilderment, as I climbed up, away from him, and knocked at the door.

My grandmother was stretched right out on the couch holding a small mirror that she held up to her face, near and far alternately. In her other hand was a pair of tweezers with which she plucked out the black hairs on her upper lip.

When she was young, the hairs had been mere down; the problem was that with the passage of time, the down had thickened, and was now as strong as actual hair, and spread out over this vital area. My grandmother had made the rounds of the clinics and practiced all the folk remedies, to no avail; nobody managed to tame this down or stop its growth. What made matters worse was that if she neglected it for a week, it became a mustache in the making. It drove her crazy, and she took to hunting it down with tweezers so as not to become the laughingstock of the women in our building.

My grandmother set the tweezers aside and turned toward me. "Why are you late, Mud? Now your grandfather's gone out without his breakfast."

I replied coldly, "What am I to do? Find someone else to get your beans. And furthermore, my grandfather told us yesterday that he was going out early and wouldn't be having breakfast with us today."

My mother grabbed me by the collar. "All right, smarty-pants. But you'll speak to your grandmother with respect."

I didn't answer her, unceremoniously shoving the dish at her. Some of the contents spilled out onto the front of her gallabiya. "What's the matter with you, boy?" she yelled. "What's gotten into you?"

Waving an arm wildly, I said, "I know what Sheikh Damanhouri's saying!"

"What is it that you've found out, Mr. Clever?"

"He's reciting the Qur'an!"

"Let him recite what he wants. What's it got to do with us?" She laid a hand on my head, saying more softly, "Don't you know, Galal, that we're Jews, and our holy book is the Torah? We're one thing, and they're another."

"Jews, huh?"

"Yes, Jews."

"All of us?"

My grandmother started to roll up her sleeves, staring hard at me. My mother nodded.

"Every last one of us?" I asked again.

"Yes: me, your grandfather, your grandmother, your aunt, and your uncle. Every last one of us."

"Me too?"

She didn't answer. My question had so startled her, she could find nothing to say. She merely looked me in the face, a smile starting to play around her lips—a puzzled, perplexed smile, a smile that hid something behind it, something that was not insignificant nor even small. Her every feature showed that she was in a bind, and that she couldn't think of a single thing to say.

I was young back then, so I had no idea of the source of her predicament, nor did I relent. My tongue ran away with me. "The kids, see, they say I'm a Muslim and I'm going to Heaven. And you're all going to Hell. Every last one of you. My grandmother, and my aunt, and my uncle . . . ." And I started counting them off on my fingers, not noticing my grandmother's descent from the couch, nor her slow, careful steps toward me, not until she had her hand clamped round my neck.

Frozen with shock, I tipped over, using both hands to catch myself against the sofa cushions. Naturally, she granted me no opportunity to flee; with a move worthy of Farid Shawqi, she twisted my arm into a half nelson. Her other hand captured my entire right ear, twisting it back and forth and pulling me down by it until I was brought to my knees on the rug, my wailing resounding throughout the apartment. My grandmother never stopped her attack until I lay on my back, both shoulders on the rug like a wrestling mat. Then she placed one knee on my stomach and started hurling insults. "What kids, you scum, son of scum? May they all burn, and their families too! And what's wrong with Jews? They're the best of all people, you son of an old boot—better than you. You couldn't dream of being a Jew!" All the while, my mother was circling, moving this way and that, trying to release me from my captivity.

It was only Divine Providence that rescued me; at a knock on the door, my grandmother took her knee off my stomach and turned toward the door, her fingers unconsciously loosening their grip on my earlobe. Seizing the opportunity, I fled for my life.

My mother made to open the door; my grandmother screamed at her not to, or the son of a bitch—she meant me—would get away from her and run off into the street. I was a couple of yards away from her, glancing about me like a mouse freshly escaped from the trap, my blood-red ear throbbing with pain. I screamed at her with all my strength, "I'm not a Jew, and I'm not going to Hell like you are, Old Beaky!" I knew that this was the neighbor women's secret code name for her, and I was so mad that it came to my lips in spite of myself. She ran for me, slipper upraised, as I scurried away before her.

"May your head split open, you and yours! And you have the nerve to talk back to me? Me beaky, you son of a rotten old shoe? Is this the thanks we get for raising you and feeding you?"

All the while, my mother was trailing around after us. "Mom, don't carry on like that! He's just a child; you can't lower yourself to his level!" And then she raised her voice. "We told you, Mom, me and Papa, stay out of it; stay out of this."

"Stay out of it? You want me to stay out of it? He needs to be taught some manners! Don't you hear what he's saying? And he must learn that he's part and parcel of his mother, his mother who bore him and bears his burden still. He's the same as she is. If she's Jewish then so is he, and if she's sky-blue pink then so is he."

We were still all chasing each other around, and the fight only ended when I sought refuge on the balcony. My grandmother was afraid for her image, lest people in the street see her in such a state, so she remained inside the apartment and merely threw her slipper, hitting my face.

My grandfather resolved the matter when he came home that evening. He took my mother and grandmother into his room and closed the door. I lay in bed, eyes swollen, my grandmother's scratches still on my face and neck. Their voices would rise occasionally, and my grandfather's voice could be heard warning my grandmother of the consequences of what she had done, and that this would ruin everything when I went with my mother to meet my father's family.

Later, my grandfather emerged, the two of them following him, and said to me soberly: "Galal, my boy, you're a Muslim. That's what it says on your birth certificate. The certificate is with me, in trust, and when you grow up, I'm going to give it to you." He swallowed and went on. "My boy, Moses and Mohamed are brothers. We will raise you, educate you, until you grow into a man. After that, you are free to choose. If you want to come into our religion, by all means, we'll welcome you with open arms. If you want to stay a Muslim, that's your choice, and we'll always be family." He told me to rise and kiss my grandmother's hand, which I did. She patted me on the head, and kissed me.

8

ONE EVENING, MY GRANDFATHER AND I went out to a wake. I saw him sitting on the couch, dressed to go out, cleaning the edges of his tarboosh with a brush. I asked him to let me come with him; he said he was going to a wake and suggested that I play with the other children on the landing. I asked him again, but he was adamant; when I became more insistent, he raised his voice: "That's enough, Galal! I said no and I meant no! This place I'm going is no place for children! Stay here with your mother or go play with the other children."

I started with the first weapon in my arsenal; I waved a hand in anger and stormed off to my room, crying out, in a voice trembling with emotion, "I hate you, you meanie! I hate you, I hate you! I'm never speaking to you again!" I slammed the door, lay down on the bed, and pulled the coverlet over my head. I was careful, nonetheless, to leave a little crack in it, so I could watch what went on around me. Not two minutes had passed when I heard the door squeak open, my grandfather looking in. "Why is Mr. Gel-gel upset? Doesn't he know his grandfather can't go out without him?"

I pretended to be asleep and not hear him. He smiled. I grew angry at his smile, and wanting to assure him that it wasn't as he thought, that I really was asleep, I started snoring loudly. My grandfather's smile became a laugh, and he sat on the edge of the bed. He slipped his hand under the coverlet to tickle the sole of my foot. As I wriggled away, the hand moved to my tummy, then to my armpit, until I burst out laughing under his gaze. Like lightning, I streaked to the hanger and retrieved my shirt; he put it on me and knelt, tucking it into my shorts and pulled my suspenders over it. He couldn't resist giving me a playful pinch in the side, or a quick pull on my ear, as I wriggled and gave as good as I got, getting in punches to his tummy and chest, and a bite to the shoulder if I could manage it.

We went out in single file, my mother admonishing me never to let go of my grandfather's hand, for it was night; my grandmother's eyes followed us, accompanied with sighs and mutterings about spoiling the child rotten. Once across al-Khalig al-Masri Street, we went through various side streets until we reached an immense ceremonial tent, at the start of Nuzha Street on the Midan al-Geish side. The tent was for the funeral of the mother of a prominent Azhar Street business-man in the fabric trade; my grandfather's shop window was opposite his store. The man stood at the entrance, receiving the mourners. He shook my grandfather's hand warmly, and looked at me in surprise. My grandfather went a little pale and he bowed his head, apologizing in low tones. "I apologize, sir. I know it's a funeral and no place for children, but what could I do? The boy wouldn't take no for an answer. I really do owe you an apology." And he looked at me reprovingly. "Did you have to insist, Galal, and embarrass me in front of this gentleman?"

The man showed no reaction to my grandfather's words, for he was busy with me. He patted me on the shoulder and bent to ask me my name. My grandfather, perking up, answered for me. "This is Galal, my grandson, the one I told you about."

The man looked at me for a moment, then placed a hand in his pocket, the wide sleeve of the gallabiya riding up to his elbow. His arm showed, plump and fair-skinned, covered with yellowish hair; on his finger was a large ring with a blue stone. He pulled out a fifty-piaster note and held it out to me. I took a step back in embarrassment, looking at my grandfather, who looked pleased and serious all at once. He said in a commanding tone, nodding and urging me on with a gesture: "Take it, Galal, and kiss the hand of Amm al-Hagg—why, we all live under his protection."

The man motioned to two seats, far from the couches at the mouth of the tent. We sat. My grandfather whispered in my ear what he had said on the way dozens of times: that I was to stay silent and not say a single word. I watched him jump out of his seat every time an Azhar tradesman of his acquaintance passed by. My grandfather would bow his head and salute them in the traditional manner, raising both hands to his head as though shading his eyes, then lowering them to his chest and raising them again several times, until they had left. For their part, they also greeted him with affection, and some clapped him on the shoulder or noticed me and favored me with a friendly glance.

Sheikh Abd al-Baset Abd al-Samad was the Qur'an reciter for that evening. As soon as he cleared his throat and his melodious voice rang out, "In the name of God, the Merciful, the Compassionate," everyone got ready to listen. Some gestured to their fellows, and to the waiters bearing trays of coffee and cold water, to be silent; even those coming into the tent tiptoed in and sat quickly on the closest seat. My grandfather took hold of my wrist, warning me not to make a sound.

One verse, then another, and a deep hush fell—not only over those assembled in the tent; gradually, the noise died down in the cafés around the tent and the houses in the street, until there was deep silence all the way to the square. Close to us sat a man who jumped up every time the sheikh would bring a musical phrase to its resolution with his renowned skill and accuracy, and call aloud for God to grant the sheikh a long life. The people around us all said, "Amen." Even my grandfather was touched by the reading, and was moving his head gently from side to side as Egyptians are wont to do when filled with listening pleasure; when our eyes met, he would comfort me with a glance, his face overcome with gentle, sorrowful affection.

We were all overcome with emotion, with an ecstasy almost magical. I found myself slipping gradually away from those around me, my heart filling with an awe I had never known before. It was as though something unseen was spiriting me away to a world unlike the world I lived in, something that flowed through my veins, engulfed me from top to bottom, right and left, relaxed me, cradled me, drugged me, melted me, made my body light. It made me weak; it made me strong; it made me joyous and filled me with anguish. Tears seemed to form in my eyelids, my eyes burned, and I burst into bitter tears: great, gulping, gasping sobs, so loud that the mourners noticed.

My grandfather bolted up in alarm, looking around him. He was afraid that the bereaved gentleman might have seen us; reassuring himself at the sight of him occupied in greeting a company of important men, he snatched me up from the chair and rushed out.

In the square was a sugarcane juice store. He took me there, splashed my face with a glass of water, and ordered a glass of juice for me. I could only manage a sip. My grandfather, reluctant to return the glass all but untouched, drank the rest of it and carried me in his arms, heading for home.

I could hear my own heartbeat. It was loud, faster than usual. I distracted myself with that, trying to forget what had happened to me; I even tried to count the beats on my fingers as my mother had taught me to do. He never stopped patting me on the back. The crying fit returned, though, when we were close to al-Madbah al-Ingilizi Street, but this time the sobs were accompanied by choking. My grandfather leaned back against the wall and splayed his hand over my head, reciting verses from the Holy Book and various prayers he knew by heart. When I calmed down, I said to him in a ragged voice, "I love you so much, Grandfather. I want you to be a Muslim so you won't go to Hell." He kissed my cheek, but said nothing. I said, "Well then, I'll be a Jew just like you."

I felt his cheek press against mine, his hands tighten slightly around me. I must have fallen asleep because I never felt him go up the stairs and into our apartment.

I had a nightmare that night. My mother was walking in a transparent nightdress, very short, in an empty street with no one on either side. Everything was still and silent—not a whisper, not a breath of anything moving as far as the eye could see: no cars, no people, not a living creature. The people were all there, above, silent and staring through the slits in the windows at her body, which was mostly exposed.

I ran behind her with all my might. Although I was panting and running faster and faster, instead of coming closer, we drew further apart. Overcome with exhaustion, I almost fell, while she almost disappeared from my sight.

Suddenly, I heard a loud, continuous clangor from close by. Before I could detect the source of the sound, a single-car tram burst out upon her from a side street. It ran her over and disappeared into the distance. My heart burst; I could hear it beating even as I slept. I fancied that the iron wheels of the tram were crushing my bones and not hers. I woke up in a fright, the clanging still ringing in my ears.

She was lying next to me. I touched her with my fingertips, my heart still pounding. The arm; the shoulder; the neck; the face. Little by little, I realized it had only been a dream, and that the wheels of the tram had not gobbled my mother up. I rose, went to the light switch, and turned on the light in the room. Undisturbed, she slept on. Her face was peaceful, her long hair splayed out on the pillow. Her lashes looked longer with her eyes shut. I noticed that the nightdress she wore was the same one as in my dream.

I went back to bed and snuggled into her, enjoying the warmth that emanated from her bare shoulders; she turned to me and took me into her arms, eyes still shut.

9

My grandmother went on drinking wine, despite her promises to herself that she would give it up. My mother would reprove her angrily, "That's enough! You're a scandal! The women of the building smell it on your breath and whisper and gossip about you!"

My grandmother, resentful, would curse their mothers. "They're no better than me. Why so holier-than-thou? Their husbands smoke hash all night at the cafés, and they wouldn't say no to opium eating if they had the chance!"

"At least don't leave the bottles out in the open when they come to visit!"

"Do you mean the time when what's-her-name came in unexpectedly?" She scratched her forehead. "Yes, yes; I remember! You mean that benighted little slip, the clerk's wife? May she have a clout over the earhold!"

"Yes, Mommy Dearest, that is what I mean," my mother said tartly, "not to mention being plastered and slurring your words when Umm Hassan was at our place the other day, or the time when they came to inquire about Papa's health, or . . . ."

"Plastered? You uncouth little thing! I'll plaster you to the wall, you and your stupid little brat—" And if my mother had not decided that discretion was the better part of valor and retreated in haste, my grandmother would have thrown the scissors at her, the heavy sewing scissors that lay in her lap.

*

My grandfather settled the matter. He came home one swel-
tering Bashans summer day—a muggy day where the very
air was a thing to choke on. It showed on his face that he
was coming down with the flu, and he was exhausted from
haggling with the customers all day. I ran to take his leather
satchel and his tarboosh, and he went into his room. We sat
waiting for him, dinner on the table. It was not he but his
shouting that reached us. We learned later that he had found
wine spilt on the bed; apparently, my grandmother had been
having a grand old time in her room after lunch, and took to
drinking toasts to herself; she would down one glass and pour
the other onto the bed sheet.

My grandfather came out wearing his sleeveless undershirt, pillowcase in hand. He flung it in my grandmother's
face, yelling at her, "Even this! Soaked in crap!"

Naturally, my grandmother didn't take it lying down. She
gave as good as she got, and sometimes more. His ire rose and
rose, and I shrank into myself in tension and fear, as he stormed
around the house, searching for the bottles. His body was thin,
with not a scrap of fat nor even a hint of muscle—only vein and
sinew—and his face was yellowed like a lemon with rage. His
voice was the strangest thing about him; I had never imagined
that his neck cords were capable of standing out that much, or
that his gullet could produce such a loud noise.

He knelt by the couch; he crawled under my grandmother's bed; he searched our room, the kitchen cupboards, the
attic, and the rest of my grandmother's hiding places. He
found ten empties that had been stored in a carton awaiting
the visit of Amm Younis, the rag-and-bone man, and in the
washing basket he found a bottle wrapped in a pair of his
trousers with a few sips left inside. It must be this accursed
bottle that was responsible! My grandfather smashed it with
one blow against the bathroom tiles and opened the door,
calling to Amm Idris to get rid of the carton of empties. As

56

for my grandmother, she settled into a corner of the couch and pulled out a handkerchief to wipe away her tears.

This was the angriest I had ever seen my grandfather. But, thank God, my grandmother never drank wine from that day on.

My grandparents didn't speak to each other for an entire month after that incident. They only properly reconciled months later, when we were sitting on the balcony with a spread of sunflower seeds, lupin beans, and peanuts. I still remember the gray pajamas with dark blue stripes I wore that night, when my grandfather walked in hiding two parcels behind his back. I hurried to him, and he said, "This package isn't for you," and he placed it before my grandmother. She opened it to find a large bottle of Stella beer, and two glasses bearing the brand name Zotos. She smiled at him, and from that day forward, she officially switched to beer.

The second package bore a knight on horseback, sword held high. It was the time of the celebration of the birth of the Prophet Mohamed, and my grandfather appeared to have sensed my wishes as I watched the boys and girls in their parents' company, carrying the confectionery dolls and horses. I spent quite a while shrieking and jumping with joy on the balcony tiles as my mother looked on in delight; my grandmother saw nothing wrong with it, although she did ask my mother to have me eat it up as soon as possible so as not to bring the ants down upon the apartment.

That wasn't the end of my grandfather's surprises, though. He asked my mother if she had told me the news of our trip tomorrow. I looked at her in surprise, and she said, "We're all going together to see your father's family."

I asked, "Every last one of us?"

She said, "No. Just you and I."

Her face was strange. Her eyes were misty. All the images I had formed in my mind of my father came to me; my mother's eyes grew distant, too, and she didn't even notice it when my grandmother said to her, "Don't you dare come back empty-handed. The boy costs a pretty penny," nor when my grandfather admonished my grandmother not to put pressure on the girl, for she no doubt knew what was best for her own son.

10

IT WAS QUITE A JOB, but we finally made it to Kitkat Square in Giza. My mother didn't want to take the privately owned microbuses that charged by the head, although they had set routes; "The government buses," she maintained, "are cheaper and safer." Some helpful fellow travelers directed her to the rickety old bus at the stop for the provinces, explaining that it was the fastest and most direct route to Mansouriya, and that it usually made the journey in half an hour.

The steps of the coach were high and worn down, and but for my mother's firm grip on my hand, I would have slipped off. Thanks to God, we managed to get on. The first thing we saw was the driver. He sat in the driver's seat, slumped over the steering wheel, head encircled by his arms, fast asleep. This was no ordinary nap attack, like the ones that came over Amm Idris, the doorman of our building, as he sat on his wooden bench; it was a nap extraordinaire, accompanied by snoring. Over and above, the poor man murmured to himself in his sleep, in between bouts of snoring, elbows convulsively jerking. He was doubtless having a nightmare, or fighting with someone in his sleep.

I stood staring at him; my mother took me by the arm and sat me down on the bench behind him. My mother was strung tight, as though she was afraid and dreading the errand. As for me, I was in another world. I sat entranced by the driver and the people boarding the bus in gallabiyas and caps, with their straw and reed baskets and containers of different shapes and sizes, which they seemed to prefer to thrust in through the windows rather than carrying them onto the bus through the door in the usual manner—in short, by every new thing I saw.

When I started to ask my mother questions, she leaned in toward me and pleaded with me, for God's sake, to keep my mouth shut.

The conductor came onto the bus. He glanced at the passengers, then yanked off the handkerchief that encircled the collar of his government-issue uniform and dusted it off in our faces. He turned to the driver, poking him a couple of times until the latter woke up and turned to look at us. His forehead was slightly reddened, an imprint of the lines in the steering wheel formed upon it. He yawned several times in succession and bent to an earthen pot next to him, splashing some water from it onto his face, then began to hum a popular song by the comedian Shukuku, which everyone was singing at the time. I was watching him, and he noticed and smiled at me, starting the engine.

He was a merry driver, and no mistake, clearly well versed in the art of driving down country roads: he took hold of the steering wheel and started off at a speed only a whisker faster than that of your average bicycle. He stopped for everyone who hailed, and each stop lasted roughly ten minutes. Sometimes he would stop quite of his own accord, once at a tea stand, whose owner brought him a full cup of tea and carried away his empty one, and another time for no reason at all. After he had crossed the train tracks, he stopped the bus beside a straw hut next to the Imbaba Airfield and called out at the top of his voice.

A shifty-looking character emerged from the hut, his trousers rolled up, in a sleeveless undershirt, his arm hair as thick as a gorilla's. The driver alighted and began to take him to task for the quality of the chickens he had bought from him the day before, which had died before dawn. They had words and the quarrel commenced; it would have escalated into a fight had the driver not returned to his seat and with great suddenness hawked and launched a gob of spittle at the man through the window. He then took off like the wind, the other man chasing the bus for all he was worth, spewing invective and curses upon the driver's religion.

Due to the sudden speed of the bus, we were bouncing up and down in our seats and colliding with them and with each other. My mother took me into her lap, screaming repeatedly at the driver to slow down. He completely ignored her, but after having gone some distance and realizing he was safe, he slowed to a more sedate pace.

Strangely, all the other passengers remained undisturbed, unconcerned even; to them, everything was proceeding in the natural course of events. There was no activity on the conductor's part, either, until we had traveled quite some distance; he took a doze by an open window, blissfully unaware of what had occurred with the driver, and only awoke when we had long since left Kitkat and the surrounding buildings, driving now on a dirt road flanked by farmland on either side. Pulling a lead pencil from behind his ear, he tapped its butt twice on the block of tickets in his hand. This was the signal for a fight with three of the other passengers, who had, it transpired, spent all their money in the big city and had none left, not even the two piasters for the ticket.

A while later—about an hour and a half—a stream appeared on the horizon, surrounded by tall Eucalyptus trees, behind which small huts could be seen on the edges of farmland. The conductor yawned and pounded his chest, producing a sound that was a cross between a moan and a deep sigh. Then he tapped the glass between the driver and the passengers, calling loudly, "Mansouriya! Mansouriya! Come on, sir! And you, madam! You, asleep over there!" Upon receiving no reaction, nor any sign that any of the passengers were getting ready to alight, he appeared disgruntled and repeated his instruction, this time accompanied by loud thumps of his palm against the glass, then walked up and down the aisle, looking left and right.

He looked disapprovingly down on two men in a unique position: the head of the first lolling upon the shoulder of his neighbor, who, in return, had pillowed his head upon the head pillowed on *his* shoulder, both fast asleep and probably dreaming. He hit one of them with his block of tickets, right on the head, but the man didn't blink. He finally awoke after several such strikes, though, and looked up reprovingly. The conductor pointed to the window and the houses that approached; understanding, the man took it upon himself to wake his neighbor, and they took to rummaging for their things under the seats, one wiping away the trail of spittle that had descended from his mouth and reached the collar of his gallabiya.

The conductor continued his rounds. Next came two women with their heads bent forward; one was performing a calculation on her fingers and thumbs, and the other waiting impatiently for the result. He said in commanding tones, "Come on, Zakiya! Come on, now! Do you have to give me a hard time every time?"

The women smiled and said as one, "Bless you, sir," and they bent together, picking up a straw box with two levels: the first empty, with a door blocked by palm fronds, and the second with two pigeons, nestled close together, resting on a small mound of straw. It was clear that these were the two pigeons left over, the ones they had not managed to sell at the Kitkat market along with their fellows.

On the bench alongside us sat a woman shepherding a whirlwind of children. The youngest absolutely insisted on sticking a finger in her eye; the second was underneath the seat, pulling on her leg while she kicked him in the stomach to get him to stop. Three, or perhaps four, on the seat next to her were fighting amongst themselves. The conductor paid them no heed and turned to us with a significant glance. My mother nodded and rose immediately, leading me along by the hand. There was no doubt that he was qualified for his job: he knew the destination of each of his passengers and the suitable moment to prompt each of them to disembark.

We stepped down from the bus and found ourselves standing next to a steam mill, once whitewashed but now faded with time. Still, it was awe-inspiring, with its smokestack from which clouds billowed, and its imposing structure, towering above the farmhouses. Spread out before it was a spacious square filled with donkeys, some of which had already been relieved of their burdens and tied by the leg to a tree, and others that had slipped their reins and were being enthusiastically chased down by their owners. Some had arched their backs and spread their legs in preparation to urinate as people hurriedly moved away to avoid the spray.

Women waddled lugubriously past, bearing reed baskets bursting with wheat or corn. To the right of the iron gate leading into the mill sat a man with glasses and long pants, a medium-sized grain scale before him. He slid the metal weight to place it at the pointer whenever a woman placed her basket in the lap of the scale, or when a man lifted his sacks from the back of his beast of burden.

Next to him was a very old man, sitting at a table with spindly wooden legs. On it was a worn glass inkwell. He held a flat paper quill in his hand, which he frequently dipped into the well. The man sitting at the scale would tell him a number, which he would jot down on a scrap of paper he fished out of the pile before him and pass over offhandedly, with sleepy eyes, to the person whose turn it was.

Close by, a number of porters stood around dressed in empty burlap sacks open at the shoulders, their arms and legs all bare, heads covered with something like a hood of thick fabric. They took turns hoisting down the sacks of flour stacked by the mill wall and hauling them toward a donkey cart that stood by the side of the road.

We didn't wait long. An old man approached us. He wore a large-beaded rosary round his neck; it hung down almost to his stomach. On his head was a dusty shawl; his gallabiya only hung down a few inches below his knees. He waved a stick made from palm fronds toward my mother. She took two steps back, and I clung to her dress. When he spoke, his jaw dangled toothlessly, intensifying my fear. "Where are you headed?"

"We want the house of Hagg Abd al-Hamid al-Minshawi," said my mother.

The dervish scratched his head, muttering incomprehensibly, then asked again, blinking rapidly. Some boys had gathered around us, yelling boisterously and shouting in his face. Some poked him in the stomach, or pulled him by the belt around his waist. He began to yell back at them, defending himself with his stick. My mother got hit in the fracas, getting a blow round the shoulders and a couple of pokes in the waist. She took to cursing my father, the day she had ever met him, and the day we had ever come here. She tightened her grip on my hand, craning her neck this way and that in search of someone to rescue us and show us the way.

Apparently, the crowd and the screaming around this madman were routine; nobody paid us any heed. We were obliged to capitulate when he succeeded in shooing off the boys and quickly emerged victorious, turning his attention back to us. We repeated my grandfather's name to him and walked with him in a small procession: him in the forefront, my mother and I behind him, and what remained of the boys following behind.

Naturally, the dervish attracted a following of children: with every step, our numbers swelled as more and more joined the procession; a nanny goat also joined the cavalcade—who knows where she came from! A boy riding a little ass came along, too; he seemed to have been on his way to the fields, but apparently, seeing us, found it more fun to join in.

We arrived at a single-story house. Despite its lack of a second floor, it was imposing, with a tall enough roof to indicate high ceilings. The gate was broad with heavy wooden double doors slightly ajar, each topped with an oval opening barred with rust-edged iron. The house had clearly not seen repair for some time: damage from rains and age marred its façade. Some of the large stones it was built with were showing, the paint and plaster eroded to expose them. On each side of the gate stood a young mulberry tree. By one of them there was a water pump with a cement trough before it, leaking in thin trails from a fine crack in its side.

We stood before the gate in a riotous procession that exceeded forty people, in addition to the two four-footed friends. The madman began to call for my paternal grandfather in a loud voice, the children yelling along.

11

No sooner did my father's father appear at the gate than an electric thrill went through me. The children rushed off, the madman with them. My newfound grandfather was tall and broad, wearing a light wool abaya with wide sleeves. On his head was a turban with fringes that hung down, tucked behind his ears. He stood at some distance from us, leaning with the palm of his right hand on a crook-handled black walking stick. Next to him was his manservant, whom I later found out was called Imam, barefoot and wearing a shirt with no undershirt. Both stared at us with eyes that bore a thousand meanings.

"Who are you?" he asked, and bent to scrape off a bit of dried mud stuck to the front of his abaya. My eyes were drawn to the back of his hand, resting loosely upon the stick. It was fleshy and freckled, with a uniform tremble as it gripped the handle, shaking the stick along with it, stirring up tiny dust motes around the base. I caught his eyes surreptitiously examining us, especially me: although they were completely obscured by wrinkles—the pupils narrowed, the whites yellowed—they were shining. The force emanating from them was piercing and said in no uncertain terms that he did in fact recognize us.

Without waiting for an answer, he turned on his heel and walked ponderously toward the door to the house. My mother and I stood there, uncertain as to what to do. I will never forget that moment, nor will I forget Imam bending to kiss the top of my head, giving me a gentle nudge in the direction of my grandfather.

We passed through the gate and walked down a long garden path flanked by opposing wooden benches, all pretty much the same size, except the last one on the left, which was much larger and was covered by two black sheepskins. It had an armrest in the center, formed of two bolsters, one atop the other, between the two skins. At the end of the path were rooms on the right and left, their doors and windows shuttered. Beyond these lay an uncovered courtyard, in the corner of which sat three brick ovens. Two of these stood empty; the third was topped by a massive copper pot, but no fire burned beneath it. In the other corner was an earthen oven, from whose mouth a light steam emanated. Atop the curve of its roof sat a large earthenware pot and an old copper washing pot, with rusted and corroded edges, and bits and pieces of empty bottles and other junk peeking out from inside it. Before the oven stood a pile of green ears of corn, which apparently had been on their way to be cooked before our arrival. At some distance from these cooking appliances stood a tallish shed with one door that opened onto a back street and another that opened onto the interior of the house. At its doorstep sat an older man with his sleeves rolled up, head slumped down over his chest. He was asleep, unaware of anything around him. In the silo, a female water buffalo rested on the floor masticating something or other, and close to her was a calf who appeared to occupy her attention.

Imam had us sit down on the bench facing the big bench, which it became obvious was reserved for my grandfather. I happened to come to sit in a corner that afforded me a view of what was going on in the barn. After a long period of silence, during which my grandfather stroked the edges of his unkempt beard and looked at me again, he addressed my mother with a muttered, "Yes?"

He followed this up with a loud cough, which startled and frightened me.

My mother said not a word. She reached unconsciously for her handbag in her lap, clasping my wrist with her other hand, eyes uncertain, avoiding contact with anything in their line of sight. She fumbled with her handbag for quite a while, until she finally pulled out a roll of papers bound together with the elastic of one of my grandfather Zaki's old socks—a roll that held my birth certificate, the marriage contract between her and my father, a check my father had signed made out to my grandfather, and the contract for the room where they had lived. My grandfather Zaki had been smart enough to prevail upon the landlord to make the rental contract out to both my father and mother, and further make a note that read: married according to the holy writ of God and his prophet Mohamed by a ma'zoun of the district, etc., within the jurisdiction of such-and-such a court.

She handed over the roll of papers, while I watched what was happening in the barn. Apparently a calf had just been born; I watched him raise his head, sniffing out his mother, then his shaky attempts to stand, time after time, so as to get to her udder. Every time, his thin legs gave out under him, and he made quite an effort to untangle them from where they had gotten twisted up underneath him. Tiring, he stopped moving and closed his eyes, falling asleep.

My grandfather placed the papers in his lap, pulled out a pair of reading glasses from the pocket of his waistcoat, and put them on, looking even more fearsome; he examined each document intently, sometimes murmuring the words out loud to himself as he read them. It was his eyes, though, that he could not control; his gaze betrayed him, going to me, time and time again. When our eyes met, he cleared his throat and looked away, upwards, looking as though he were thinking of something else, that what I had seen were mere imaginings.

My mother's face was pale, and she looked worse off than a mouse in a mousetrap.

After some time passed, my grandfather looked at my mother, as though expecting more explanation. One of the closed doors opened. A thin woman emerged, wrapping a black shawl around her head. She had sad eyes. It was my grandmother. My grandfather motioned to her to sit down. My mother stood immediately at her approach; my grandmother passed over her and sat down by me.

My mother told the story of her marriage to my father, all the way back to when he had first come to buy the wool from Sednaoui, until the last time she had ever seen him, when she was pregnant with me. That day he had said to her that he was going home to his village and that the next time, he would take her with him; but he had never come back. My grandfather watched my mother as she spoke, never taking his eyes off her face. My grandmother's ears were with my mother, but her eyes were on me.

I heard the click of a window latch. One of the window shutters parted a few inches, and from behind them appeared a woman who stared intently at us. My grandfather recognized her although the window was not within his line of sight. He bellowed out to her, and she came in answer to his call, draped all in black. By the hand she held a little girl who looked at the ground shyly. My grandfather motioned to her to sit down beside him. The woman and the little girl sat at the other end of the bench. To my mother, he introduced them as my father's wife and her daughter.

A heavy silence fell, broken only by the sounds of two children who had sneaked in through a door that had been left ajar. They took to crawling up and down the length of the path, back and forth, laughing all the while.

After a while, we began to hear mutterings and murmurings behind the other windows in the house. When my grandfather clapped his hands, the hubbub died down completely; but the murmuring returned again, and my grandfather couldn't shut them up this time. He motioned to my grandmother to call the others to come as well.

The wife of my uncle Ibrahim arrived, with a gaggle of children, as did two of my father's sisters from another room, and a third sister who was staying in the house with her children until such time as her husband, a tradesman, returned from a business trip to Upper Egypt. An old servant woman called Umm al-Kouz—"Mrs. Mug"—stood at the end of the passageway. My grandfather waved her away. She took a couple of steps back, waited a moment, then took a step forward. In another minute, she returned to her original position. My grandfather, angered, shouted at her, but she didn't budge. She did not leave his sight, in fact, until he bent in search of something to throw at her. In spite of all that, though, I saw her coming back; she sat alongside a door that hid her from my grandfather, watching us through its narrow opening as it stood ajar.

My grandfather motioned to my mother and told the people who thronged the seats: "This is the lady whom the late lamented was married to, in Cairo." He looked to me. "And this is his son . . . ." he stared at my mother, prompting her for my name.

"Galal."

Silence reigned.

12

WE SPENT THREE DAYS AT my grandfather's house as though in exile. They opened up an attic for us that had previously been used as a storage room and pantry. They blocked up the openings that used to let in mice and swept, cleaned, and furnished it. All this, though, didn't do a thing for the odors that filled it, especially the stink of old mish cheese and buttermilk. They told us before shutting us in, "You've got two windows. The first opens onto the street; open it, but just a crack. The window that opens onto the rest of the house, though, leave that one shut."

At mealtimes, food would be carried in to us on a tray borne by Umm al-Kouz, whom they had charged with seeing to our needs. At first she looked at us with such resentment that it seemed she had a personal quarrel with us; if we asked her something, she would not answer, merely bringing in the tray in silence and coming to take away the empty plates in equal silence. Then, though, she took to hanging back, sitting on the bed without asking permission, then drawing up her legs to perch cross-legged on the bed next to us. Bowing her head, she rummaged in the neck of her dress and pulled out a scrap of handkerchief, hawking and sneezing and spraying us with spittle. My mother was overcome with disgust, but she couldn't say a word.

When the woman was done, she would ask if the food was enough for us, or if we wanted our clothes washed. She would pat my shoulder and say I was the image of my father, which never failed to bring a smile to my mother's face. Then the woman would start to talk, chatting with my mother of trivial matters. She appeared to imagine that she could draw her out and get her to slip up and divulge the reasons that had brought her here, and spill the secrets unknown by the family about my mother and her own folk. But she had met her match in my mother, who deftly steered the conversation into unrelated topics, never giving her the information she wanted. If the conversation turned to my paternal grandfather, my mother would ask the servant-woman of his temperament, and how he and my grandmother spoke of us; the woman would just look at her without letting anything slip, and if she did talk, she didn't say much. It was a well-matched tournament: I sat there, head in my hands, boredom eating away at me.

Once I hung onto her gallabiya and asked her to take me outside with her to play with the other children. She hesitated, saying, "I'll ask your grandmother first." My mother reproached me and yanked me back by my pajama sleeve so hard it almost came off in her hand.

Nobody told us not to leave the room. My mother understood it of her own accord. For two days, we stayed inside, only leaving the room for absolute necessities, such as using the toilet.

The toilet!!!! Oh, the toilet. I had never known the value of our bathroom until I went to the countryside. It was indeed a restroom, a life preserver for those in a fix such as us. Our mealtimes and diet were different from what we had been used to in Cairo; breakfast and lunch were lighter than what we were accustomed to and did not require much coming and going to the toilet. The main meal of the day, though, was dinner. A brass tray would be brought in to us, upon it a single serving dish, large enough for ten, bearing an entire goose or large cubes of meat that wafted steam. Surrounding the main dish would be half a watermelon with a knife stuck into it, dishes of vegetable stew and salads, and another tray bearing an earthenware dish full of rice with nuts and raisins fresh out of the oven, or something like a pastry cooked with raisins and milk.

We were unused to this hearty fare. My mother knew it was too rich, but every time the food arrived, we nevertheless grabbed our spoons and set to it as though it was our last meal on earth. One pitcher of water wasn't enough for us after a meal like that; we needed two. Naturally, we would start to go out to the toilet. Not once, twice, or thrice, but more. And when they would turn off the spirit lamp outside and the house quieted, we lay down, not to sleep but to quench the inferno raging in our bellies. We both, I especially, felt we had a lot to empty out! My mother would go a couple of times in the middle of the night, but then forbear for shame; but for me, there was ceaseless coming and going.

When she grew tired of this, she would say threateningly, "That's enough! This is the last time you leave the room, you uncouth boy! It's pitch black outside, and the wicked witch has diarrhea same as you. I could see her going into the bathroom. Do you want to go to the toilet with her? Do you?"

Once I was properly petrified with fright, my mother would then start to take security precautions, first making sure that both windows were securely shut, both glass and shutters, and capable of keeping out any would-be intruder. Next, she would draw the dead bolt all the way shut, then pull up every chair and movable piece of furniture in the room against the door. She would stand still for a moment, her head moving gently from side to side as she recited some verses from the Holy Book while I watched, wide-eyed.

My grandmother started coming into our room. She would stand at the doorstep and ask my mother if she was comfortable. My mother would indicate 'yes,' whereupon she would steal a glance at me, then leave us alone. Once she came in, and I ran to her and kissed her hand as per my mother's previous prompting. That time, she came in and sat on the edge of the bed next to me and my mother and placed a hand on my shoulder. Her silk head scarf touched my face: it was smooth, and tickled, so I started playing with its edges and stroking a hand over it. She kept looking at me, something playing around her lips, like a smile. She mentioned my father to my mother, and they both burst into tears.

On the third day, I had had enough of waiting. I tried—an independent initiative—to break the siege and go outside. I pushed the door ajar and slipped warily out. I took two steps out, eyes latched onto the sunlit space in front of the barn. The calf was lying there, eyes looking in surprise at this world into which he had come. I only made it a third step—after that, all I felt was a sponge-broom landing on my head and a pair of older boys landing on top of me and bearing me to the ground. A third boy—no, a girl with short hair, wearing pajama pants so that she looked like a boy—seemed to have sprung up out of the earth, stamping her feet and pointing a small stick in her hand at my head, screaming at the top of her voice for me to put my hands in the air and turn myself in!

They had me, the imps. The only insult I managed to choke out was met with a volley of insults. Everyone came at the hullabaloo. My mother didn't say a word. She snatched me out of their grasp, as the wounded are lifted from the field of battle, and closed the door against any child who might wish to sneak in and repeat the incident. It was my grandmother who took it upon herself to defend us: she brought a stick down on the back of the eldest boy, whereupon commenced a battle between her and the boys' mother—her daughter—that lasted an hour. We could hear her saying that I was the son of her son, and that I had as much right and more to the house as her children.

When night fell, my grandfather learned of what had happened, and he made my aunt come into our room and apologize to my mother. He sent instructions that we were to come out and partake of meals with the family.

Morning came, and we came out for breakfast. My grandfather sat on his seat with a tray before him. On the ground, the length of the path, were three trays: one for my grandmother, along with us; the second for my uncle Ibrahim's wife and her children—my uncle had been up late in the fields last night, and was still asleep in bed—and a tray for my two aunts, accompanied by the third aunt and her children who had attacked me. At dinner, upon orders from my grandfather, I moved to sit by him and eat at his tray. I ate a piece of testicle and oxtail with him, which were delicacies reserved for him alone. The boiled meat was for everyone.

My uncle Ibrahim came over when we were having tea. He ignored us, and my mother and I, for our part, did not look at him. When my grandmother admonished him to say hello to my mother, he made as though not to hear her and entered into conversation with my grandfather. In spite of this, he never stopped stealing glances at us surreptitiously.

I didn't see him much after that. He was always either busy in the fields or fighting with his wife. My mother didn't like him and would not leave her room if she heard his voice outside. The times I did see him, we ignored one another roundly. He would pass before me as though he didn't see me, while I would stand stock-still as soon as I glimpsed him, letting him pass in peace. This was how we were all the time, and yet I was drawn to him, staring at his back every time until he was out of sight, fascinated by his broad shoulders and extraordinary height, and wishing I could have such a build when I grew up. My mother's family was not as tall as this: even my grandfather Zaki wasn't as tall as all that.

My uncle remained an enigma to me. To this day, I do not know whether he loves me or hates me. I remember him patting my head once, when I was sitting on the step of the outer door, playing with my grandfather's rosary. As soon as I raised my head, he left. Another day, he was handing out pennies to his children and called me over to take a penny too. I held out my hand to him warily, and he looked at me strangely. He raised his eyebrows, looking long and full at me as he gave me the penny.

13

As soon as my grandfather was done with the afternoon prayer, his favorite ritual began: Imam, carrying a mat and two cotton bolsters on his shoulders, would hurry ahead of us to the western wall of the house. The shade would by now have covered the stalks of greenery opposite us and crept up to the middle of the wall. In the distance, the Eucalyptus trees stood clustered round the creek at the entrance of the village. The rings of black smoke that ascended from the mill would have started to fade, and the number of donkeys outside it decreased to four or five at most, and even those, by this time, were being readied for return, bearing sacks of flour.

My grandfather would be pliant in Imam's hands: Imam would take him by the shoulder and armpit and lower him to the center of the mat, placing a bolster at his back and another as an armrest. He would then start sprinkling water on the earth of the clearing that separated us from the plants. My grandfather would look at me for a moment, but no sooner did I return his glance than he would suddenly become absorbed in stretching out his legs, then pull his rosary out of his waistcoat pocket. Next, he would take off his turban and place it at his side.

I had found it strange at first to see him bareheaded: his face looked different when he exposed his head, shaved completely bald with a razor, not a single hair on it. I would feel that he had lost something of his stature and look with awe at the turban that had the magical power to transform him utterly. How I wished, back then, to put it on my own head, even just for a moment, when he wasn't looking!

My grandfather never seemed at ease while Imam still held the water pitcher. He never took his eyes off him while he moved, and unconsciously fumbled for his turban whenever Imam sprinkled near, pulling it toward him. If it did get splashed with water, usually mixed with mud, my grandfather's face would cloud over and he would fling something or other at the man: a slipper, an empty glass, the cover of the water pot, or indeed the water pot itself, yelling at the top of his voice, "Look where you're working! Are you blind or what?"

Sometimes he would pull his stick toward him and half rise, whereupon Imam would drop the pitcher and race off. I would be scared too and stick my feet out in search of my sandals.

A stone's throw away, an old dog lay asleep. He slept all the time, only waking at this noise, whereupon, ascertaining the cause, he would rise upon his two front legs and start barking at Imam, in homage to my grandfather. He would only stop barking when my grandfather would wave him down, saying softly and somewhat melodiously, "That's enough, Artichoke." This was his name. He had grown up with my grandfather and obeyed only him. They had been together so long that they had come to understand one another, and they had their own language, a kind of code.

The fight quickly over, Imam would return, his tread careful, warily eyeing my grandfather's stick. He would then kneel on the edge of the mat and set down a copper tray bearing glasses, a teakettle, a sugar bowl, a packet of tea—a brand called al-Sheikh al-Sharrib, or The Sheikh Who Likes His Tea—and an ancient Primus stove the like of which I had never seen before. They said it was the only thing that remained of my grandmother's trousseau and that when my grandfather had found it among the pile of old odds and ends in the storage room, he had insisted upon getting it repaired, and kept it for himself.

Imam would bend over the stove, turning off the gas valve, then pump the air compression valve inward several times, until a thin jet of gas burst out of the mouth of the stove. This he lit with a match, and little by little the flames would grow higher.

This was not an easy process for Imam. The poor man would be dripping with sweat at the effort it took to light this ancient stove, which was four years older than my uncle Ibrahim. He did not dare to say so, though, for fear of the stick that lay across my grandfather's lap, especially since my grandfather kept a close eye on his movements. The fault, Grandfather would always say, lay with Imam, not the stove.

Imam would finally breathe again, after reassuring himself that the stove was hissing strongly and continuously, and the steam was rising in a low whirr from the teakettle upon it.

The place where we sat was out of the wind—not a breath of air could reach it. My grandfather sometimes stretched out his legs and pulled out a handkerchief to mop the sweat that had collected on his head, or hung in droplets from his eyelids, or trickled down behind his ears. Suddenly, he would lean forward, taking hold of the back of the collar of his gallabiya, shaking it in annoyance, whereupon I would guess that a drop of sweat was trickling down his back.

In spite of this, he never changed his spot: he said that it was well out of the dust of the path, and away from the doorstep and all its comings and goings. Also, a strong breeze would occasionally spring up, coming over us, shaking the leaves of the mulberry trees next to us, making them whisper. When this happened, my grandfather would lose control of his gallabiya; it would fly up, and I could see his legs, naked up to mid-thigh, and note with surprise his right knee, swollen much larger than the left. In such moments, I would be overcome by my childish feeling of how nice he was, how amiable and innocuous as he found the same joy I did in the breeze slipping into the crevices of his clothing and blowing his gallabiya around. I would follow his head tilting backwards, the shadow of a smile on his face. But whenever he saw me watching, he would frown and cover his legs up, pinning the hem of his gallabiya beneath his heels.

Once, at my mother's behest, I asked him to take me to visit my father's grave. But he shook his head without looking at me, then put his chin in one hand, and stared off into space.

Imam came to us, saying softly, "There now, Hagg! It's God's will after all!"

I sneaked a glance at my grandfather, noticing the tic in his left eye. He stayed silent and unmoving. I grew flustered, unsure of what to do. I found myself shuffling on my rear a few inches away from him and watched a lame goose lurching by in front of us, a line of featherless baby goslings tripping along behind her, stumbling and struggling to keep up.

The tension was only broken by the arrival of two friends of my grandfather's. His face lit up at their approach.

They were about the same age as him. One of them sat next to me, the other coming to rest cross-legged in front of my grandfather, having first taken off his slippers, slipped them neatly into one another, and placed them beneath him. The man next to me was quite dark-skinned and almost toothless. As soon as he sat on the mat, he pulled out a packet of Abu Ghazala brand tobacco and a small pack of rolling papers. He pulled one out, trimmed it with his teeth, and started to stuff the tobacco into it. His companion—fat, with a face as round as a loaf of pita bread—sat watching him until he had completed his task, then pulled out a pack of Hollywoods and took out a cigarette. They lit up together, my grandfather fanning the smoke away from himself, and from me, as best he could with his hand.

The two men started to talk, especially the darker one sitting by me: he never stopped talking or gesturing with his hands. Naturally, I was unable to avoid being bumped by his elbow, which hit me on the shoulder on the rare occasions it missed my head. I followed the conversation avidly, though, mesmerized by the country dialect they spoke. The darker man sometimes used words I did not know, and followed them with a wink of his left eye, saying to my grandfather, "Remember, man, when we—do you remember, or do you need me to remind you?"

My grandfather would relax, throwing his head back, and grin. "Remember? How could I forget, Abu Rizq!"

"Or when . . ." the fat man interjected.

My grandfather, enjoying the conversation, would say, "And who could forget that!"

The darker man let go completely, enjoying himself so thoroughly that he let loose and started to jab my grandfather playfully in the stomach with the small cane in his lap. My grandfather's face darkened, and he whispered to the man without looking at me, "The boy!"

Noticing me for the first time, the man felt my head and said, "Who's your father, my fine fellow?" Finding me silent, he added, "Are you Ibrahim's boy?" Then he turned to my grandfather, smiling. "Or is he your boy, Abu Mahmoud, and I didn't know? Tell us the truth, man; go on!" The fat man elbowed him, whispering in his ear. "Ah!" cried the darker man. "The Jewish woman's son! Well, well, well! So this is her kid, then?"

I trembled, and everyone fell silent. Close to me, I noticed a faint motion between the plant pots. I looked hard at it. The air was misty with late afternoon, the sun's disk almost gone.

My grandfather gave me a penny and told me to go and play with the other children.

They were all the way on the other side of the house. I approached them, and they paused in their play, watching my approach with silent glares of derision. I turned away from them and headed for our room.

I told my mother about what had happened with the other children, and she said comfortingly, "You've got friends among your own kind. Rachel, your cousin; and David, Mr. Samaan's son; and Marika and Cookie, Auntie Hanna's children. The kids here are backward clods; they're no use to anyone."

"What about Hassan?"

"Hassan? Hassan who?"

"Hassan, our neighbor. Umm Hassan? Did you forget them?"

She started guiltily and shook her head. "Yes," she said almost inaudibly. "Hassan, too."

14

I HAD BEEN DRESSED SINCE sunrise, in my shirt and short pants, and my shoes with the buckles. My mother wrapped a dark shawl around her dress and wore black shoes and stockings. We sat on the edge of the bed, awaiting a signal from the passageway. Then we heard two rapid, stentorian coughs outside our window that indicated my grandfather was calling for us.

We emerged to find him at the outer door, leaning on his stick, watching Imam place the velvet saddle on the she-mule reserved for his personal errands. Artichoke was by his side, pacing back and forth with uncharacteristic vigor.

We heard a faint squeak from the catch of the window where my father's wife was. It opened, and she looked out in her nightdress, her expression not merely angry, but venomous. My mother avoided her gaze. She moved away, leaning one hand on a doorjamb, her other hand curling around my wrist.

My grandfather turned toward us, and in a flash, my father's wife closed the crack in the window. My mother and I readied ourselves, and he threw us a silent glance.

I pulled my wrist out of my mother's grasp and approached him, hearing her soft reproach as I did so. Grandfather noticed us and looked down at me, a faint smile playing on his lips. Then my mother pushed me toward him and he picked me up, his breath covering my whole face.

His brows were thick, more white than black. I took a long look at the scar beneath his neck, which showed clearer as the neck of his gallabiya slipped down. I felt it with my fingertips as he gazed at me pensively. It was the first time I had been so close to him. When I touched the button of his turban, he showed no anger. It was my mother who froze, petrified with fright. She bit her lower lip warningly and hurried forth to take me. But he waved her away, laughing, and bent his head to allow me even better access.

Afterward, he looked at his bedroom and cleared his throat twice. Clearly, this was the signal for my grandmother: her voice immediately sounded from within, saying, "I'll be right out!"

"Shouldn't you have worn a good peasant dress, Umm Galal?" he said to my mother.

She looked down, saying nothing. My grandmother had arrived and indicated to him that he should ignore this matter, so he said no more. My grandmother noticed my father's wife looking at us through the crack of her door and said in surprise, "Still in your housedress, my girl?"

"Sorry, Aunt; I've a headache," the other woman replied indolently.

My grandmother appeared incensed. "Girl, you were fine a moment ago! Now you're using your women's wiles? Go on; get dressed. You're coming with us."

She came out. "Coming?" she snapped. "Coming where, Aunt? Why, even God's law says that infidels aren't to enter the tombs of Muslims! And you want me to come as well?"

My mother hung her head. My grandmother shouted at my father's wife, "What's with you, you little snot? Is this what we agreed? Right, back to your apartments, and I'll have words with you later, daughter of Marzouq."

My grandfather cleared his throat warningly, whereupon everyone fell silent. He made for his mule.

Grandfather mounting the mule's back was no simple matter. Imam tried to accomplish this task and failed twice, all the time being reproved by my grandfather because he had not brought one or two able-bodied men along to assist him. Artichoke made matters worse with his ceaseless barking, which attracted other dogs who took to barking, too. He growled at them, as if to say this was an internal affair concerning him only, and none of their business.

Rescue arrived, in the form of a passerby who took hold of my grandfather low down around his waist while Imam held onto his shoulders, both pushing him up: the mule took a step forward, though, and only Divine Providence saved Grandfather from sliding off the animal's rump.

Imam ran to and fro, my grandfather's shouting echoing far and wide behind him. Artichoke, understanding the problem, barked loudly in his wake. Finally, we were joined by a man built like a bull, accompanied by a boy from a neighboring alley. The boy held onto the rope around the mule's neck, while the three men gathered round my grandfather. One good push, then another, and he was perched atop the beast.

After a moment, my grandfather, supremely unconcerned with the hubbub that had centered on him, opened his umbrella to shade himself from the sun, whereupon the mule moved off of her own accord.

We walked in a small procession: my grandfather on his mule, with Imam's hand on its neck, while my grandmother, my mother, and I followed on foot. Upon seeing Artichoke in our company, my grandfather commanded him to turn back. He gave a doggy frown, growling resentfully, then obeyed, lying at the gate, looking at us until we were far away.

The graveyard was all the way at the other side of the village, and the only way to get there was through its streets and alleys. My grandfather took the lead, greeting all who passed in a booming voice. Men congregated at the steps of the mosques, on street corners, and in front of shops, said hello back, and made way for him. They weren't really watching him, though: they were too interested in the people following behind. They made us out at a distance, and then the whispers would start. As soon as we drew close to them, they fell silent, then began to talk again once we were past. Through the window shutters and slits in the casements moved shadows of women and older girls, some looking behind them and calling to the others to come and look at us, increasing the number of faces looking down at us. The women's voices rose, then subsided suddenly. The older women only watched us silently, without making any movement. When I pointed out to my mother two women pointing at us as they sat on the roof of one of the houses, she poked me in the stomach to shut me up.

News of our procession reached every corner: there was not a villager, young or old, who had not come out to watch us. Even the dogs that lay in the street raised their heads to look at us: some rose to their front paws and barked at us until we had moved away, while others contented themselves with looking up at us and sinking back into sleep.

The strange thing was that my grandfather had disappeared; we couldn't see him moving ahead of us any more. This concerned me, and at every turn of a street or alleyway, I looked as far as I could in search of him, but it was no use. I could find nothing for it but to suggest to my mother that I run on ahead quickly to see if I could find any news of his whereabouts, whereupon she hit me in the back, saying, "Oh, God; that's all I need." She tightened her grip on my wrist, while I tried fruitlessly to wriggle out of her grasp.

"Easy, now," said my grandmother. "She turned her head and addressed herself to me. "Don't worry about him. You see, sonny, your grandfather prefers not to be seen traveling with women. It's the village custom."

I remained unconvinced, though, and kept looking ahead, hoping to catch a glimpse of him from afar. I don't know why Naguib al-Rihani crossed my mind: I was overcome by the fear that my grandfather would drop dead suddenly, as al-Rihani had.

Two streets and four alleyways later, we saw the cemetery in the distance. We sobered, one and all, especially me: I was overcome with an unfamiliar, unprecedented sensation, as though I were being led to a world unlike the one I saw and experienced every day, a world I had feared since I was little, ever since I had found out that once friends and family went there, they never returned.

The gravestones became clearer before my eyes the closer we came. I looked at them with eagerness and awe. A tear sprang to my mother's eye, and she palmed it away, bowing her head, her neck looking even thinner than usual. Her hands lost their resolve, swinging back and forth more slowly. My grandmother's face stilled. Neither of them spoke.

I was still a child, with a child's quicksilver emotions. I forgot my sober mood when I saw a gaggle of children my age, standing in a line on the side of the road. They started to lift up their gallabiyas in unison and took to urinating simultaneously, as though in some kind of contest. I was entertained by what they were doing and asked my mother to be allowed to join them, for which I received a slap on the nape of the neck.

Then I asked her about the goats, sheep, donkeys, and everything else I saw on the road, especially about the woman walking next to us—who, as soon as one of the buffaloes dropped a cow pat, soft and odoriferous, pounced on it, picked it up joyfully, and placed it in a bowl she carried on her head—all the while receiving pokes and pinches on the ear from my mother. My grandmother watched in silence, her fatigue starting to show. My mother slowed her pace out of consideration for her.

When we were almost at my father's grave, we found my grandfather sitting on a seat made of palm fronds. He was bent over, such deep sorrow roiling on his face that he did not notice our arrival. Imam had a stick in his hand, at the ready to defend him against any dog or cat that might think to approach. Flies filled the place: strange flies, much larger than houseflies. They had no respect for my grandfather: they buzzed around his face, and he shooed them away mechanically with a hand, eyes half-closed.

At the edge of the neighboring field, a donkey nibbled the grass. Another donkey approached, challenge in his eyes. The first donkey snorted, pawed the earth twice, and prepared for combat. In a moment, they were exchanging kicks. My grandfather, displeased, bent for a stone, which he then threw at them. Imam ran toward them with a stick, whereupon they ran off after one another, trampling flower beds in their path.

My mother and grandmother sat, cross-legged, at the grave. Out of the blue, a Qur'an reciter appeared, although today, we had been told, was not a visitors' day. My grandfather motioned to him, and he sat at some distance away, singing his verses from the Qur'an, dispelling the silence around us. The words broke softly upon my heart, flowing upon my soul in the same rhythm I had heard from Sheikh Damanhouri on my journey to get the beans every morning. I found myself dreaming, clasping a fistful of the sand spread out in front of the grave, letting it flow out from between my fingers. Again and again, grasping the sand and watching it flow. I felt a weight on my heart, my chest tight, as though the world didn't have a breath of air left in it. My grandfather appeared to hear the voice of the reciter: he leaned his chin on his stick, allowing his eyes to roam over the graves that stretched out before him. Paces away from him, the mule lay on her side motionless, eyes open.

My mother was saying prayers under her breath: she only stopped when my grandmother whispered to her that there should be no talking during a reading of the Qur'an.

Atop the grave was a marble tablet, inscribed with a verse from Surat al-Qamar: *As to the Righteous, they will be in the midst of Gardens and Rivers / In an Assembly of Truth, in the Presence of a Sovereign Omnipotent.* Beneath that was an inscription: "Here lies Mahmoud Abd al-Hamid al-Minshawi, Martyred in the Tripartite Aggression on November 3, 1956." My mother contemplated it, grief writ on her face; with the hem of her shawl, she wiped away the dust that covered it. My grandmother shooed away a column of flying insects making its way to the mouth of the tomb.

When my grandfather rose to his feet, that was the order to return. My grandmother asked him to stay a while, but he ignored her request and headed for his mule. Imam rushed ahead of him, looking about him for a savior who would relieve him of the task of getting my grandfather back up onto the mule. My grandmother looked very pale, a light sweat on her brow, looking to my eyes as though she had grown older on the way. She hid her face in her black scarf, muffling stifled sobs. My mother clung to her arm. Her eyes, too, were filled with tears.

On the way back, I decided to split off from my mother and grandmother and join the front of the procession. My grandfather had no objection and ordered that I be placed up on the mule behind him.

Before we went to bed, my mother told me, "We'll be leaving in the morning."

"Can't we stay?"

She was stunned. "We don't need to stay any longer." Then she explained that we had visited my father's grave and met my grandfather, plus Hagga Umm Mahmoud had promised to see to our expenses. Why, then, should we stay on?

15

GRANDFATHER'S HEADDRESS WAS OFF, AND he was lounging on the bench. Uncle Ibrahim, wearing a long-sleeved undershirt and tight cotton long johns, sat half-reclined on the bench opposite, taking tea with my grandfather as they talked of laborers, melons, watermelons, and zucchini, and the shocking dearth of profit these had made, or rather not made, this year.

My grandfather's face lit up with smiles as he saw me coming toward him. He picked me up and sat me down beside him, occupying himself with adjusting my clothing. He tied my shoelaces tight and said, patting my hair, "You're really going, Galal?" He took a sweet out of his pocket and put it in my hand, stroking my neck, now fast, now slow, as I leaned this way and that in delight at the tickling. When I told him to stop, he said, laughing, "All right, I will, but on one condition. You have to stop here with me—stay with me here for good! You let your mommy go home all alone, and I'll have a peasant gallabiya made for you and take you out into the fields with me!"

Even at my age, I understood that he was only kidding, and I leaned my head back and shook it no. "Are you sure?" he said, tempting me. "I'll let you ride the mule every day!" I shook my head. "And I'll let you play with Artichoke!"

"Yeah, why not, Dad?" my uncle cut in. "Have him stay."

My uncle's face did not show any of the joking mood evinced in my grandfather. I shuddered at his words and turned to Grandfather. He pressed a reassuring hand to my chest, then looked up at my uncle as though to say, "Say something nice or say nothing."

My uncle seemed not to get it, though. He sat up, going on, still deadly serious: "Yes. Yes. He'll be brought up with the others."

Grandfather sent another look his way, clearly telling the man to stop scaring me, but said nothing. My uncle, though, kept talking. "It would be better, after all. They're saying he's our son, aren't they? He can just stay here and be raised with us. Yeah, be raised with us. Or are you going to let him go back with that witch, Dad? Some dubious woman we don't know anything about?"

Grandfather's face darkened, and he huffed audibly. My mother appeared, bearing her suitcase, accompanied by my grandmother. Silence reigned. The inner rooms were still. Every woman sat glued to her window, watching us through it, although neither I nor any of those assembled could see a single hair of their heads nor hear a single whisper indicating their presence: they were too experienced at these matters.

My grandfather waved my mother to a seat opposite him, and every eye clung to him. He picked up a roll of paper by his side and offered it to my mother. He told her to open it and count the money inside. When she demurred, he insisted.

There were pound notes, and fifty-piaster notes, and twenty-five piaster notes, and ten-piaster notes, and two five-pound notes. She counted it all, twice, then looked up at my grandfather. He indicated to her that she should count it a third time. She did so, and banded the notes with a thin elastic band from her handbag. Then she said to my grandfather, "This is a hundred pounds, Uncle!"

Uncle Ibrahim was visibly taken aback at hearing her say 'Uncle.' He looked from her to my grandfather in surprise, then half-turned to my grandmother, dusting his hands in disgust. She frowned, and I saw her raise her finger to her lips to silence him.

"How many months will this last you?" my grandfather was asking my mother.

She politely declined to reply, saying instead, "I'm very grateful to you, Uncle, of course. We have enough for our needs, praise the Lord, and my father doesn't let us want for anything."

"My dear, this is only my duty, and this boy—" he patted my shoulder—"is my responsibility. I'm the one who must provide for him, not anyone else." He took a breath. "And you, too; as long as you're raising him, and taking care of him as the Lord would have it, I must support you: your food and drink and clothing, that is all my duty to provide." He leaned forward on his walking stick and used his fly whisk to shoo away a fly that was buzzing around my face. Then he scratched his head and said low, almost in a whisper, "My dear girl, haven't you yet . . . ?"

"Do you mean, I haven't converted yet, Uncle? No, not yet. I have decided to do it, but there hasn't been an opportunity yet. I had agreed with—" And my mother was seized with a violent fit of coughing. My grandmother hurried to her with a pitcher of water, and my grandfather indicated to her that she should catch her breath and not speak. She went on, though, in a choked voice, "Don't worry about Galal, Uncle. Galal's a Muslim, and I have a neighbor called Umm Hassan whose husband is an Azharite sheikh. She takes him into her house, and the sheikh educates him on fasting and prayer and teaches him the Qur'an by heart." She added enthusiastically, "Why, he has many chapters committed to memory already!" She turned to me. "Isn't that so, Galal?"

I knew my mother was lying, but I went along and said, "Yes, it's so."

My grandfather was silent a long time, then said, "My daughter, you are free to do as you please when it comes to your own self; my only concern is for Galal. It's not the time for such talk, though. With God's will, we will speak of this again in the future. Let's talk of the present. How many months should this money last you?"

"It'll last five months, maybe even longer."

"That's what I thought."

My uncle, apparently, still had not taken it all in. He suddenly burst out, interrupting: "Listen, Umm Galal! I think the best thing would be for you to get lost, and leave Galal here to live and be brought up with us. I've just been discussing it with my father."

My mother did not reply, seeking rescue in my grandfather's eyes. He cleared his throat and said, weighing his words, "That won't do just now, son. The boy is still a child, and he's still attached to his mother. The future is before us, and God will decide in the fullness of time."

My mother added, "He's starting school this year, too. His uncle Shamoun has enrolled him already."

My uncle turned right round to face my mother. "Shamoun? Shamoun who?"

My mother was taken aback. "Shamoun is my elder brother."

Loudly, he exclaimed, "For God's sake, you! What kind of a name is that, woman? And this Shamoun, is it a man that walks and talks like us, or what?"

My mother cringed. She seemed to shrink within the dress she wore, her fingers interlacing and twisting as I had seen her do before when she felt vulnerable and helpless. My grandfather, finally at the end of his rope, bellowed at my uncle, "Enough, Ibrahim! Say something decent or shut the hell up! What the hell business is it of yours if his name is Shamoun or Maymoun or Zarzour?"

"But, Father, you see—Are we to leave the boy in the clutches of those people? Why, even God's law says—"

"No, I don't see," my grandfather roared. "And furthermore, why are you sitting around like that? Get inside and put on a gallabiya like decent folk! Can't you see your sister-in-law is with us? For heaven's sake, have some couth, you great oaf!"

My uncle appeared taken aback. He still made to speak, though, which drove my grandfather over the edge. He bellowed like a bull: "I said, GO! Get up and make yourself decent!"

My uncle rose and walked off, muttering, my grandfather still shouting in his wake, "And before you spout off about God's law, go ask the people who know of such things, and get yourself some education first! Go to Sayyidna, the teacher at the kuttab, and ask him! Have him teach you your Qur'an all over again, because it's pretty obvious you didn't learn it the first time! Have him teach you that these are the People of the Book and we are bound unto them by a sacred covenant!"

My grandmother went off in my uncle's wake, then came back. The easy atmosphere of before was gone, though, and for the first time I could make out the forms of some of the people lurking behind the shutters: I heard them moving about, and I heard whispered curses and imprecations against me and my mother, accompanied by mutinous mutterings that we were infidels after all and that the so-called covenant was a figment of my grandfather's imagination.

Looking at my grandmother, my grandfather said, "There; they have enough for five months, and every month after that, remind me to send them twenty pounds with young Imam." He nodded, concluding in a voice thick with emotion: "Remind me? Could I forget? And when I'm gone—"

My grandmother interrupted him with the traditional, "Long life to you." And she pulled a small handkerchief from her clothing, wiping away a drop of sweat that clung to her eyelashes.

"—I entrust you to send the money every month after I am no more. And tell Ibrahim."

"I will. I will. Ibrahim has a kind heart—he's hotheaded and ill-spoken; that's all."

"I know," he answered her absently. "I know."

Imam arrived in the taxi that was to take us home to Cairo. My grandfather insisted that he wouldn't have his daughter-in-law going to the bus stop and taking a public bus like everyone else. Imam seemed unhappy to see us go. My grandfather said to him, "When winter comes, come to me at the start of every Islamic calendar month, and I'll give you something to deliver with your own hand to Umm Galal at her home. Do you know the house where she lives?"

"Yes, I do."

"What do you mean, you do? Of course you don't! Saying any old thing just to please me and hang the consequences; that's the way you've always been, lying cur!" And there was almost a fight—as usual—between him and Imam, had not my grandmother intervened and let him know that this was no time for fighting. My grandfather relented and said to Imam, "You take the cab to the door of the house. Take down the name of the street and the number of the house on a piece of paper, and you hand it to me as soon as you get back."

"Yes, Hagg."

My mother bent to kiss my grandfather's hand. He hesitated a minute, then let her. He patted her shoulder, then held out his hand to shake hers. It was the first time he had ever done so: since her arrival, his hand had not touched hers, and he had only spoken to her at a distance.

My mother nudged me forward, telling me to kiss my grandfather's hand. I did; not only that, I flung myself into his arms and he lifted me up high. I clung to his neck as he shook with laughter and kissed every inch of me his lips could reach. My grandmother did the same, her eyes filling with tears.

Uncle Ibrahim arrived, wearing a freshly ironed gallabiya and a woolen cap with a crease like a knife-edge. He said goodbye with a glare, then took me and placed me in the cab without a word.

When my mother and I were seated in the backseat, the women of the house clustered around the gate, surrounded by the boys and girls. They kept staring at us, but we exchanged no words, nor even gestures. The car drove off, and I looked at the shops, at the children running alongside the cab, at the chickens and ducks sauntering in front of us, heedless of the automobile and its horns. When we crossed the bridge beyond which the route began, I looked outside the car, losing myself in the fields, which spread out thickly on both sides, and the people coming at us on foot or on donkeys' backs. Little by little, the car picked up speed; I relaxed into the seat, looking out the window at the trunks of the Eucalyptus trees speeding by.

16

MY GRANDFATHER ZAKI SAID MY mother wasn't to pay a penny toward the household expenditures, and that was final. "The money you got from Galal's family goes into a post-office savings account in his name for a rainy day."

When school time approached, as was my grandfather's wont, he bought me a shirt whose sleeves, fully extended, dangled off my fingertips by a full two inches, and a positively dismal pair of pants. The school's instructions were, "Shorts should fall two inches below mid-thigh," whereas my grandfather believed they should, in the name of future expansion, fall three inches below the knee and he saw no harm in them being as big as pajama pants.

The shoes, though, managed to get past him: in the store, I tried on the larger sizes he pointed out, feeling my feet getting lost inside them and trying and failing to keep them on. For my part, I exaggerated the absurdity of the situation with my lurching gait and my hands, which I placed on the salesman's shoulders like a baby learning to walk and about to fall at any moment, my grandfather half-watching and shaking his head.

He leaned toward my mother and told her to ignore my antics, and that the shoes on my feet—two sizes too large— were the best, and if I used them well, they would last me three years. He suggested stuffing a piece of fabric or an old sock into the toe of each shoe to keep my feet securely wedged into them. She remained unconvinced, though; after much discussion between them, he gave in and I walked out of the store in a pair of shoes that were my size.

My shoes were a continual headache to my grandfather. He bought such cheap shoes that I would come home a month later, sometimes a scant two weeks, with the sole coming off from toe to heel, or else missing entirely. He would then make the rounds of the stores to get them repaired. One time I came back with only one shoe on; I had kicked a stone in the street, whereupon it had flown off and fallen into an open manhole.

My grandmother nearly killed me that day, grinding a coin into my earhole and twisting it mercilessly while I howled at the top of my lungs. Angrily, she commanded my mother to go and withdraw the cost of a new pair of shoes from the savings account with the money we had gotten from the village, for my grandfather—as she said—would not buy me anything out of his own money in the future. Meanwhile, I ran from her, being chased all the while, crying, "You stay out of it! My grandfather loves me, and he'll buy me everything I want, you nasty old meanie!"

My school days were not entirely free of unpleasantness. On weekly uniform inspection day, during the morning lineup, the first pupil their eyes would light on would of course be me: I was conspicuous, a skinny child swimming in a shirt so big it resembled a straitjacket more than anything, pants that would have fit one of the teachers, and men's socks that fell dismally from my knees, where they should have rested, and flopped limply over the front of my shoes, exposing the broad elastic that girded the openings. They would crook a finger at me, always first in the penalty lineup. Then they would go up and down the lines.

I would generally be joined by the child who brought his books to school in a pillowcase, which his mother had hemmed on both sides with thick black thread and fashioned an outer pocket of an old woolen rag to hold his pens, rulers, and the rest of his school supplies, then added a handle made out of cord, transforming the pillowcase into something like a schoolbag. They would then pull out a further ten to fifteen pupils for various reasons: a tear in the pants or the shirt collar, the smell of eggs or garlic lingering about them, and shoe irregularities, which naturally took the lion's share.

Always, the distinctive odor of fesikh wafted out, ripe enough to make the revered headmaster choke; he would make a face, which was the signal for three teachers who were always at his side to fan out and form a search party. The source of the stink remained a mystery at the start—even to us pupils. The teachers would take to sniffing at us and shoving us in a bid to make us confess, looking around in all directions, as though in a race with one another to find the culprit.

Mr. Leheita, the P.E. teacher, was the quickest, clapping a hand on the shoulder of the son of Amm Girgis, who had a fesikh store at the corner of our street. Two rotten fishes, each nestled in half a loaf of pita bread! Green onions! A rotten tomato in the other pocket of his school smock! They would hold up his hand, proclaiming him "the dirtiest boy in the school!" The P.E. teacher then took him by the ear and dragged him bodily, handing him over to the headmaster. The latter would not deign to touch him, but pushed him with the point of his stick into the center of the quadrant formed by the four lines of students so we could all see him.

This was where Amm Tolba, the janitor, came in: he rolled up his wide sleeves and drew near with hurried steps, then picked him up with practiced ease, placing his rear end in an accessible position for the headmaster. That worthy blew into the palm of his hand, took a step back, then brought his cane down upon the offered posterior ten times, more if he happened to be in a bad mood.

After this, they would turn their attention to the pupils in the punishment line. We would hold out our hands, as we were accustomed to doing, and receive several strokes with the cane or the ruler. The strokes were not painful, for when the headmaster was done with Amm Girgis's son, his enthusiasm would wane—they would sometimes even go on with morning assembly, forgetting all about us and saluting the flag, while we would stand there unable to believe our luck at having gotten away scot-free.

This was nothing—indeed the arithmetic teacher's cane in class was also nothing—compared to the inescapable, insoluble issue of my schoolmates, who had found out somehow that my mother was Jewish. Hassan, myself, and Fahmi, the accountant's son, kept the matter silent like a military secret, and we never breathed a word of it. If it did occur to me, it merely flashed across my mind, after which I would quickly become distracted by the things that interested a boy my age.

But what could I do about the cousin of Zakariya the tailor, who lived in the building next to ours? Angered when I took Hassan's side in a quarrel between them, he kicked me, yelling derisively, "Get lost, son of a Jewess!"

I was dumbstruck, unable to think: I withdrew without another word. When the news spread around the school, the world became a cold and unfriendly place. I slept and woke in a constant state of misery and hung back, every day making a new excuse to avoid having to go to school. When my mother shouted angrily, I would take my book bag and set out, dragging my heels. Later, she would ask me the reason, but I would not reply. When she'd grow tired of asking, she would leave me alone. I'd stare after her retreating form.

I began to watch her when she was not looking. I would take long looks at her as she came and went in the house, as though rediscovering a thing I had not really fully known before. In the evenings, when she sat on the couch in the hall, reading from her holy book, my eyes were always on her, as though observing her committing a sinful act. I peered at her as she sat before the mirror in our room; I watched her every move, her hands as they combed her hair, or when she bent to pick up something she had dropped. When our eyes met in the mirror, I looked away.

Although I was very young, my heart began to chew upon things that must not be said. A strange grief would sweep over me, and on its heels, a sensation I could not place. I would rise and embrace her for no reason, and with a reproachful smile, she would always take me in her arms. Part of me would be consumed with regret and relax upon her shoulders, but another part would remain as it had been before.

I came to fear school. Some boy or other, it seemed, was always dogging my footsteps, but when I looked behind me, no one was there. I developed a fear of someone suddenly yanking down my shorts and exposing my nakedness to the other boys, or punching me unawares. I began to fear the boys sitting behind me in class. Feeling their presence, I was prepared to swear that not a single one of them was paying attention to the teacher: it was me their attention was focused on; they were whispering about me, and I was helpless to do anything about it.

There were fights, too. Bags, rulers, and the various objects strewn about in the school yard were all used as ammunition. Hassan and Fahmi, always on my side, stood by me, defending me: but what could they do against so many?

One day I came home from school after a huge fight, and insults that never stopped until the very mouth of our street. Imam was there. It had been months since he had been. He was uncharacteristically solemn. He said that my grandfather had passed away. His glass of tea had fallen out of his hand as he sat among friends, and he had passed away on the spot.

Unable to help myself, I blurted out a question: what had become of Artichoke? He said the dog had gone blind with grief, and then they had found him one morning on the doorstep, dead.

Imam asked of my mother that she come to the funeral, for my grandmother's sake. He offered to come and bring her by car, and drive her back the same day, but she declined. She was insistent as I looked on balefully, astonished.

17

MY LATE GRANDFATHER CAME TO me in a dream. It was as though I was playing with the calf in the barn back in the village. I spoke to it, and it answered. I made to pull its tail, and it ran away and hid. From outside, my grandfather's voice came to me. He sounded weak, pausing every few words to catch his breath. In the brief days I'd known him, I'd never heard him sound like that. Then I heard him coughing painfully, calling on my grandmother to bring him some water.

I went out searching for him, following the sound of his voice. I thought he might be in the room where my mother and I had slept. I headed for the room, the sting of fear inside me. There was not a sound in the house, not a movement, and the air was soft and misty.

I stopped at the door to the room. There were two dogs there, growling at one another, preparing for a fight. I turned away, into a corridor.

The benches were all packed with people: people not like us. They had long hair, like women's hair, hanging down to their shoulders, and they had catlike whiskers. My grandfather was not among them. When I approached, they fell silent. I stood apart, at some distance. Their eyes were all on me, staring. I had not noticed before that they glittered, too, like cats' eyes. One of them—I think it was the group's elder— invited me to come forward, but something whispered in my ear, *Get away. Run for your life, quick! Get away from here; run, run!*

But my feet wouldn't move. They were dead; the ground clung to them, and I no longer had any power over them.

I only remembered the dream as I was on my way home from school the next day. It came to my mind when I saw Muallim Habib, in his gallabiya and turban, on his usual seat outside the sugarcane juice store. I took the steps three at a time and flung myself upon my mother, pouring out my dream to her, panting, my heart bounding with emotion.

She looked at me. Lightly rubbing her forehead with a finger, she said, "I wish I hadn't been too shy to remind Imam of the money your grandfather promised."

Still breathing hard, I said, "I recognized my grandfather's voice, and his cough. I know them. And the people on the benches are bad people. They look scary."

My mother frowned, whispering, "It'll be a problem if that Ibrahim tries to hold back the money."

"It was him, my grandfather, I swear it! My grandfather Abd al-Hamid! I'm sure of it, and he was calling for my grandmother in the dream!"

When my grandmother Yvonne came to ask what was going on, my mother made a sign to me to go and change. I hung back, but she yelled at me to go on, and I heard her saying to my grandmother as I went into our room that she didn't know what was the matter with me, that she was at her wits' end: hardly eating and always daydreaming, and every night moaning in my sleep, getting startled every time she woke me.

I closed the door and stood there listening to what they had to say. They were speaking of my paternal grandfather: they said he was an ignorant yokel, and if my mother hadn't been in possession of official documents, he'd have thrown her out of his house and denied he so much as had a grandson. Then they took to cursing him in his grave, as well as his wife, saying she was 'a smarmy old biddy' and 'butter wouldn't melt in her mouth,' and they cursed 'that useless scarecrow' Imam for good measure. My mother then said that a billy goat had more sense than my uncle, and thanked the Lord that my uncle didn't have horns, or else he'd have surely butted her when she was in the village. She wondered at the Islamic religious law that deprived her of the right to inherit any of my grandfather's property.

"Weren't you married to his son? You had a child by him!" my grandmother railed.

"What about Galal's rights to his grandfather's estate?" my mother moaned.

"Yes! He gets part of everything! The fields, the house, the cattle, even the ducks and chickens and geese, too! And every little thing in that house!"

"And who dares tell them that?" my mother asked.

"I know they're fuckers. There's nothing for it but for your father to hire a lawyer. But there's the time factor. I'm afraid there'll be no time for that."

"I know," said my mother. "I wish I'd never made this miserable match! I could be getting ready to leave the country with you!"

When they were done talking, I stood silent for a while, then lay down on the bed in my school uniform. My mother called me to dinner, but I told her I wasn't feeling well and spent the rest of the day in bed, saying I had a headache.

Days passed, days when I couldn't stop seeing my grandfather, not just in sleep but in my waking hours too. He didn't come to me; I summoned him in my mind's eye. Our first meeting; the time he carried me aloft as I played with the button on his turban; the afternoons sitting next to him as the wind blew up his gallabiya. My grandmother: her calm face and high cheekbones, and the small mole next to her cheek. It wasn't black, but only very slightly darker than the rest of her skin, completely unnoticeable unless you really looked closely at her face.

After that, I never stopped talking about my paternal grand-father—not just to my mother or to my grandfather Zaki, but to the other boys. I said he was the umda of the village, and that he had guards and a jail where he could put you, and endless acres of land. I said that my uncle Ibrahim was the village elder now, and that the village people respected and feared him. I described what I imagined of his big house, and the elder's home, and the barn, which held fifty head of cattle—maybe more!—and the towering Eucalyptus trees all along the stream, and the women who went there carrying clothing and utensils for washing, and the boys who sneaked there to swim naked in its waters.

Hassan and Fahmi never tired of hearing about the country-side, of which they knew nothing, especially as I embroidered the tale with something new every day. Upon finding them impressed with something I said, I would give myself leave to expand, giving my fertile imagination free rein.

This vainglory affected me, all unawares: I first noticed it the next time one of the bullies confronted me. He cursed me as the son of a Jewess. I returned it with an even more heinous insult upon his own mother, and added, my voice rising, that I was the son of a village elder. I returned punches with kicks, and anyone lying in wait for me would be attacked without fear. Hassan and Fahmi spread the news and told the other schoolboys that my family back home in the village had big poles and stout sticks, and if they came to visit they would surely break some bones. Even the headmaster himself, they said, would not escape their wrath.

Things started going my way. I was no longer easy pickings for the bullies. The one thing that still made my life unpleasant was the stares I got for my too-large clothes.

Imam paid us another visit at the end of the school year. I came upstairs to find him sitting in the hall with my mother. His smile upon seeing me did not entirely conceal the ire on his face. When I came in, their conversation cut off abruptly, and the three of us were silent for a few moments. My mother was red in the face, and Imam busied himself with smoothing out the yoke of his gallabiya, a bit crumpled around his neck. White hair had begun to creep up the front of his hairline and appear at his temples. Surreptitiously, he stole glances at my mother. Seeing that I had noticed, he became suddenly very interested in his cap, jamming it down on his head, then pulling it off again, smoothing the edges and finally placing it on his lap.

I smiled, remembering how my grandfather used to take off his turban and keep it in sight at all times for fear of the water pitcher in Imam's hand.

Imam coughed twice, rather artificially. Then he offered to take me to visit my uncle—an offer directed to my mother, of course. He said beseechingly, "Just a day or two, Umm Galal, and I'll bring him home myself."

"No," she said. "Anyone who wants to see him can come here." When I made to speak, she made a gesture to me for silence. "I said no and that's final."

Before Imam left, he gave my mother the money for the months he had missed. My uncle kept up the payments after that, but he never came to visit us, not once.

18

Every Friday evening I would stay out in the street playing from the time the call to afternoon prayer sounded until after the evening prayer call, whereupon my grandmother would call down to me from the balcony to come upstairs. I would look up resentfully, not answering, whereupon she would call again, louder and angrier. I would play deaf. She would bend forward, a tell that she was taking off her orange slipper. At first she would just threaten with it, waving it in my face and that was all.

Her tactics changed, though, starting that summer; she began to throw it at me without warning, and the funny thing is that she never, ever missed, though her vision was cloudy at best. I hardly ever avoided the flat slipper with the red bow: it unerringly hit me in the head or side, or any other painful place she aimed at.

One time, I got lucky and evaded a body blow, instead catching the orange slipper in my hands like a ball. I went upstairs and threw it at her feet. My nervous system was on high alert. Sure enough, that was when her fingers, as of old, reached for my ear.

But that was in the past, Old Beaky! I was already gone, flown off to shower, eat dinner, and watch the Egyptian movie on television.

I liked to watch Fairuz, the child star: I would imagine myself in her place on the screen, dancing and singing and driving Anwar Wagdi, the star playing opposite her, to distraction. And yet, I never stayed long enough to see "The End." I would start to doze off around the middle of the movie; that is, if I managed not to fall asleep—deep sleep, complete with snoring—during the opening credits. If my mother or grandfather were still awake, one of them would pick me up and carry me to bed. My grandmother never did, saying that she had back trouble and that I weighed as much as a young calf, and that if she tried to pick me up, it would be curtains for her.

If a horror or action flick came on, though, my grandmother would lose her mind, dropping her work and planting herself squarely in front of the screen, her every sense aquiver with excitement as she hung onto the edge of her seat. As for my grandfather, he would stick his lower lip out in a kind of facial shrug and head off to bed, followed closely by my mother. When the evening was over, my grandmother would poke me in the chest and scream in my face to wake up. Naturally, I would bolt up in alarm, and she would lead me to bed by the hand, like a stray goat, and push me down to fall asleep by my mother's side. I would remain asleep until the call to Friday prayer rang out.

But this night was different. I woke in the dead of night with an urgent need to use the toilet. I felt for my mother, but she was not there. The hall light was on, and sounds emanated— sounds of bags being dragged—as silhouettes came and went against the glass of the door to our room. I could make out the voice of my cousin Rachel. She was talking to my grandmother, then she hurried toward the door to the apartment, followed by my aunt Bella, her high heels clicking as she said to my mother, "There's no time to take the photographs off the walls. There's no room for them in the suitcases anyway."

I got up out of bed, caught between surprise and sleep. Pushing the door open a crack, I stood there, watching.

My grandfather sat there in his navy blue suit, his gray tie unknotted, its ends hanging unevenly round his neck, the fabric slightly darker in the spot where it was usually tied. His shirt was dirty, collar half-off, the other half caught under the jacket collar, unnoticed by him. His tarboosh teetered precariously half-on, half-off the edge of the couch, wobbling at every movement.

My grandfather himself was gray in the face, as though he had aged ten years in an instant. His eyes were screwed up, his head bowed. I had seen this look on him before, when some disaster had struck. My grandmother was flitting about like a sparrow from room to room, giving instructions to my mother to take the savings club money from Umm Fouad, the midwife, and send it to her in francs with our relative Artin, who was going off to join them soon. Then she rushed to the balcony, answering the call of Haroun, her daughter Bella's husband, from downstairs in the street. Then she pressed my mother's shoulders instructing her to 'get that lout's permission for an exit visa for Galal' as soon as humanly possible. I had no way of knowing that 'that lout' was my uncle Ibrahim.

My uncle Shamoun came upstairs, taking the last suitcase. He said to my grandfather, panting, "This is no time to sit on the couch! Hurry up! Planes don't wait, you know!"

My grandfather got up. It took him three tries to do it. When he stood upright, he took to staring at his own photograph, the one that hung on the wall. It hung slightly askew, to the left. He adjusted the frame, and it tilted, now skewed to the right. He stepped closer, adjusting the frame with tiny movements of his finger.

My grandmother flew into a rage, screaming and pulling him by the sleeve of his jacket, but he ignored her completely, bending to take his tarboosh. She snatched it out of his hand, ranting that they were going to Paris, not to the sticks, and that if they saw that thing on his head there, he'd be the laughingstock of all and sundry. Then she told my mother to throw it out or give it to some unfortunate, such as the doorman or the man who fixed the gas burners.

My grandfather took my mother by the hand and said in low tones that that wouldn't be necessary. The tarboosh had been on his head for thirty years and wasn't fit for a dog now.

"They don't even wear them here any more," my mother responded tenderly. "I'll keep it for you and bring it with me when I come, and I'll bring all the pictures on the walls, too."

He smiled and embraced her, turning his face toward the door to our room. Our eyes met, and I rushed to him, bawling. He lifted me into his arms and pressed me close to his chest. It was the first time I had ever seen him crying and wiping away his tears with the heels of his hands the way I did.

My mother disengaged us, lifting me out of his arms when the car horn from below sounded louder. I looked around, hardly believing it. He seemed like another person, not the grandfather I knew and loved. He was silent, eyes lost, puffy, without even a hat on his head, clothing in disarray. He was in a pitiable state.

My grandmother took hold of him and led him out the door. With the creak of the closing door, he turned to me for an instant. He seemed to be trying to say something, but the words wouldn't come.

19

After my grandfather's departure, the household died; my mother lost her bloom. I went off to school while she was still asleep, and came home to find her still in bed. I would buy whatever from the grocery store to keep body and soul together, and she and I would spend most of the day without a word: she in her room, only emerging when there was no way around it, and I in the hall, either lying on the couch or doing my homework. I didn't have the heart to turn on the television.

Sometimes I would hear the click of the door handle to my grandfather's room and look up from my copybook. It would be my mother, who had gone in and left the door ajar. Without conscious volition, the fingers of my right hand would creep backwards, and the pencil end would come to rest between my lips, as I cautiously craned my neck to follow her movements. She would head directly for my grandfather's bed and stand looking pensively at it. It was high, the heavy quilt hanging off both ends, the quilt he always used. Its four brass posts stood there silently, the brass knobs on their ends, formed like a face with protuberant eyes, seeming to look at her wherever she went. My mother would adjust the quilt—an inch on this side, an inch on the other—and turn the pillows over. When she turned to face the wardrobe, our gazes would meet. Then, I would take the pencil out of my mouth and go back to my homework.

One evening, hearing the creak of the door to the wardrobe, I went back to looking. I saw her taking out my grandfather's tarboosh. She gazed at it, then placed it on her head. I smiled and looked at her even more intently. She took it off and stroked its sides with her palm, then replaced it.

She looked toward me, but I knew enough to appear occupied with what I was writing and not let her notice that I was watching. She bent to take one of my grandmother's old dresses out of the bottom of the wardrobe, briskly brushing off whatever clung to it, then dusted it with quick strokes of her hand.

In the silence in which we now lived, the blows rang out loudly, and in the daylight, with the sun streaming in through the shutters, I could see a fine cloud of dust ascend, then descend again, fine dust motes floating in the sunbeams. I could sense the warmth and heaviness of the air from the room coming toward me, as though I breathed my grandfather and heard his voice.

My mother came out, tears falling. She asked me if I missed my grandfather. I nodded yes.

As I sat there, hearing the children playing outside, I missed going out into the street. I went out onto the balcony. One of the children caught sight of me and yelled at the top of his voice, "Gel-gel! Come on down, Gel-gel!" They paused in their play and waved to me, calling to me from downstairs.

I made some excuse and went back inside. I thought I was keeping my lonely mother company by doing so, but when the children called to me repeatedly, she made me go out into the street and play.

When I went out, though, it was with no joy; it was as though I was ill and couldn't play. The truth of the matter was that my mother was not the only reason I stayed inside; I missed my grandfather, too.

Nobody knocked at our door for ten days. All the neighbor ladies were mad at my mother for not telling them when my family was leaving, thus depriving them of a chance to say a proper goodbye to my grandmother and my aunt Bella. My mother's apologies didn't appease them, and they'd suck on their lips disapprovingly or make faces when she came out onto the landing to call down to the doorman or put out the garbage.

We remained cut off from everyone, and might have remained so if it hadn't been for Umm Hassan. Although she reproached us first and loudest, she came to visit us, and the others followed suit.

Once she said to my mother, "Camellia, I'm afraid we'll wake up one fine morning and find you and Galal gone as well."

My mother did not answer, busying herself with tying the scarf tighter around her head, and asked me to go and get her a couple of pins from the dressing-table top.

"Where have Mr. Zaki and the rest of the family gone off to, then?" added Umm Hassan. Leaning to one side and scratching her side, a knowing expression coming over her face, she went on, "I hope, my dear, they haven't left us for that benighted country, Israel!"

My mother leapt to her feet, saying she heard something scratching around in the kitchen—probably the mouse that came into our apartment every day through the window onto the back stairs! With that, she rushed into the kitchen, slipper in hand.

Umm Hassan bent to take her own slipper off too, and I, believing my mother, flew off on their heels, armed with my grandmother's old slipper, whose toe I'd spotted peeking out from beneath the sofa.

In fact, that was the moment I discovered those orange slippers were still in the house. I wanted very much to throw them into the trash or toss them out into the street, the red bows and pointed heels buried under garbage and gone forever, but I relented. I couldn't get rid of them. When all was said and done, she was still my grandmother.

The window was closed. We turned the kitchen upside down. No mouse, not an ant, not a creature was stirring, not even a cockroach. The pots were all upside down, empty but for a lone pot in a corner giving off the smell of food gone bad. My mother shook her head, saying, "What on earth was that sound, though? It might have been the wind rattling the pots, I suppose!"

Umm Hassan looked over at the closed kitchen window and said, in a pointed tone that wasn't lost on my mother, "Could be. Could be." Then she added, chuckling, "What would a mouse find in here, anyway? The kitchen's cleaner than fresh-washed china! Really, Umm Galal, not even a crumb of bread in the house?"

That night, she came bearing a hot meal, and the same the next day. I was grateful, for it had been a month since my mother and I had eaten anything but beans, eggs, and tinned sardines.

20

My mother stopped making hot meals entirely up until my grandfather's first letter from Paris arrived. It seemed so impossible to me: my grandfather, who would take me to the movies, where we watched actors sing and dance in front of painted backdrops of the Eiffel Tower or the Arc de Triomphe, now lived in that fabled city, that setting of romantic fantasies. But the strange stamps and oddly lettered postmark on the envelope stood as proof. My grandparents really were in Paris. The first person he asked after was me, then my mother, and finally his friends, especially Muallim Habib.

He said that they had stayed for two weeks at the apartment of Mr. Labib Museiri, who was related to an aunt of his, and that he, my grandfather, with this accommodating gentleman's assistance, had been the first in the family to find work. He was a cleaner in a large fabric store owned by a wealthy Jewish gentleman in a district called Barbès. He and my grandmother now lived in a small apartment they had rented close to the store, on a street full of Arabs from Algeria, Morocco, and Tunisia. My grandmother didn't trust them, though, he told us, and had taken an especial dislike to the Tunisian who lived on the first floor.

My uncle Shamoun had not managed to find work for the longest time, until just a couple of days ago, when he had been taken on as a bellhop at Hotel De La Gare, by the St-Lazare railway station.

Grandfather had, he wrote, seen the Paris Opera twice—once, of course, from the outside—and found it a magnificent structure the like of which was not to be found in Egypt, but what was it, in his heart, compared to the Cairo Opera House? Forty years he had been coming and going in front of that grand hall, in all his comings and goings to and from Ataba Square!

He also asked my mother after the ten pounds owed to him by his ex-apprentice, who had bought the storefront from him, as though there was anything she could do about it now, and other trifling matters that he had left behind with us in Cairo.

A month later, another letter came, full of emotion. In it, he begged my mother to investigate the truth of a rumor that was being bruited round by the Egyptian Jews in Paris. It said that the Egyptian Ministry of the Interior had stripped Jews who had left the country voluntarily of their Egyptian citizenship and issued an ultimatum for them to return—a summons roundly ignored.

My mother went to see a Jewish friend of hers, a lady who worked in the home of Salvatore Cicurel, owner of the renowned upscale department store Cicurel's, hoping to get information, but the lady knew nothing. She went to our neighbor, Mr. Husni the accountant. He took down the names and particulars of my grandparents and all those who had left along with them and promised to inquire about the matter.

A long time passed, but whenever she passed the man in the street, all he would say was, "Things are very unstable, Umm Galal. Be patient; God grant you patience!" He would then clear his throat and excuse himself, saying he was late and his wife would be waiting.

Finally, there was a letter from my grandmother. Naturally, she never asked how I was, nor any of her ex-neighbors. The first few lines were all about the money from the savings club that had not yet reached her, and she cast some aspersions on the honesty of our relation, Artin, saying his morals were "elastic, just like his father," but that he couldn't give her the slip and that the moment she saw him, she would spit in his face and get the money back from him plus interest!

Then she said that my grandfather had sent his second letter to us behind her back, and when she learned of what was in it, she had spent an entire night fighting with him, and that furthermore, he was a senile old fool and my mother wasn't to listen to a word he said.

My uncle Isaac had finally come from Israel to pay them a visit, she said. He had married a Moroccan Jewess he'd met with her family on the boat out of Marseilles when he had immigrated to Israel. He was healthy and wealthy, praise the Lord, and had a good job over there. My aunt Bella, Grandmother wrote, was thinking of joining him there.

It was my uncle Shamoun who worried her: his employers had dismissed him from his job, saying he was negligent, plus they accused him of stealing a bath towel from one of the hotel rooms. But our relation Busiri, bless him, had found him another job at a well-known fabric store—not the one where Grandfather worked, this one was on the Rue de Rivoli—as a porter, again, although at a lower salary.

My grandmother expressed her astonishment at Shamoun's reluctance to immigrate to Israel, despite his brother's urgings. She and my grandfather, though, were not inclined to leave, preferring to stay where they were, at least until such time as my mother could rejoin them. She asked if my mother had done anything about finalizing my exit visa from my uncle Ibrahim, not forgetting to call him 'scum, son of scum' and a few more insults thrown in for good measure.

My mother's state improved with the arrival of these letters, and life gradually began to return to our apartment. The neighbor ladies began to visit as they had before. The conversation always started with them asking her if she was all right for money, and if she needed a loan or anything of that sort. One or two of them even fumbled in their bodices as though to take out their pocketbooks. My mother always waved these offers away, recognizing that they were merely for form's sake, dictated by custom, and had no real intent behind them.

After offering them something to drink, usually green tea, she would sit up straight for all to see and say softly, "I want for nothing. My father has left me a tidy sum in the savings account, quite enough to cover my expenses and Galal's." She never volunteered information about the money that came to us by way of my uncle Ibrahim.

If they kept talking, asking about sensitive issues such as our absent relatives, she never grew flustered. As though she had been rehearsing, she would say softly, "My mother is always complaining of how hard it is to live away from one's own home. All the world, she says, would never mean as much to her as a single day here, in the bosom of Egypt! The thing is, my father slipped and fell on the stairs of the building they're staying in over there . . . ."

At this, the neighbors would be hanging on her every word.

Sighing, she would go on, voice lower and unhappier than before, "Now he's gone and broken his hip, and he's had to have a pin put into his knee! That's what comes of leaving the place where you belong!"

Silence would reign for seconds, and then the neighbor women would hasten to offer get-well wishes of the stripe of, "May he soon be well! Zaki is older, after all, and not fit for these tribulations! The soul of decency and courtesy is Amm Zaki!" This came from the heart, for my grandfather was well loved by all on the street. The one they had reservations about was my grandmother.

One day, one of the women asked about my uncle Isaac, who was universally viewed with suspicion.

My mother cringed only a moment, then said, smiling, "Isn't he the lucky one! Living in Tunisia with his own carpentry business! He's really in clover! Why, he's the one paying all

Papa's doctor bills and supporting him, may God repay him for his kindness!"

One of the women looked up in astonishment. "Supporting Uncle Zaki? But where's Zaki, then? In Tunisia, or where?"

My mother nodded, seizing upon the response. "Yes, in Tunisia."

Another woman said suspiciously, "But Mr. Husni's wife says that Amm Zaki's gone to foreign parts, not Tunisia!"

The woman looked around for corroboration, and was joined by another, saying, "Yes, we heard that he was in I don't know, France or what d'you call it." And, with a nudge to the woman next to her: "What's it called again, Umm Abbas?"

When my mother answered, I noticed her hand wrapping around her left wrist, ceaselessly scratching at it with her thumb. She did this when she was lying, along with looking down and blinking more rapidly than usual.

The women fell silent, looking at one another surreptitiously, exchanging messages in code.

My mother eventually sensed their skepticism, losing patience with the game of cat-and-mouse. She began to make excuses not to meet them, and no longer opened the door when any of them came calling, except for Umm Hassan. That lady never badgered her with questions, and my mother still felt affection for her. As for me, I knew I was as dear to her as her own son Hassan.

One night, when my mother and I were chatting about my grandfather, I learned that but for my uncle Ibrahim, we would have been able to go with him. They had told her at the Passport Authority that as a minor, I could not leave the country, nor even have a passport, without the approval of a member of my father's family.

When she had sent this request with Imam, he repaid her in the same coin she had paid him before: no and a thousand times no.

21

I WAS A BIG BOY now: I was now in prep school. Still, all I knew of prayer was what I learned in religion class.

I would stare at Sheikh Zaki avidly when he said to us that prayer was the pillar of religion, and that those who failed to perform it were to be counted as infidels who had abandoned their faith. I watched him intently as he rolled up his sleeves and showed us how to perform ablutions, washing our hands and arms up to the elbows, and took off his turban to show us how to pass a damp hand over our hair. He taught us prayer times and how many prostrations for each one, and the prayers we must recite in times of trouble, when traveling, and before bedtime.

But no sooner did vacation roll around than I forgot everything I had learned, as schoolboys forget their arithmetic. It was summer, and in summer all thoughts of school are forgotten.

One of the boys, joking, asked me how many prostrations were in the sunset prayer. This would usually be in front of someone new, or when the mood had grown too serious in an attempt to lighten the mood.

"Three," I said.

He smiled, but there was something malicious in his eyes.

Confused, not knowing if he was encouraging me or trying to trap me, I amended hastily, "Just two."

He asked again, accompanied by others around us, and I remained steadfast in my response, swearing to it by God.

More questions would follow: "What is the difference between shaf' and witr prayers?" and, "Are they a fard or a confirmed Sunna?" or, "Can you explain Chapter 30 of the Qur'an?"

I was left stuttering, unable to answer. I only knew three short suras: al-Duha, al-Layl, and al-Tariq, and some scattered verses from al-Baqara and al-Rahman, which I knew like the back of my hand and flowed from my lips like water.

Funnily enough, when I, out of all the other boys, read these verses aloud in the religion class, a hush fell over the class, and all the boys stared at me, open-mouthed.

Sheikh Zaki frequently looked at me in admiration. Frequently, he asked me if I could recite the verses I had just spoken in the melodious fashion of professional Qur'an readers. I would nod and begin my recitation for all the world like a young Sheikh Abd al-Baset Abd al-Samad. The surprise usually turned to admiration for the rhythm of my oration, and Sheikh Zaki tilted his head from side to side in appreciation and shouted, "Wonderful, wonderful! May God reward you for your wonderful skill!"

One time he was so taken with me that he patted my back and said affectionately, "Bless you, Galal! May God keep you ever thus, a strong pillar of Islam, and bless your worthy and righteous family!"

Sniggers reached my ears: one of the boys who lived in our alley was in my line of sight. He clapped a hand to his mouth, shoulders shaking with laughter. I understood.

Memories of elementary school rushed back to me. What made matters worse was a loud guffaw from the back row, followed by laughter and whispering. The class degenerated into chaos.

Sheikh Zaki straightened up and, gripping his stick, walked among the rows sternly, and silence fell once more. The boys' eyes followed the path of the stick: the sheikh was known for this, that if he set upon a boy with his stick, he would never stop hitting until the stick snapped.

The lesson ended, and we went our separate ways, but the incident was not so easily forgotten. The sheikh's curiosity was roused, and he spent a few days inquiring about me.

The results did me no favors: the little rats caused a rift between the sheikh and myself, telling him a twisted and distorted version of my story, sprinkled with scandalous inventions made up from whole cloth. The sheikh ended up convinced that I was no Muslim, but Jewish through and through, and that my mother took me to the synagogue every Saturday to recite the psalms of David. Indeed, they told him, I was a card-carrying member of the choir!

The good, trusting man believed them and began to single me out, seizing every opportunity to break his stick over my head, out of a conviction that I had been deceiving him all this time.

I was unable to stand up to him, but with the passage of time, his good nature came to the fore: his conscience appeared to have pricked him, and he ceased his harassment of me. Still, a barrier remained, and he never ceased to follow me with accusatory glances.

I will never forget, though, what he did when I came in top of my class in religion. He came toward me, his kind, affectionate face embracing me. He patted my head and pulled an entire ten-piaster note out of his pocket, giving it to me, and prayed that I might remain steadfast in my faith no matter how sorely I was tempted.

I knew what he meant, of course.

Elementary school had come and gone. I was now in preparatory school, and still without a copy of the Qur'an, a visit to the mosque, or a day of fasting. At home, my mother closed up her holy book for good. She wrapped it in silken fabric and preserved it in the wardrobe together with what remained of my grandfather's belongings. She did not go to synagogue once after he left. "When I was young," she said, "I used to walk to the Nessim Ashkenazi Synagogue on Kuwah Street, me and your grandmother . . . ." But after it closed down, she found the way too far to Abbasiya, where the Karaite Synagogue was located, and the duty devolved upon my grandfather.

And so my mother and I lived in our apartment, as though neither of us had any religion at all. Every Friday I would look out of the balcony at the boys walking in their fathers' footsteps, off to the mosque to pray. I heard the echo of Sheikh Damanhouri's voice, which had held me in such thrall when I was younger, and I remembered the day I had wept on my grandfather's shoulder and he had carried me out of the funeral tent by Midan al-Geish. Silence would enshroud me, as though I were in the thrall of a thing I did not yet fully understand. The sound of the call to prayer would ring out of the mosque, stealing my heart away. Yet my feet would not move; I did not join the prayers. I would pull my chair up, lay my arms on the banister, and rest my head on them until I saw the Friday crowd of men and boys walking back from the mosque.

Then I would get up and walk aimlessly about the apartment. Bereft, I would look at the photograph of my absent grandfather. I would open his wardrobe, gazing at what remained of him: the tarboosh, an old pair of shoes and another of threadbare socks, and the empty case in which he had kept his glasses. When I went back into the hall, I would see him before me, closing his holy book, curling a hand around mine, pressing it kindly, and taking me out. My grandmother Yvonne would be seated in her usual spot on the couch, eating lupin beans, the shells falling into the lap of her house gallabiya. The day she had attacked me when I had told her she was going to Hell. The slipper that, praise the Lord, I had grown skilled enough to evade. All this I would remember, leaning on the kitchen doorjamb.

Often, I would see my mother, her back to me, elbows bent, her arms, showing in her housedress with the shoulder straps, white and plump. Higher up, near her shoulders, beads of sweat were starting to multiply from the heat of the kitchen and the steam ascending from the pot in front of her. No matter how busy she was, she would always sense me standing there. She would turn to me, motioning with her head to come in, inviting me to pull up a chair and sit with her and keep her company and talk. I just walked away, her voice calling after me, full of surprise. I would not answer, though, going to my room and lying on the bed, eyes fixed on the ceiling.

My paternal grandfather would come to me. When I heard the call to Friday prayers and neglected to go to prayer, he would materialize before me with his impressive bulk. His eyes would be piercing, fearsome, and sometimes he would wave his stick in my face. I'd push him away, but he wouldn't go: I would be reduced to an empty husk in his thrall, unmoving, knowing what brought him to me: I did not pray, nor did I fast. My paternal grandmother's shade would appear, floating before me, and I could breathe again. She would pray for me to find the right path, take my grandfather's hand, and lead him away.

22

THE FIRST DAY OF RAMADAN, as always, we came to iftar at Umm Hassan's. My mother recognized her knock on the glass in the door, and her silhouette impatiently fidgeting behind the little window.

My mother bent to find some slippers, while I was faster, already opening the door.

In a second, Umm Hassan was sitting beside us, still wearing the clothes she had had on while cooking: a short-sleeve gallabiya, plastic slippers, and a head scarf that appeared to have been hastily thrown on, for it did not cover her arms, while most of her hair poked out from beneath it, all unkempt.

The smell of meat soup wafted off her as she said to my mother, "Iftar today at our place, Umm Galal."

My mother knew that there was no arguing with that: like every time, though, she attempted to decline politely. Shyness filled her face as she said, "You really shouldn't. Galal can go; that's enough."

Umm Hassan would laugh out loud. "Galal? Who's this Galal I hear you talking about? What use is Galal without Umm Galal? You wouldn't want to offend Hagg Mahmoud, now, would you?" Patting my mother's shoulder tenderly, she would say, "May we always have these times together."

And off she flew, my mother calling after her to stay and getting the answer from the landing, "I've got things on the stove! And you know how useless my daughters are in the kitchen!"

I hurried through my homework and planted myself in front of the television, eager to watch the daytime soap operas: as usual, it was something about how the Jews had persecuted Prophet Mohamed when he first moved to Medina. My mother sat perched opposite me on the other side of the couch, some knitting and yarn in her lap, working on the as-yet palm-sized kernel that would grow into a sweater for me.

The soap opera started. My mother stole fleeting glances at me out of the corner of her eye, and then returned to the screen. Her face was intent, unblinking. She didn't change the channel, knowing I was watching, but the events on the screen were more than she could bear. Her face flushed, her hands moving jerkily over her work. The ball of yarn bounced, sometimes falling off her lap and rolling onto the floor in front of us. Naturally, she dropped a stitch or two and huffed in irritation.

The soap opera placed us in an embarrassing situation. We could not meet each other's eyes, nor could we say a word. After a while, I sensed rather than saw her rise and withdraw, going into her room and closing the door, only emerging after the afternoon prayer call, dressed to go out.

Unlike Umm Hassan, who would come to our house wearing any old thing, my mother was something else entirely. When she set foot outside the house, she was careful to always look her very best, whether she was headed for a reception at the Maccabi Club or to buy cheese and olives from the grocer's. She asked me to dress to go out as well.

I gestured to her to wait a moment—the soap opera was just about to end. With an angry look, she marched over to the television and snapped it off.

I made to go out in the pajamas I wore around the house, but she remonstrated with me and made me go get dressed, while I dawdled and protested all the while. In the end, I gave in and got dressed, and we descended the flight of stairs to Umm Hassan's apartment.

The woman's face lit up at the sight of us, and she welcomed us warmly. Hagg Mahmoud, in his gallabiya, was sitting on a couch in the hall. He nodded a greeting to my mother as Umm Hassan led her in and invited me to sit down beside him, asked me how I was doing in school, and whether I was fasting like Hassan, then went back to the rosary in his lap.

The smell of incense filled the house, the Qur'an recitation that preceded the call to sunset prayer just beginning. Although Hagg Mahmoud's television was a Grundig with a big screen and far superior to our own, he preferred to listen to the Qur'an on an ancient, funny-looking radio. It sat on a shelf on the wall, two large batteries sitting next to it. Seeing me staring at it, he pointed to it and told me and Hassan, "It's our lucky radio. My father bought it just one month after the Egyptian Radio Broadcasting Company was launched. The day they broadcast the first recording ever of Sheikh Mohamed Refaat—I was a young man then—everyone in our alley was invited to come listen at our house."

"Here in the apartment?" I asked.

He sighed. "No, my boy. In those days we lived in Abbasiya. Then, when I got married, we moved to this building. Your grandfather moved here in the same month as us. Your mother was still a little girl." Then he went back to talking about the radio, saying that you could not find its brother in all the length and breadth of Egypt.

Umm Hassan poked her head out of the kitchen door, dripping with sweat from the high temperatures and steam of the kitchen, laughing. She yelled at the top of her lungs—imagining that we, like her, were deafened by the hissing of the two gas burners in the kitchen—"And did you remember to tell them that your priceless treasure barely makes it through Ramadan, and as soon as it's over you have to cart it over to Amm Abu Shifa the electrician to get it fixed? Make sure you tell them that last time, he said he wasn't fixing the stupid thing again because it was a jinx and it brought bad luck on his store, and don't leave out how you had to beg him and plead with him so he'd agree to fix the thing!"

Hagg Mahmoud smiled. "Easy with the kidding! The children might believe it!"

The sunset prayer was drawing near. Hassan and I could tell from the tone of the Qur'an reciter, and from the way the light changed outside the glass of the closed window. Hagg Mahmoud looked at us, saying, "The first day is something special. You'd never hear of me, nor any of the old folk in our street, starting iftar without hearing the call to sunset prayer from Sheikh Khalaf!"

This was the signal to go! We got ready, reaching for our discarded sandals where they lay by the feet of the chair.

Umm Hassan motioned for us to wait: she'd washed her face and changed and looked very different from the way she had looked half an hour ago. Meanwhile, her youngest daughter rolled in the tabliya, a low, round wooden table, on its edge while the eldest followed, the tray of food on her head wafting steam and delicious aromas. Other hands rolled a second table toward the room where my mother sat. Hassan and I stood on tiptoe to try and divine what was in the tray. The eldest sister noticed: she was about our height, so she grinned and stood on tiptoe herself, to make sure we couldn't see.

"There's no need to take the children running about, now," Umm Hassan remonstrated. "They're fasting, after all. Any minute now we'll hear the call to prayer from the loudspeaker of the mosque next door."

He waved away her protest. "No, no, Hagga; we can't be breaking tradition now, can we?"

We didn't listen to the rest of the dialogue: in four bounds we were downstairs.

Said, Hassan's elder brother, was just coming home. He was a young man now, with a job in a workshop on Ahmed

Said Street. Although Said was Hagg Mahmoud's firstborn, Hassan had emerged victorious in the mysterious sweepstakes by which one's mother is called by one's name. We never called her by Said's name, just as we now roundly ignored him as he came in, rushing instead from street to street, joined by more and more boys about the same age, running alongside us, and younger little boys and girls all with the same goal.

A loud "Allahu Akbar" sounded from the microphone of the neighboring mosque. We slowed down, exchanging glances, then redoubled our pace, running full tilt to the tiny zawya, or prayer nook, run by Sheikh Khalaf, ignoring the prayer call that sounded from the official mosque run by the government authorities. Upon arriving, we found a horde of children had arrived before us, clustering around the building.

Sheikh Khalaf was an elderly gentleman, well over seventy. He had built the zawya with his own money over thirty years ago and spent most of his time there, either sleeping or cleaning it and performing the functions of an Imam, leading people in prayer. He refused to use a microphone, not for prayer calls and not for the Friday sermon. He would climb an interior staircase that took him to the roof of the building. First his head would appear, topped by a turban with a small tassel, then the rest of his body. As soon as he was properly situated, we would look with awe upon his round face and white beard, and a sigh of contentment would ascend from the assembly simultaneously.

As was often the case, we were accompanied by two or three old men, homeless street beggars. One said, "I've seen him wearing that heavy thing on his head all my life. Shouldn't he do better to wear a white cap in this heat?"

"Shut up," said another, elbowing him.

Sheikh Khalaf was, as always, expecting our presence. He looked down on us from above. The roof of the small building seemed to shake under the weight of his footsteps as he advanced toward the side where we had congregated. The microphone's call to prayer had already died away.

"Now," we said amongst ourselves, "now he'll start." The little ones got ready to shriek along with him after the first "Allahu Akbar"—but it didn't go as planned. He bent over one bare foot, scratching at it irritably, visibly disgruntled. He must have been bitten by an insect that had then made good its escape.

He stood straight again, staring still at the sun's descending disk. The men standing amongst us looked at each other and nodded approvingly. The man who had spoken first said, "His prayer call, I swear by God, is in accordance with religious law, for everything errs but the sun."

The sheikh cleared his throat twice.

At the first "Allahu Akbar, Allahu Akbar," we lost all control, especially the younger ones. Their shrill little voices screamed out, "Yay! Yay! Yay!" and they ran home.

Hassan and I, as well as some of the other children, were older: we didn't do that. We preferred to walk home relatively sedately, so as not to look too eager to eat. But no sooner were we out of the street and inside the building than it was as though our feet were possessed by demons, bounding high up the stairs as though we would never get another chance to eat in our lives.

Hagg Mahmoud and his son Said were seated at the table, the plum parts of the meal all but gone. All that was left was fat, gristle, and two small pieces of meat. The stuffed eggplant was almost gone, and the same for the lovely green mulukhiya soup and the peas and pickles. However, there was still enough rice and bread left to feed us and the neighbors as well.

We had been duped! There was treachery afoot! They had started to eat when the government prayer call had sounded, and this Sheikh Khalaf business had all been a trick to cheat us out of our share!

We refused to greet them. We instead sat grim-faced at the table with them, so that they would feel the weight of the injury they had done us. They blithely went on with their meal, not acknowledging our arrival as we sat, nor seeming to realize we were even there.

Unconsciously, without prior agreement, Hassan and I started to eat in a way that threw all etiquette out the nearest window. We would seek our revenge for the parental perfidy: if we only could, we would have done as cats did and snatched a piece of meat from the hand of Hagg Mahmoud, or his eldest son, without hesitation.

Luckily, Hagg Mahmoud was in clover, blissfully lost in the food he was consuming, and too busy to notice us.

Said, having filled his stomach, looked oddly at our antics. He elbowed his brother, telling him to have some table manners, and looked at me as if to say the same thing. We paid him no heed at all and carried on regardless.

However, he who crosses the finish line first wins: having eaten their meat and vegetables first, they set upon the tray of sweets that sat beside us, which threw our thoughts into disarray: should we keep on eating the remnants of the food they had left for us, or abandon it and start to fight them for the sweets? This question became more pressing as it appeared that Said was determined to polish it all off, and he had the capacity for food of a young, healthy water buffalo.

I was invited to iftar twice after that, by friends of mine from the street; I went, naturally.

I asked my mother if I could invite them over for iftar as well. She feigned a sudden interest in whatever she was working on and pretended not to hear me. However, I insisted, and she finally, grudgingly, agreed.

I met them and extended my invitation. They said nothing, just looked at me. When I insisted, they said, "We'll ask our mothers if it's OK."

Days passed, and I received no reply. It was then I realized that they would not eat food prepared by the hands of my mother.

23

I WAS THE ONLY ONE of our little gang to make it as far as secondary school. Hassan failed his exams twice and then apprenticed to his father at the family spice store. Fahmi, the accountant Husni's son, moved to Nasr City with his family. Two of the boys from the building next to ours went into vocational school.

I had never even noticed Nadia, the daughter of Madame Subki, who lived upstairs, until we bumped into each other one day at the outer door of our building.

One of the pair of iron gates was closed, unusual for our building, and I was bounding downstairs as I did every day. Inertia propelled me like a projectile into the open door just as she was coming in, and I barreled straight into her.

Her schoolbag was knocked out of her hand, as well as her little pocketbook, a ruler, and other small things she had been holding. Flustered and embarrassed, we bent together to gather her things from the floor.

The top button of her blouse must have been hanging by a thread, for it, too, fell to the floor. Her blouse gapped open slightly to reveal a thin black band, and the beginnings of a budding, perky breast. She gave a little moan and bent her head, pulling her blouse closed, a slight blush coming over her cheeks.

She was down on one knee, as I was, looking away in embarrassment. Both she and I seemed to be drugged somehow. When she reached out to pick up her little comb that had fallen by my foot, I was overwhelmed with the scent of pure femininity pouring out of her whole body. It was an innocent, virginal scent, or so it appeared, but its freshness belied its power to utterly enthrall and captivate.

I looked away modestly, saying, "The button, right—just a second; I'll find it for you."

"Oh—oh, that's right, the button! Where did it get to?"

We stood. She said, panting, a light dew sparkling at the parting of her hair, "So, hi, Galal!"

"I'm sorry. I didn't mean it! I was in a hurry."

"It's OK. What a nice surprise to see you!"

"What year are you in, now?"

"Second year, secondary school. Literature division."

"I'm in third. Sciences."

She held out her hand to shake mine. I felt the sensation of her small, smooth hand, soft and pliant in mine.

She walked away, up the stairs, leaving me gazing after her, my heart remembering when she would come to us as a very little girl, holding her mother's hand. We had played hide-and-seek and chased one another incessantly, shrieking all the while. Sometimes we would sit on the balcony quietly, building houses out of the empty cigarette boxes my grandfather used to keep, for some unknown reason of his own.

Once, with a single swipe of her hand, she had demolished the house I had spent a whole hour carefully building and bolted away on the balcony, running as I chased her. When I caught her, without thinking, I kissed her on the cheek.

Back then, she stared at me with her big black eyes, surprise filling her little face, and said in piping, angry tones, "I'm telling!"

I took her hand, scared, and begged her, stammering, not to tell her mother on me. Adamant, she kept threatening me and saying I'd get it from my grandmother when she found out.

I don't think she ever told. I don't think she forgot what happened, either.

Perhaps she could feel my eyes on her, my gaze that took her in from behind as she climbed the stairs; perhaps she was thinking the same thing that was going through my own head. At the curve of the stairwell, she paused and gave me a nod and a smile.

I couldn't get her out of my head for weeks. I couldn't stop hanging around the door of our building in hopes of meeting her. For hours, I would sit in the balcony, waiting for her to come in or go out.

Once, I caught sight of her. I grabbed a shirt and pants from the hanger, pulling them on as I hurried toward the door, jammed my feet into my shoes that lay next to the couch, then burst out onto the landing, looking around after her.

I never made it any further, though: I encountered Hagg Mahmoud, ascending the stairs in a small procession that included himself, the doorman, and Amm Marzouq the iron-monger, accompanied by his apprentice, Shalabi al-Latkh, the pair of them toting half a sackful of cement, a wrench, a ham-mer, and some nails for the purpose of repairing the water tank. They were accompanied by a fellow who lived on the top floor, plus four of the boys from the building, three of whom were barefoot and the fourth in only his slippers and under-wear, clearly there for the spectacle.

I greeted Hagg Mahmoud, and he asked me how I was and where I was off to. I said loudly, my eyes on Nadia as she tried to make her way past the sea of shoulders that had paused along with Hagg Mahmoud and were now blocking the stairwell, "I'm going to the bookstore, Hagg Mahmoud. I want to get a book of study-aid questions to help with the Arabic language program for the second year of secondary school."

He looked puzzled. "Aren't you in your final year?"

Smoothly I said, just as she slipped by us, looking at her meaningfully, "I could never forget the second year; how could I do without it? It's the fundament, you see."

He nodded his agreement and said in fatherly tones, "You are so right. Bless you, my boy."

As for the old doorman, he pushed his cap a little back on his head, smiling at me and saying, in his Nubian accent, "Be strong, Galal! You have hard time working! God be by your side." He gestured at the open door to our apartment, mischief in his eye, "But be careful to close the door! You is so eager, you was going to leave it wide open as you rushes out!" He looked at my shoes. "Not to mention the shoelaces, Galal, young sir. Tie them, I begs you, lest the young master trip on the stairs and fall on his face. Tie them, tie them now; there's a good boy."

I ignored him, turned tail, and retreated, fuming and cursing inside at this old fox who had popped up out of the blue. Had he noticed something?

My mother was out. I was half-mad, at my wit's end, unable to find a pretext to see Nadia. I paced the apartment, sat down only to stand up again. I wanted to see her, right now. Now, now, not a minute later!

I changed my clothes, a mad idea forming in my head. A fresh shirt and pants, new shoes and socks: I looked at my appearance in the mirror—my height, my figure, my hair, the color of my shirt—and the next thing I knew, I was knocking on Nadia's door.

Madame Subki opened the door in an apron. "Why, it's Galal! You don't usually come calling, my boy!"

I blinked, smiled, and stood there, rooted to the spot, like the village idiot, inspiration resolutely refusing to strike. My brain hung out an 'Out of Order' sign, and my tongue seemed struck by terminal paralysis. All I could think was 'Now I've gone and done it! Now I'll get what's coming to me.'

"What's wrong with you, my boy? You look quite pale! Is something the matter with your mother?"

"My mother? Oh no, she's fine. I just wanted . . . ."

"Yes? And what's the matter with your voice? Are you coming down with something, son?"

144

"Yes. I've a bit of a cold. And—I wanted to borrow a book from Miss Nadia."

"Oh, I'm sorry to hear you're unwell. But what book? You're not even in the same year!"

"No, that's true, but as you know, it's all connected, and they build on what we learned the year before."

Madame Subki was a trusting soul. She believed my story, and called loudly for her daughter. Nadia came out right away, but when she saw me, a faraway look came into her eyes, and she paused.

Her mother looked at her in surprise. "This is Galal, Madame Camellia's son. Don't you recognize him? Why, many's the time you two played together when you were little."

"Sure I recognize him." Her brow furrowed in concentration, as though casting her mind back. "I don't remember playing with him, Mom, though," she added with an apologetic smile.

"Well, anyway, let him into the sitting room, do, and see what he wants. I've got to go back into the kitchen."

I followed her. She led me to a chair near the sitting-room door and asked me, her eyes dancing, "Did we play together when we were little? I don't remember any of it."

She cast a look at the kitchen door and asked me what I wanted; then, when I'd choked out the name of the only text-book I could think of—*Arabic Grammar*—she left.

I was enormously impressed by the sitting room: formal, ornate, and smart. The chairs were old-fashioned, but they were all gilded, their gilt still pristine, underlain with silver. The table was black marble, with a crystal vase upon it, and there was wall-to-wall carpeting on the floor. A small curio cabinet with a glass door sat in the corner. Inside it stood a doll in the shape of a bride and various other pieces of small statuary. They were clearly much better off than we were. Her mother's family were businessmen and Azharite sheikhs—good family of good stock, who clearly took care of them.

After a little while, she came back, bearing the book I had asked for. She was preceded by a delicate perfume—it was clear that she had just put it on—and wearing a different dressing gown from the one I had seen on her minutes ago: a light silvery gray one with a small, dark red floral pattern. I don't know what she had done with her hair: it was prettier. I must admit, it tickled my vanity when I realized that she had done all this for me.

She sat on the chair next to mine, where she could see the kitchen door. We took to looking through the book together, turning the pages. I didn't have a particular question in mind I wanted answered, but I appeared serious and intent on my study for her sake.

Finally, I pointed to a page, and she said, "Is this what you wanted to find out?"

I nodded. "Yes, yes."

"What part of it don't you understand?"

I had no answer for that. Instead I took the book from her and leafed through it.

When I stopped again, she said, "This one? It's a blank page, Galal."

My eyes were fixed on her lips as she spoke. Whenever our fingers brushed together, unintentionally, she became extremely flustered. I noticed that she sneaked occasional peeks at me, and her eyes told me that she minded not at all that all I was doing was nothing but a ruse, and a flimsy one at that.

I laid my hand over hers. She withdrew it immediately with a reproving glance. I returned my hand to the arm of the chair, as though I had not meant to do it at all, and we kept talking. I did it again. This time, though, I couldn't control myself: I laid my entire palm over her hand, and without even knowing what I was doing, I pressed it softly, raising it to my lips.

She bolted to her feet, and so did I. She took a step back,

but I didn't retreat, moving closer. Her cheekbones were dusted with freckles. I brushed my lips over them. My breath mingled with hers. I kissed her on the same spot where I had kissed her when she was very little. I plucked the book from her hand and rushed for the door.

Before I had gone down two steps, I looked back. She said before she closed the door: "Send me the book with Auntie Camellia. Don't you dare bring it back yourself." Then she added, coyly, "Is that clear?"

I flew down the stairs, my heart fluttering in my chest and calling out to me, while I admonished it to calm down and wait until we were alone in the apartment.

At the curve of the stairs, in my haste, my confusion and joy, I slammed into Amm Idris, the doorman, coming up with a bucket upon his shoulder, dripping water onto his gallabiya and his boat-like footwear.

Laughing, he cried out, "What's with you today, Mr. Galal? Always in a dream! Where has you been, naughty boy?"

24

My MOTHER WOKE UP AT exactly a quarter to six each morning. She started her day by making sandwiches: beans, cheese, sometimes halva and boiled eggs, with kosher bread. She wrapped them in newspaper and put them in the outer pocket of my schoolbag, which I packed at night and left by the door. Yawning, she opened the balcony doors, flooding the hallway with daylight, usually faint at this hour, especially in winter.

The light, of course, made its way into the room where I slept, through the pebbled English glass that formed the upper part of the door. The darkness in the room would grow less deep, waking me; I don't know quite why, although I tend to be a sound sleeper. Things always looked indistinct to me at first, the eye unable to comprehend them. Sounds filtered up from the street: Amm Subhi with his monotonous call, "Fresh milk!" He took great pride in his wares, which he carried in two great jugs fastened with iron hooks to the rear wheel of his bicycle. He would only call out once or twice: he had a spot at the corner of every street, where the doormen's wives would gather, holding tin mugs and pots.

Then there was Amm Hilal, who never stopped yelling, hawking his newspapers and magazines. These he carried in a cardboard folder under his arm, hanging from his shoulder by a length of cord. Pity us the day there was something new in the headlines—an accident, or an attack by the military police on what, in those days, they called the New Feudal

Lords, or perhaps a fiery statement made by the president to the foreign press! The man would take to stamping his foot, or yelling with feeling, until the whole street had heard him. Back then, he seemed to us no mere traveling newspaperman, but a mover and shaker, a maker of news.

Then, there was the duo Said and Zakiya, coming occasionally on their donkey cart. On it was every stripe of fruit and vegetable that the regular fruit stores didn't carry, like guava, mulberries, and sycamore figs. They would station themselves outside our building, whereupon Zakiya would stand calling out their wares in a melodious voice not unlike song. Many times I saw her on the way to school, planted on her cart, dusty feet stretched out in front of her, swollen, her neck cords standing out while her head, a little larger than a cabbage, turned left and right in time to the off-key calling emanating from her mouth. As for Said, leaning with one elbow on the driver's platform, he stared admiringly at her, licking his mustache with the tip of his tongue. When her vocalizing was over, he would place his thumbs below his earlobe, tense his palms that reached mid-turban, and start calling out, too. To tell the truth, his call was sweeter and more mellifluous than Zakiya's, which was a bit too shrill for my taste.

The comedy would be complete if the donkey pulling the cart joined in. It was a dwarf donkey with an unusually large belly and flanks that were not round and taut like other beasts', but almost rectangular, with scattered black patches that had increased with the winter until they almost reached his stomach, perhaps a form of scabies or a result of malnutrition. The donkey appeared to be musical, too: we could see his long ears wiggle along with the song, especially when it was Zakiya singing. His spindly legs would shift and prance in time to the music, and from time to time he would fall completely still, raising his head, flaring his nostrils and turning his lips outward. I imagine that in these moments, he was at the pinnacle of musical enjoyment. Indeed, he would suddenly preempt Said, taking the metaphorical reins of action, and respond to Zakiya's call with a long aria of braying.

It would be unfair to dismiss the sounds produced by that donkey as 'braying,' as though it were a sound made by any other donkey. It was tuneful, melancholic, a sound that could only be produced by an ass of uncommon talent. I do not think that anyone in the street could get back to sleep after that performance, not unless you were a special case like myself.

All these sounds would come to me muddled, unclear. I could hear my mother as she moved about the apartment, but I would never be certain if this wasn't all happening in a dream. There were these seconds when my attention would drift, and I would slip back into sleep, feeling as though I were falling into a dark void.

My mother would go into the kitchen to make herself a big cup of coffee with milk. This was a beverage as yet unknown to the inhabitants of our building, indeed to the entire Daher district, except for the few houses where foreigners lived. It was my grandmother who had first introduced it into the house after learning of it from a friend of hers who worked as a maid in Qattawi Pasha's home. The women of the building exclaimed at it, saying, "Who ever heard of such a thing? Milk, Umm Isaac, milk that calms and relaxes the children, and you put it on coffee, the coffee that you drink to perk up and get your brain working?"

In fact, Umm Hassan told my grandmother that when she had spoken of it to her husband, he hadn't believed her, and when she asked him to try it, he responded mockingly, "Look, you may know all there is to know about meat and okra and zucchini, but when it comes to coffee, you stay out of it."

My grandmother had looked at her with astonishment, and Umm Hassan had added, "Well, that's understandable. He's a man who likes his coffee fix, and he won't touch it unless it's good Turkish coffee, with cardamom, and he always

151

drinks it black. And God forbid it come to him without foam on top: he yells and makes a fuss, and sometimes throws the cup on the floor."

My grandmother, unable to keep her mouth shut as usual, said, "And of course he needs his opium fix alongside."

Umm Hassan gave her a black look. But for the fact that she was friends with my mother, she would have had a thing or two to say to my grandmother. But even respect for my mother didn't stop her from some light artillery fire, followed by a strategic retreat in the form of storming off in a huff. Umm Hassan refused to set foot in our apartment afterward until she had received appropriate and fulsome apologies—and she did.

Next, my mother would sit on the couch in the spot formerly occupied by my grandfather, which had become her regular spot. After two or three sips of her coffee, she would call out to me to wake.

At first she would call softly, using my first name. "Galal, wake up! Galal. Galal." Then her voice would ratchet up several notches, with a sharp tone, and my name would be replaced by names.

"You, boy! Wake up, you stubborn mule! Wake up, you spoiled brat! Wake up, I said, you blot on the universe, or I'll come and wake you up with my slipper!"

She would catch her breath, then add, in a long-suffering tone: "Oh my, what is this suffering every day? Every morning I have to go through this song and dance? Wake up, you slugabed!"

Meanwhile, I would be dead to the world. The funny thing was, my mother knew full well the futility of her shouts and imprecations: I was not one to be awakened by the sound of a mere voice, and a voice from the other room at that!

But she had gotten used to the ritual, or perhaps she considered it a warm-up. In any case, she would soon spring up, sometimes knocking over the coffee as she did so, which added to the total of insults raining down on me.

She would barge into my grandfather's room, which had eventually become my bedroom. The alarm clock would have started by now as well—alarm bell and mother ganging up on me, until I raised my head off the pillow.

The alarm clock, surplus from the British Army, with brass bells that could be heard in the street outside, seemed to have been specially fashioned for lazy soldiers, or perhaps as an instrument of torture. My mother, meanwhile, would angrily pull the blankets off me, dropping them to the floor, while she'd scream and slap loudly on the headboard.

Today, even before the first sip of her coffee with milk, my mother found me yawning at the door to the room. She stared incredulously. I came toward her and kissed her at the part of her hair. She smiled, goggle-eyed, as I drew even closer and bent to kiss her hand. I had not known before how wonderful love was, or that Nadia could do all this for me.

I flew off to school. It was a Monday. Monday was either bright and cheerful, or unhappy and ponderous: it all depended on the emotional state of Mr. Busrati, who had us first period for double Arabic. He was a teacher/supervisor who had been passed over four times for the position of deputy headmaster, despite his seniority, and it was said that his colleagues at the same level of age and experience had received their due promotion to headmaster last year; indeed, Murqus Effendi, the administrative head of the school, assured anyone who would listen that the district director of the Ministry of Education had been his classmate in freshman year at Dar al-Ulum, the faculty of sciences, but that Mr. Busrati had not graduated with them in the normal course of events, rather preferring to take his sweet time graduating, finally getting his certificate seven years plus a term later.

To console him and give him the illusion of importance, the powers that be had conferred upon him the title of 'general school monitor,' an honorary title the most important part of which, for a teacher, was to sit alongside the headmaster on special occasions and festivities and when handing out cups and prizes. Out of respect for him—or rather, to keep him happy and out of their hair, as the other teachers whispered—after the headmaster had presented the cup to the winning team at the awards ceremony for some school championship or other, he would occasionally call upon Mr. Busrati to present one or two medals—to the losing team, of course. He never realized it, though.

The first ten minutes of every lesson were wasted in his boasting about his new job. In his capacity as general school monitor, he had decided to implement so-and-so and such and such, and he had given Professor So-and-So a dressing down because the latter knew nothing of the principles of education. He was pleased to say that Professors Mahdi Tayie and Fahmi Nashed, who were retiring next month, were most responsive to his ideas and praised them to the skies. The school, he said, had changed completely since his appointment to the position.

We would show polite admiration, saying, "You're the right man for a difficult job, sir; may the Lord give you the strength to see it through!"

His voice would change as he began to mimic the high-ranking government officials who spoke on television. His eyes acquiring a faraway look, he intoned, "It is a duty I have been charged with. Should I shirk? No, a thousand times, no!" With a yawn, he would add, in tones suggesting that their owner had been exhausted and taxed to the limit, "Do you know, my boys?" We would open our eyes wide and lean forward. "I have been staying up till dawn for a week!"

He would fall silent. As one boy, we chorused, "Whatever for, Mr. General Monitor, sir?"

"Because I have been thinking up a splendid scheme to make this school run like a dream! It will be like the schools in Europe! And I, my dear, industrious boys, will not reveal this plan to anyone but His Excellency the minister himself! Yes, the minister, and no one else! That was the advice of one of my retired colleagues. This, my boys, is a secret, so don't you dare tell it to anyone, for we live in wicked, wicked times!"

We would be shaking with suppressed laughter at this point. One of us would ask him suddenly, "Is the general monitor higher up, sir, or the administrative director?"

The man would look at the boy who had asked, openly disgusted at such a show of ignorance. Immediately he would respond decisively, "The general monitor, of course, you fool." Then, lowering his voice, "Did you know, boys, that the latest pedagogical research shows that the general monitor is far more important than the headmaster?" Upon finding us still silent, waiting expectantly, he would plant his forefinger squarely in the center of his own chest and say even more decisively—but in much lower tones—"In my opinion, this position is of far more importance than that of the director general of education himself!"

We would all play dumb, saying as one, "How true! How true! How could we not have realized it?" And one of our number would invariably bounce out of his seat, saying, "Maybe better than the minister, too."

Mr. Busrati would look embarrassed, saying softly as he patted that boy on the back, "Well, I wouldn't go that far. A general monitor is a bit like a deputy minister, or a counselor." He added enthusiastically, "Do you know why, boys?"

We would ask in unison, dragging out our syllables so as to sound appropriately impressed, painting a false expression of astonishment on our faces, "Why is that, sir?"

He would smile as though amused by our simplemindedness. "Because," he said, "I live only to accomplish the sacred duty entrusted to me: I care nothing for official positions."

He would stick out his lower lip in a kind of facial shrug, waving a nonchalant hand: "What is it to be a headmaster, or a director, or even a minister? I am a pedagogue: I call for high manners and I cure troubled morals."

Pretending to believe him, we would say, "That's certain! May the Lord shower his blessings upon you, O Greatest of all Professors!"

Someone in the back row once though asked suddenly, "How do you cure morals, then sir? With pills, or injections?"

The boy had said the final phrase under his breath. I think the professor heard it, though, because he went very red in the face, and he growled, "What did you say, boy? Raise your voice, coward!"

So as not to upset the professor's mood, we all took his part, upbraiding the boy who had spoken. Crisis averted.

There was one unforgettable incident with Professor Busrati. It involved me and another boy in my class, named Khairi.

It was like this: once, as he was teaching, we heard a slight noise from the music room; it was some students from another class playing some instrument in the periods set aside for extracurricular activities. It was a regular thing, and we never paid it much mind when another teacher was in.

In this class, though, with Mr. Busrati in particular, things were different.

We looked at one another. Quickly, most of us raised our hands in complaint. The professor tried to convince us that this was hardly a noise loud enough to make a fuss about, but we stood firm, saying that we could not hear the lesson properly.

One student said, completely straight-faced, "Sir, it's not right. The people around us should know that when the general monitor is in the vicinity, everyone should be quiet and behave themselves. For heaven's sake, it's the general monitor we're talking about!"

The professor could vacillate no longer: it was his dignity on the line, especially as we started to shoot him disappointed looks accusing him of failing to take appropriate action and suggesting that this was behavior unbecoming of the general monitor of the school! He looked around him and motioned to me and to my classmate, Khairi, and told us to go to the music teacher to kindly request he keep the sound down a little—being sure to speak to him politely and tactfully because we were not representing ourselves in this matter, but speaking for the professor himself. He was, as we knew, entrusted with a sacred duty, bearing the torch of education upon his shoulders.

However, we knew what his request for politeness really meant. Mr. Somaa, the music teacher, was irritable and tetchy, and picked fights with the very flies that buzzed in front of him. He was narrow-minded and always spoiling for a fight, and Mr. Busrati doubtless knew this and wished to avoid a confrontation.

We hurried over, whereupon Mr. Somaa met us with a scowl. We said provokingly, in a tone more like an order than anything else, "The deputy monitor of the school says you'd better stop that din you're making or else. Sir."

He looked us up and down and took a step closer. We took a step back to maintain our distance, for neither of us could be sure of his reaction. "Din? I'll give you din, you insect! So that useless figurehead is sending threats now, is he? 'Or else!'" He huffed a laugh. "Or else what, you little louse, you street urchin, you and the other one there?"

I answered coldly, as though it were the most logical thing in the world, something he should have divined himself, "Or else he'll take action against you. Severe action, no doubt."

"He said that himself?"

We nodded yes. Khairi added: "You'd best knuckle under, Mr. Somaa! You know that the general monitor is very strict."

Whereupon I added, "You said it, Khairi, man! And you know Mr. Busrati has no mercy, and he's got a heavy hand!

Remember when he grabbed ol' Hamid under his arm and laid into him with his cane?"

Khairi, completely on my wavelength, went on smoothly: "Who could forget? They say he had to be carted away by an ambulance, and the doctors said to pay our final respects, and that they'd better take him home so his mom and dad could say their last goodbye!"

"And remember when he hit Zanati and made him fall on his face?" I added, one eye on Mr. Somaa, my finger all but pointing at him. "Truly, sir, you should keep your distance! He's vicious! He's not afraid of anybody, man! He'll beat anybody, anybody at all, to a pulp!"

"General monitor my foot!" burst out the music teacher. "A pox on you two and your general monitor into the bargain! Standing here singing a duet! The nerve! Go on, get lost, you and the other ass!"

And when we tarried, requesting an answer to take back to Mr. Busrati, the response was a fist flying toward my eye with deadly accuracy. I was prepared for it, of course, and dodged, but he followed up with a kick that dropped me to the floor. As for Khairi, he was already running for dear life. I rolled out of the way as he was gearing up for another kick, got to my feet, and ran like the wind.

We ran back in a panic, preceded by our yells of alarm and cries for help. Busrati stood listening to our complaints and looking at the footprint on my pants. I noticed that his feet were fidgeting, ready to go, and his face was so agitated he couldn't maintain the same expression for a moment. His nostrils had flared, and he was snorting loudly. We had clearly awakened his vengeful glands and excited their secretions, whereupon these had pumped him full of vigor and prepared him for battle: especially as the whole class had urged the professor not to let it go, and that his dignity—to put it bluntly—was hanging by a thread. The guilty party must receive his just deserts; there was no way around it: an insult to the messengers of the general monitor was an insult to the general monitor himself. QED. And, as one of the boys called out in dramatic tones, "Proper respect must be shown by everyone in the school, no matter their position!"

The man grew livid with rage: he kicked the classroom door open and stormed off in the direction of the music room. We all clustered at the windows, eager to watch the Clash of the Titans about to start. Less than a minute later, shouts and yells were heard, as well as the crash of musical instruments falling out of students' hands. Janitors and office boys poured in from all directions. The venerable headmaster himself was seen hurtling toward the music room, a number of teachers in tow. He was a sight to behold: some of his shirt buttons still undone, shoelaces untied, and the man himself busy pulling up his suspenders. I think he had been in the toilet when they raised the alarm.

After a long investigation, they discovered the culprits. Five marks were taken off everyone in the class for general bad behavior. As for me and Khairi, we got ten days' suspension with a warning of final dismissal. Hagg Mahmoud had to come to the school and sign an affidavit that I would behave in the future and not do such things again.

25

THAT WAS THE START OF last year. Mr. Busrati took to coming into our classroom breathing fire, a countenance that said he was quite prepared to murder any one of us.

If any student should so much as make a move, such as we used to in the good old days, Mr. Busrati would grab him, twist his arm up behind his back, and drag him to the headmaster's office, suggesting that he call the police. The headmaster would try in vain to calm the man down, but he would never rest until the student received a three-day suspension. Mr. Busrati would then hurry into Murqus Effendi's office, looking over his shoulder as he wrote the letter, insisting he add one or two stern phrases to the traditional form letter.

My friend Khairi and I knew our limits with him. We stayed completely silent, not paying attention to what the teacher was saying, instead keeping a watchful eye on the teacher himself.

Our only concern was following his movements as he circulated around the class, especially after we had committed his tactics to memory: he would teach while moving from his position at the chalkboard to the center of the classroom where we sat. At that point, he would be suddenly afflicted with a malfunction of the nervous system, and his hands would start to shake, his eyes, in spite of himself, never leaving us, following our every move from above the glasses perched on the bridge of his nose.

Naturally, he desired to keep these tics a secret from us and tried in every possible way to have us believe that he held us in the same regard as every other student. But he couldn't. Perceiving that his earlobes had gone blood red, or his fingers were shaking worse, I would take this as a danger sign, elbowing my friend, who took my meaning.

On the days when the teacher was able to control himself, he tried to mislead us, either by looking at us neutrally or asking us a question. Whether we answered right or wrong or not at all, he rewarded us with a fatherly pat on the shoulder and walked away, imagining that we had bought it and that he had lulled us into a false sense of security. He would walk back again whence he had come, turning his back on us for a long time, addressing himself to the front rows, hoping for us to crawl out of our holes and make a slip. Then, he'd whirl upon us.

We would be waiting: hands at our chests, faces polite and submissive as two little angels. The only smile was in our eyes.

When the end-of-year exam arrived, it proved the worst punishment for the entire class. But for the intervention of the headmaster and the clemency committee he quickly convened for the express purpose of raising all of our grades, not one of us would have passed.

Things changed that year, though, after our old classmates were scattered. The students from 2D were either gone or farmed out into other classes. Khairi and I went into 3J—a class with an awful reputation, filled only with those who had had to be re-enrolled after failing too many times to stay on, those with something terribly wrong with them, and the most troublesome students. Not a single boy from that class, it was rumored, had ever gone on to university.

When we asked the deputy headmaster the truth of this rumor, he leaned back in his chair until it hit the wall, exposing a pair of pants so filthy it looked as though he'd been wearing them for three months straight, sagging socks, and virtually colorless shoes.

He looked at our expectant faces, breathed on the lenses of his spectacles, and took to cleaning them with a dirty handkerchief that had been in his lap. "The documents I have say that only one boy managed it, seven years ago. He scored 44 percent on his final exam, and the placement authority sent him to a polytechnic in Damanhour."

"What about the rest of them, Murqus Effendi? Where did they go?"

"Go? Into the streets, of course. Some became laundrymen, some have kushari carts, some apprenticed to a fesikh maker—what a stink!—some peddle hash . . . ."

"So only one was successful enough to get into a polytechnic?"

"Who said anything about success? I heard from his family that he was booted out in his first year after exceeding the maximum number of times for failure."

The next day, I went to school and sat next to Khairi. No sooner had we started to chatter than Mr. Busrati came in. A student in the last row, by the name of Leithi, screamed, "All rise for the general monitor of the school!"

We rose and looked, not forward, but back, where Leithi was. Everyone wanted to watch Leithi's antics on the few days when he did come to school. He only came two or three days a week at most. The attendance sheet was taken care of: Leithi paid the janitor who came by with the sheet a monthly salary, and if there was too much talk, Murqus Effendi would intervene and always rule in favor of Leithi. He had other ways, too, ways of which we knew nothing. Leithi, to be honest, was a special case, and his word was law in the school, just like the headmaster's.

Anyway, when Leithi was in attendance, he would clear his throat and thunder, "Hold your positions, class!

Hold—hold—hold—don't move! Don't you breathe, soldier!"

Then he would start to march, military-style, to the teacher. As he marched, he raised his arms very high, kicking up his knees and feet, Third-Reich style. Our eyes would remain riveted to him as he marched before us like a Nazi soldier from a Second World War movie. As soon as he drew level with the teacher, he would stamp his foot loudly on the floor and perform a flawless military salute, not forgetting the vibration of his palm as it sprang up into position, in dead earnest. Then another scream: "Reporting, Sir Monitor General sir! Complement: forty-one students! Seven on suspension from the headmaster, nine asleep, one in jail at Waili Police Station, the rest present and accounted for and ready to receive instruction SIR!"

Mr. Busrati would fidget in place with annoyance but never made any visible remonstration. He would mutter, "Dismissed," clearly praying for the ceremonies to conclude without casualties. He knew that before him stood not a student there to learn, but a criminal in student's clothing.

Leithi would turn on his heel and march back to his seat in the same style, all eyes on him, including the stunned gaze of the teacher. Leithi would then proceed to yawn loudly several times and lean his head back, napping until class was over.

On the days when he was tired from a late night or some such, the student next to him would leave the desk for him, whereupon he would draw his legs up onto the seat, stretching them out, and wedge his head and shoulder against the wall, or rest his head on the desk, and fall into a deep sleep. When this occurred, the quadrant where he slept became a no-fly zone, where no teacher could approach.

There was no way this could possibly be a student: tall, broad, a mustache that curled up at the ends, a scar above the left eyebrow from a knife wound, and married, so they said, to not one but two women. Leithi wasn't even in our school;

he was the son of a Rod al-Farag businessman, transferred out of his school in that area when he and his gang entered into a fight with sticks with the itinerant street salesmen who blocked the entrance to the marketplace. He got out on probation and was almost barred from sitting for his thanawiya amma exams, but his father got the minister of education to grant him an exception, and so he ended up here.

One of the school workmen swore on his mother's grave that Leithi's reputation was hotter than fire in Rod al-Farag, and that when the sun set, he would put on a peasant gallabiya and a traditional men's shawl like an adult and mind the store with his father. He affirmed that he also had a cudgel to keep order and get rid of intruders and trespassers.

Mr. Busrati started the lesson entitled "Analysis of a Poem." He explained each verse in succession, until he came to a verse I have no idea why they didn't censor from the Ministry reader. The very opposite of chaste, it described womanly charms in a way that set us young men chattering like mad. The teacher tried to rush through it, hoping to avoid our comments and talk, but I was lying in wait for him. I raised a hand and, all innocence, asked what the poet meant by that verse, and especially what *that* word meant, sir?

He looked at me, biting his lip, his eyes saying, 'You again, you bastard?' No doubt he was remembering our shared past, especially as my friend Khairi joined me in professing his incomprehension, followed in turn by Leithi, who, apparently, hadn't quite fallen asleep just yet, and whose interest was piqued by our talk.

The teacher realized that I had him by the short hairs and drew near to me, snarling hysterically, "You don't get it? What do you mean you don't get it, you young scoundrel? Up to your old tricks, you and the little beggar with you? Go ask someone in your family! I'll tell you what—go ask Golda Meir. She'll tell you what it means!"

I have no idea how he had found out that my mother was Jewish. There was nothing in my file at school to indicate that. He must have asked about me at school after the incident last year, or perhaps followed me home and conducted his own investigations.

The funny thing was, I wasn't shaken by this surprise attack, the way I had been in my primary and middle school years. I had no sense that this man whom they called a teacher had insulted me or humiliated me. Calmly I said, "Do you mean because my mother is Jewish, so you're using that to shame me?"

"God forbid!" he replied at once, waving his hands apologetically, "God forbid! I . . . I . . . ." Flustered, he fell silent.

26

My heart beat faster whenever I stood at al-Nasr tram station. For two weeks—say, three—I had been knocking, now at the deputy headmaster's door, now at Mr. Busrati's, now at the door of Mr. Shenouda, the supervisor of that floor, asking permission to leave after third period.

They would look up at me in annoyance, and I would meet their gaze with sorrow that I strove to make plausible and truthful. The problem was my eyes: they would not be controlled, and gave me away. To make it more convincing, I would sometimes lift my lower lip and shake my head as though I were in real trouble—not forgetting, of course, to look down and fold my hands over my stomach, as people are wont to do at funerals.

Their ire would rise, and they would urge me angrily to spit it out, boy! Mr. Busrati was always the loudest at this. I would glimpse his hand skimming the surface of the desk in search of a sharp object or something to use as a weapon. When his hand fell upon the ashtray, formed of a huge conch shell weighing at least two pounds, I would take great care and anticipate his probable reaction to anything I might say. Who knew but that he was planning to fling it at my face if I should say something to disturb his mood?

In a low, intense voice, I would say that I had just heard that my grandfather had been bitten by a stray dog, or butted by one of the rams that were allowed to roam freely outside

Amm Zenhom's butcher shop at the end of our street, and that I wanted to go and see him at Dimerdash Hospital before he met his maker. Or I would say that I was going to accompany my mother, who could hardly see, to Sayyid Galal Hospital to have drops put in her eyes—or that a child had fallen into the manhole outside our building, and that it was only gallant to stand by one's neighbors in times of trouble. Often, tired of my whining and anxious to get rid of my presence standing there, they would grant me permission. If they proved stubborn, they left me no recourse but trickery, bribery, or slipping out when the lumbering doorman, Amm Sayyid, wasn't looking.

Our classmate Leithi—may God grant him good health!—was especially useful when it came to things like this. When I looked unhappy, he'd nod confidently and say, plucking out a white hair from his beard with a pair of tweezers, "Don't worry about a thing, kid. And if you want to cut school altogether, go right ahead and I'll take care of it. You know I've got the whole school in my waistcoat pocket." I would rise, and he'd catch me by the arm, going on contemptuously, "Bunch of thoughtless, unfeeling jerks, the pack of 'em. No clue what it means when your heart's burning with love, or how it crushes a fellow. I don't see why they couldn't have a class or two every week on Love and the Loving Arts! All they're good for is X and XY! Y and YZ! Square root this and cube root that."

I withdrew my hand, and he grinned. "No one's gonna teach you this stuff but me, kid. I've been in love three times besides my wife, and still thirsty for more. Right, go on, get out of here, son!"

Waving at him and grinning, I hurried into the school washroom, where I withdrew my freshly ironed shirt from a pocket in my schoolbag.

In a second it was on. Then I'd comb my hair and style it with a dab of my mother's hair cream I'd sneaked into my bag that morning. A spritz of lavender cologne or even my mother's perfume, whichever had been easier to take with me that morning, and I was ready to go.

With a move worthy of Anwar Wagdi in the movies, I flung the bag upwards with all my might to one of the boys who lived near us. He made a spectacular catch, with the understanding that he was to give it to the doorman of our building for me to pick up when I came home. Then I was off like the wind, running from street to street to the tram stop, where I got lost in the crowds.

Sweating with anticipation, I stared at the tram coming in from Abbasiya.

When I saw its yellow cars, its clanging bell announcing its arrival at the station, I lost my mind a little: I would gaze around, looking for her among the schoolgirls alighting from the first three cars, or the ones who got away, even now crossing the street toward the sidewalk.

From afar, I could see some girls coming out of the bookstore on the other side of the street, or buying sunflower seeds and ice cream at the stores adjacent to Cinema Misr. I would rush hither and thither, searching, but not finding her.

I would go back to the stop, waiting for the next tram among a fresh crowd of people, longing searing my heart. I would look once again in the direction of Abbasiya: perhaps the next tram, or the next . . . . But no luck, and I would return home empty-hearted.

Days passed, my heart still longing.

One day I even resolved to take her apartment by storm, as I had done the last time. Any excuse: English books, Arabic lessons, anything. I actually put my clothes on and made to go, but what remained of my sanity stopped me, for fear of alerting Madame Subki and bringing disaster down upon myself and her too. The street, I said to myself, is safer.

So I loitered around for hours in hopes of seeing her in the street, or perhaps looking off the balcony. I would go nearer to Amm Idris, sitting on his bench alongside him and chatting with him: we spoke of soft ice cream, Nubia, the Sudan, and our street, which was much less clean now that Amm Tolba, the street sweeper, had retired.

I would talk to him while he listened and fingered his mustache or pushed the ends of his large white turban away from his ears, scratching it as he gritted his teeth. When he got tired of me, he would stretch out his legs as if to rise and say, "Why don't you go upstairs and study a bit, young sir? It might do you good when exam time comes around, instead of sitting here just blabbering and chattering."

I no longer saw her before me from time to time as I had before. Her image now haunted me continuously, sleeping and waking. Her voice rang in my ears: "Hello, Galal. The button . . . . Oh! Oh! Where did it get to?"

I asked myself if she was as much in love with me as I was with her. Didn't she feel the same way about me? Her eyes said that she did; her flaming face spoke for itself; our fingers that had touched, accidentally and on purpose—or was it all an illusion, a fantasy that I was living in alone?

When it grew too much, I thought of asking my mother: she was, after all, an expert in matters of the heart.

I hurried to her. She was reclining on the couch, reading glasses low on her nose, holding an old copy of an imported fashion magazine that my grandmother had bought when she was still a star of the dressmaking world.

She did not acknowledge my presence, so I stood right at her head, reading over her shoulder.

She was looking at a full-page horizontal spread of a bevy of 1950s models on a catwalk modeling two-piece bathing suits. Opposite this was a brightly colored advertisement for a type of aged liquor, the English inscription beneath it proclaiming that he who had not tried it did not know the meaning of life.

I sat facing her and coughed delicately.

She looked up, turning her attention to me, and I started out by talking of superficial matters.

She replied in monosyllables, saying "Yes," "No," and "I know," her eyes still on the magazine.

As soon as I broached the subject—without mentioning Nadia's name, of course, pretending that I had a friend who had this problem, not I—she put down her magazine and turned completely to face me. A little sharply, she said, "That's because Egyptian girls are a race of luckless unfortunates. They fall in love like we Jewish women do, maybe more, sometimes. But the thing is, they're downtrodden and powerless: they have no way to express their love. And if a girl should dare, she'll be ruined—and that's if they don't smack her down with slippers and lock her away in a room and bolt the door to keep her in like a prisoner."

I said, to give myself patience and to explain away Nadia's absence from me all this time, "I thought maybe it was that she was shy." She shook her head. "Shyness, Mom, shy—Didn't you ever feel shy, when you were around Dad?"

"Shyness? Don't be a fool! It's fear, son. Fear!" She looked at a patch in a corner of the ceiling where water damage had peeled the paint and exposed the base layer, which told me she was remembering her old world, and I made to return to my room. But she motioned to me to sit down, leaning in and taking hold of my wrist.

Her voice fell upon my ears, low and tender. She spoke of falling in love, that it was she who had been in love with my father first, and that she had loved him more than he had loved her. If she could turn back time, she said, she still would not have chosen anyone else, in spite of what she had suffered, and being torn apart from friends and family. I listened, and looked at her tenderly, and kissed the hand that still held my wrist.

She withdrew her hand, startling me with a note in her voice unlike any I had heard before. "If I hadn't given your father a clue, he'd have bought his bolt of fabric and gone off and I'd never have seen him again! I had to say, 'Come back next week; I'll show you the new stock that's coming in,' or, 'Don't buy it today. The sale's starting next month. It's a secret; I heard it from the secretary of Khawaga Samaan, the proprietor, and I'm not allowed to tell the clients.' I looked down and said," her eyes turned coy, younger suddenly, "'But you're not a client. You're different.'"

She told me of the times she had taken him by the hand around the shop, to show him shirts, socks, and shoes.

She expected him to ask her out on a certain day after her shift, and sure enough, he did. They ate alfresco, then had juice at Wilson's in al-Ataba al-Khadra. They took a stroll on Mohamed Ali and Abd al-Aziz streets. She said that she had planned his move from al-Hussein, where he used to live, to Daher. Her face shone with joy as she recalled, "You know when we had our first kiss?"

I looked down at the rug, embarrassed, fiddling with my overturned slipper with my toe.

She paid no attention to the blush creeping up my cheeks. "I kissed your father on the cheek as we were unpacking his furniture in the room he rented on the roof. When he turned to me, I slipped away. Do you know," she warmed to her topic, "that Amm Idris, that cadaver, caught us kissing?"

"Mom, don't talk about things like that!" I begged, mortified.

I tried to go back to the original topic of conversation. I was adamant in my opinion and made fun of girls who were forward, but with care, of course, out of respect for her.

Angrily, she said I was stupid, would never be a man of the world. "That peasant blood is still in your veins yet!"

Then, she deliberately turned the conversation to topics that I knew little or nothing about—I was still ignorant of my religion, so I was unable to make a counterargument back then—and she kept cornering me, making me out to be a

Muslim stick-in-the-mud. I was so frustrated and beleaguered that I started to raise my voice to shut her up, and it degenerated into a fight.

After each of these fights—for more followed—we never stayed mad at one another for more than half a day, after which one of us would take the initiative for reconciliation. I would wait for a moment when she was at the other end of the house and drop something heavy. When she came running, I would hop on one foot, holding my ankle with the other. She would understand, and smile. Or I would go to her directly where she sat and kiss the parting of her hair, whereupon she would hold me tenderly. Often, she would come to me.

Then would come the skirmishes, usually performed by the party taking the peace initiative. The skirmish always began with an attempt to sound out the other party. I would say, as though in the course of normal conversation, "Those people look wonderful, coming out of Friday prayers: rich and poor, old and young, the ones who pray inside and the ones who spread out mats in the street—look at them all shaking hands after prayer!"

She would make no response, respecting the reconciliation that had taken place just a few moments ago.

I would then hold forth, in snatches of phrases, about the tolerance of Islam, about how it was the one true religion and how humans, by instinct and intelligence, gravitated to it, phrases little more than headings I had heard in religion class or from the religious clerics I watched on television: in my ignorance, I ran out of things to say quickly. I stood there, watching my mother's face to see what effect my words had had on her. It would be stiff, void of all expression: even her eyes were dull and unblinking. I would remember the verse of poetry we had long memorized at school:

I have lent you an inattentive ear;
The heart stays deaf, though the ear may hear.

*

Understanding, I fell silent.

For her part, she would speak to me of Paris, City of Beauty and Light, where my grandfather now lived, how Jews now fully owned half the shops in the Rue de Rivoli and Osman, how the Jewish voice was making itself heard in America, and how there were Jewish-owned banks, factories, and fortunes, plus a few words about Einstein, Freud, Marx, and so-and-so who had earned a Nobel Prize for Medicine, Literature, or Science. Sensing me looking at her, eyes widening, her expression would calm and relax, as though her heart was telling her: *A few rounds more, and you'll win.*

She would change her voice, making it soft and convincing, reminding me of what she had taught me as a child about Jacob and David, and the angel who brought the ram to Abraham. I would say, "But it was to save Ishmael!"

"What did you say?"

"Sayyidna Ishmael."

"Where did you get that? Ignoramus, the ram was to save Sayyidna Isaac." She would repeat it again for emphasis, taking my ear playfully: "Isaac. Isaac. Isaac."

I would insist I was right, and so would she. Seeing that her reconciliation initiative was on the verge of collapse, and that we were on the brink of a fight worse than the previous, she would blink, smiling in my face, but her trembling lips and dark expression said otherwise. I would see it, going along when she said, by way of a compromise: "Ishmael or Isaac, both are Sayyidna Abraham's children." I would nod by means of reconciliation.

And so it was that each of us realized the cold reception our words were having on the other's ears, and so fell silent in anticipation of some future opportunity to reopen the subject. But that was before the incident that forced us both to mark the whole matter of religion 'Off Limits.' Afterward, we dared not broach the subject again, even to hint at it.

174

I took it into my head to bring home a sheikh to persuade my mother to convert to Islam: a real sheikh in a gibbah and a caftan, holding a copy of the Qur'an, knowing all about religion, for I, ignorant and unconvincing, was no good for the job. And why not? Especially as I had once heard her telling my grandmother about Esther, who had worked at the haberdashery counter at Samaan's general store. Esther, my mother said, had converted to Islam from Judaism when she married her neighbor, whereupon my grandmother responded bitterly, "Isn't she Hanna's kid? Hanna, that no-good masseuse who does waxing and bathing for the ladies door-to-door?"

"Yes, Mom."

"And her father, isn't that Greis, who worked at the Greek hospital?"

"That's the one, Mom."

"I wouldn't put it past them. They'd do it, too, that and more! They're filthy slime, not a principle to their name. Don't you dare look her in the eye again."

I was only eighteen. I had no experience, and this was an extremely delicate matter. Whom could I talk to? Who could help me find this sheikh? Hagg Mahmoud? He was like a father to me, but I was ashamed to broach the subject with him. Hassan? Hopeless and useless, just like me. This was the moment when I had no one in the world to turn to, save my mother: no aunts, no uncles, no loving embrace in which to find refuge. That made me think of Umm Hassan, and I went to her at once.

Her face lit up with pleasure, and she laid her head bare in front of me for the first time since I had hit puberty, taking off her head scarf in her passion as she prayed to the Lord to crown my efforts with success. She was so delighted that she kissed me on the head, and on both cheeks. She even bent to kiss my hand, breath hitching and eyes bright. "There's no one else for the job but the sheikh of the zawya! We'll go there together, son! Just give me a minute to get dressed." She took a deep breath. "And if he's not up to the job, we'll take you to al-Azhar with your uncle Mahmoud and we'll get another sheikh, and another and another until God sees fit to grant her that blessing!"

"The sheikh of the zawya? Which zawya?"

"Come on, Galal! The zawya that you and Hassan always used to go to on the first day of Ramadan! You'd hear the call to prayer and come back with the good news, remember?"

I furrowed my brow, remembering Sheikh Khalaf, the good man who had climbed up onto the roof of the zawya to sound the prayer call, and how we had watched him from below in awe. "You mean Sheikh Khalaf?"

"My dear boy, Sheikh Khalaf is far too old to leave his house now. The people of the street went to Basatin and hired a new sheikh. His name is Salamoni Abu Gamous. He eats, sleeps, and wakes in the zawya."

I said OK.

We went there together and waited for him after the afternoon prayer. He was noticeably short and fat, and he held a cudgel in his right hand as thick as a bedpost. His beard was unkempt and dyed with henna, according to the custom of some men of the cloth. It was distrust at first sight—a feeling I believe was mutual. I kept looking at him with distaste as he walked ahead of us. It was like following a railway engine, not a person walking. He would not stop coughing and spitting in the street. Umm Hassan gave me a nudge, as if to say, *Go to him.*

"Go? To him? You've got to be kidding me! Nothing good will come of that guy! He acts like a thug!"

"My boy, don't be unfair; don't judge by appearances."

"Can't you see the cut over his eyebrow? Or the bandage on his hand? He looks like he's always in a fight!"

"Now, Galal! Don't make me regret coming with you. Are you going to speak to him, or shall I go home and leave you on your own?"

I went to him and asked him to stop. He turned to me rudely. "What do you want, boy?"

His voice was so gruff that I fell silent. Umm Hassan came over, and we stood off to the side of the road while Umm Hassan told him the story of my mother. When I interjected to clarify a few points on which her information was incomplete, he jabbed me, saying, "Shut up, boy. When elders speak, see, it's time for you to shut up and listen."

I looked at him resentfully and would have retorted, but Umm Hassan nudged me in the knee for silence.

After she was done with her tale, he turned to me. "Go on, boy, say your piece."

I waved a hand in refusal.

Nostrils flaring, displaying pin-like hairs, he said, "That's good. The summary I got from your aunt is enough. I've no patience for kids' chatter." He pushed his turban back and said, in classical Arabic, licking his mustache, "Fear not, woman, for this task is mine! Tie the yoke around my neck, and place your trust in the one who sleeps not, neither does he slumber."

"What was that, Sayyidna?"

"He says it'll be easy, Umm Hassan."

"Easy? What are you saying of easy, boy? Did I say that, liar? This is a job, a big job, I say, and I'm a pro! Besides, easy or difficult, what's it to you? This is my job, see, and results are what you want, and results are what you'll get." He snorted, "The lousy characters I have to deal with in this line of work!"

I bristled at that and waved a hand, but before I could say a word, Umm Hassan jumped in. "But do be careful, Sayyidna; she's stubborn, and her head's hard as a rock!"

"Rock? Ha! I'm Abu Gamous, the one and only! You got no idea who you're talking to! She'll be putty in my hands."

We headed for home, the three of us. He was forever listing sideways, bumping into me without apologizing, to say nothing of the spittle that issued from his mouth and splattered my clothing. I tried to avoid him as much as possible. Umm Hassan hurried on ahead. His eyes were fixed lasciviously upon her rear end as she walked before us, leading me to finally give him an elbow in the ribs. "Hey, Sayyidna! I'm over here!"

He stopped at the first juice store we found, ordering a glass, then another. He burped, motioning to me to pay. He suggested that we not start the job until we had had a meal of hot liver sandwiches. I remonstrated. "The vending cart isn't far, boy; it's just at the street corner."

"There's no time."

"Time? What are you talking about, time? It's tradition! I don't want to break tradition. Whenever I get a new customer, I take him to the kebab place. That's a kilo of meatballs just for me. Then there's the combo: liver, sweetbreads, testicles, and some fat meat, and then there's the sweets and a fresh pack of smokes. That's just for openers. I'm savin' you money, see? I'll settle for just some liver off of the cart, 'cause I feel sorry for you! You look like a migrant worker. Say, what do you do anyway, boy? Baker's boy? Cobbler's assistant? Or maybe you just go 'round in the street with a pot of beans?"

Another peep out of him and I would have pushed him down on his face. I knew without a doubt he'd prove unequal to the task we had for him. It was too late, now, though: I would have to go through with it so as not to disappoint Umm Hassan.

I refused to go along with what he asked, though. "No liver and no nothing, Sheikh Halmous," I said in a tone that indicated that this was final. "We go straight to the house."

"What's this Halmous? My name's Sheikh Salamoni. Isn't it enough that you're a dirty miser and won't lay out a penny; now I find out you're deaf, too? I don't want any liver from your filthy hands anyway, you little creep! You look like you could jinx a whole neighborhood." He stomped on, and grabbed my wrist at the gate of the building. "Before I go in, we have to reach an agreement."

"An agreement? Over what?"

"My fee, my fine fella. Did you think you were going to cheat me out of my rightful due? Twenty pounds and not a penny less!"

"Fine," I said, humoring him.

"And you'll need to slaughter a cow or a big, fat sheep."

"OK."

"And I have to be the one standing at the pot and handing out the meat."

"Just as you say, Sheikh Salamoni."

"Call me Amm al-Sheikh Salamoni; have some manners!"

"Just as you say, Amm al-Sheikh Salamoni. Do you want that set to music?"

"Keep a civil tongue in your head, boy! Do you think I'm playing around?"

The trouble started as we were going up the stairs. He eyed the steps and risers balefully. "Isn't there an elevator?"

"What?"

"An elevator, ignoramus. Don't you know anything? Do you not know the meaning of 'elevator'? A device that takes people upward, and every person is then elevated to his apartment."

"Ah! You mean a lift! Sorry, Amm al-Sheikh, you're flat out of luck."

I was obliged to offer him some assistance, especially where the stairs curved. It was like pushing a barrel of oil up the stairs, or an especially well-stuffed sack of cotton, as he cheered me on: "Yes, that's it! Push! Put some backbone into it! Down by the kidneys!"

At the second landing, he turned to me. "What's your mother's name?"

"Camellia," I said, almost at the end of my patience.

"No Camellia, no famillia, nosiree Bob! After I'm done with her today, we'll rename her Long Tail Woman, like they used to call my mother. How do you like that?"

I responded, longing to spit in his face, "You bet, Sheikh Salamoni; sure thing!"

When we reached my floor, he hurried on ahead of me and took to banging on the glass of the apartment door with both hands.

"Whoa there, Sheikh Mud! Show some manners! Show some common courtesy! I'll knock, not you! I go in first, not you! And anyway, there is a doorbell, Sayyidna!"

"It's a strategy, you dunce! We have to take her by storm! She must be shocked, overwhelmed, no time to think! She won't know what hit her! We just storm the house like the police coming to arrest some miscreant!" And then, he realized what I'd called him. "Wait, you ill-mannered brat! Did I just hear you call me Sheikh Mud? I, Mud, you son of a—"

We had almost come to blows when my mother opened the door, and with it, the door of every other apartment swung open, little children bursting out and running toward the source of all the excitement. I could hear Hagg Mahmoud huffing and puffing up the stairs, closely followed by Amm Idris, brandishing the stick he used to shoo away the stray cats that made their way onto the back stairs.

My mother screamed, face pale as a sheet, "What's going on? Who is this man? Talk to me, Galal!"

Hagg Mahmoud caught him by the sleeve of his gibbah. "What are you doing here, Abu Gamous?" He turned to me. "And you, Galal, why are you associating with the likes of him? How on earth did you meet him?"

"What am I doing?" retorted Abu Gamous. "I'm not here begging, Hagg Mahmoud! This lousy little brat here," he pointed to me, "he came to me—along with just the most delicious hunk of woman with a jiggling bottom the size of a sack of cotton!—and begged me on bended knee to come here and do what must be done to save this godless woman here."

He motioned to my mother. "Isn't this your mother, brat? It must be this heathen that I'm here to snatch from the jaws of perdition! And you, woman, what's with you, standing there wiggling your hips and flirting with your eyes and waggling your eyebrows like some common tart? Take yourself off into the sitting room, go, and find something to cover up your hair! Make yourself decent before I have an audience with you!" He turned to me. "And you, boy! Go get me a soft drink now, and have a cup of black coffee ready for me right after!"

That was it: I grabbed him by the throat.

"Heathen?" My mother was shrieking. "Perdition? Godless? I'll give you wiggling and waggling, you good-for-nothing lout! You're not even fit to be called a man! Shame on you, using such language, and you a man of the cloth—with henna in your beard, yet! Bear witness, Hagg Mahmoud, bear witness!" She rounded on the sheikh again. "You, a sheikh? You're nothing but a manky old boot!" She whacked my shoulder. "For shame, Galal! I thought I raised you better. How could you do a thing like this? You've made us a laughingstock!" She shook her head. "I'll deal with you later; this is not the time or place!"

"There, there; it's all right." Hagg Mahmoud said, placating her. "As for you, Abu Gamous, just leave quietly, my good fellow."

"Yes, you leaves quietly or else . . . ." said Amm Idris, taking several steps backwards to give his stick a better swing. "Here is a respectable building. Honorable people. You can just get out, Abu Gamous. Why, there is only five or six people praying in the zawya after you is landed there. And you is coming here to raise a ruckus in my building?"

"Shut up, you golliwog! And you, Hagg Mahmoud, what do you mean, go home? Go, without a penny? I haven't even gotten my down payment!"

"Down payment? You're a disgrace!" Hagg Mahmoud said. "Did you come to paint a room, man? You're here on a mission of mercy! Here's twenty-five piasters; now get out of here."

My mother's voice rose, remonstrating with Hagg Mahmoud. "Mission of mercy? Really, Hagg Mahmoud! What's that supposed to mean? You watch your language!"

"I'm sorry, Umm Galal! I didn't mean anything by it! I promise, I mean no offense. For pity's sake, go inside and close the door and let me calm things down my way."

After Abu Gamous had stuffed the twenty-five piasters into his pocket and gone, Hagg Mahmoud said to me, "What were you thinking, Galal! Why would anyone with a brain in his head go and get a sheikh, or anyone else, to convert another person? Faith is a gift from God, my son. More important, though, your mother is not godless, no matter what that low-life fraud said! Your mother is one of the People of the Book. She's a good woman, and her father is a good man. I've lived with your family for thirty years now. Damn Abu Gamous, anyway!"

He took my hand. "Do you know what that dirtbag originally was? He was a robber baron! I swear it! He was a gravedigger with over fifty arrests on record at the Basatin police station, for jumping over the graveyard fences and stealing the marble headstones and plaques! Heaven preserve us, he even used to open up any grave he could get into and steal the bones inside—a leg, an arm, any old thing he could get his hands on—to sell to medical students!

"In fact, I even heard—although God alone knows how true it is—that last year, the other gravediggers got sick of his misconduct. They ganged up on him and beat him up—broke his arm! God forgive whoever hired him to preside over the zawya! I wish it had stopped there: now I hear there's some new scandal with some woman, right here in the neighborhood—but I won't spread gossip, my boy. God the Merciful One is the preserver of reputations. Suffice to say that it's like the old proverb: he's like the tail of the dog, once crooked, always crooked."

Before I went inside, Hagg Mahmoud took me aside, lowering his voice. "I beg of you, convey my apologies to your honorable mother for the words I said without thinking. You know I hold your family in the highest esteem."

I nodded, assuring him I would do so, and made to leave. But he held me back. "Wait, wait! Come here; I forgot to ask! Who's that woman you were with, when you were going to Abu Gamous? That woman with a bottom the size of a sack of cotton? He's an old rogue, won't keep his eyes or his hands to himself! We really need to be careful of him!"

"Woman?" I said. "There was no woman! He's making things up out of whole cloth, Amm Mahmoud!"

"Ah! That certainly makes sense. I know he's a liar, Sheikh Mud—always has been."

But my mother didn't let it go so easily. She didn't speak to me for two weeks after that.

27

AFTER THINGS SETTLED DOWN AND my mother and I were back to normal, I said to myself, 'What about Nadia? How long am I going to go on like this? It isn't doing me any good to cut out every day after third period and hang around by the tram stop! I don't see Nadia any more on the stairs or in the street, and the balcony doors are always closed in the daytime.' I had no choice but to cut school altogether and beard the lion in his metaphorical den, at the Abbasiya Secondary School for Girls.

I still remember that day. It was a Tuesday. I jumped out of bed early, before my mother could call for me or the alarm could ring. I was lighter than a feather, and running through my head was the song *I'm Yours Forever, Be Mine* by Abd al-Halim Hafez, the most famous pop singer of the day.

A trip to the bathroom, a comb-through, a close shave followed by a splash of the Montego aftershave my grandfather had sent me from Paris, and when I was satisfied with my appearance, I opened the door to my room, eyes going cautiously to the room where my mother slept.

Closed—good. Everything was quiet—just as I wished.

I drew back the bolt and in a second was on the stairs—not, of course, touching the dusty banister so as not to ruin my appearance.

Before I stepped out of the building and into the hustle and bustle of the street, though, my name was called sharply. I took several steps back and looked up, searching for my mother. She stood at the door in her dressing gown, her hair still uncombed, holding my schoolbag and sandwiches. Sunnily, I sang out, "Good morning, best mother in the world! I won't need the bag; it's a school trip today! But the sandwiches are good."

I went upstairs to get them, but she met me with a scowl. "What's this trip that's come up all of a sudden, then? You and I were sitting on the balcony all of yesterday evening and you didn't say a word about it. What's more, I saw you arranging your books in your bag before you went to bed. How is there a trip, then?"

"I was just looking for my math book to go over something before I went to bed."

"Go over something? Go on."

"I forgot to tell you, Mother. I simply forgot. To err is human, after all! You know I'd forget my head if it wasn't attached. I forget my Arabic, I forget my chemistry, I forget my English. The teachers are always scolding me. I think I need to go to a doctor and find out what's wrong with me."

"Galal, behave! Don't play dumb with me, and tell me right this instant what trip it is you're going on."

I knew she wouldn't quit till she got what she was after, so I started to prevaricate. "It's a religious trip. We're going to visit the Islamic mosques: Azhar, Hussein, and Sayyida Zeinab too. If there's time, we'll visit the Sayyida Nafisa and Imam al-Shafie mosques as well. All of them, all of them."

"Is that so?"

"Yes, it's so."

I had led her onto forbidden ground, and she could only look at me suspiciously, but not speak. She went back inside, leaving me alone.

I lingered at the door to the building, hoping to see Nadia coming out: but I turned tail and made tracks when I saw Madame Subki leaning on the balcony sill, her eye on me. I ran through the streets to the tram stop and sat on the wooden seat, catching my breath and calming the suspicions that ran through my head. One tram passed, then another, while I said to myself, "Put a stop to this, Galal. Be careful, or her mother might show up right behind you, suspicious and following to see what you're up to."

When the third tram arrived and the whistle sounded, I found myself running for it like the wind: a couple of elbows, a shove here and a shove there, and I had cleared a place for myself on the outer stair, hanging on alongside the young men doing their military service, heading for the camps in Abbasiya and Nasr City.

In the blink of an eye, I was on the sidewalk facing her school.

Noise, motion, klaxons, and girls, girls, girls, all in navy blue uniforms. Some tall, some short, some veiled, and some with long hair flowing down over their shoulders, some serious, walking along like soldiers, and some laughing and playing. Some coming alone from side streets, and some arriving in a chauffeured car. And then there were those who gathered up the hem of their skirts as they stepped out of the tram.

When morning assembly started, I crossed the street, taking up a good spot at a gap in the school's wooden fence. It wasn't a bad gap, as gaps go: I could have gotten my whole head through it if I wanted to. I suddenly found myself joined by a one-armed man in pajama pants and an army surplus khaki shirt, and two women whom I judged to be doormen's wives. There was also an older boy who, it was evident from the grease all over his overalls, was an apprentice on his way to work. We all stood there, watching the assembly take place.

The headmistress was an admirable figure, formidable and smartly dressed. She wore gold-rimmed spectacles, had pale pink skin, and was a perfect 36-26-36: a model, shapelier than Sophia Loren.

She had come out of her office, and began to walk back and forth before the rows of girls for all the world like she was the minister of education. At her heels walked a lady teacher in black pants, a cane in her hand. She was short and squat, but it was all muscle. She must have been the P.E. teacher.

By her side walked a reptilian male teacher, looking like a crocodile: he panted incessantly, a copybook in hand in which he took notes.

The headmistress looked at him, pointing out one of the girls, and he said, "I know, I know, Madam, and if I've told her once, I've told her a hundred times! I've told them your instructions are that the hem of the skirt should come down to mid-calf!" He paused, whereupon she nodded for him to continue. He said, panting, "Yes, yes. Just let me catch my breath. I've told them and done my duty; it's no fault of mine. What am I to do with these wretched girls who won't do as they're told?"

"That's enough, Mr. Lamie. That's enough. Since they're so recalcitrant, a letter must be sent out to their parents. Today."

"Yes, Madam."

"You're aware that this isn't my idea. It's the ministry instructions. The ministry decree says that skirts must fall at mid-calf, not like that little hussy. And that girl in the second row! She's practically wearing a microskirt! Is she coming to a school or some discothèque? And that girl with a dark blue bow in her hair, Mr. Lamie? And the one in the last row?"

"I see her, Madam, I see her." He gritted his teeth and bellowed at the girls, "See? You see how disappointed the headmistress is? Haven't I talked myself hoarse telling you all this? Well, you'll be bringing letters home today, and don't say I didn't warn you! Starting tomorrow, if you don't follow the dress code, you won't be let through the gates of this school!"

The man next to me left, followed by the boy. Only the two women remained. One of them said to the other, "Look at that! A great big man like him, cringing like a barnyard hen when that woman yells at him! And him with that big, manly mustache!"

"Can you blame him? Why, this is her on a good day! You should see her when she's in a mood! She rants and raves and flattens everyone in sight! And that broth of a boy just cowers in front of her, he doesn't even dare breathe. She's hard as nails and that's the truth! That is one strong woman!"

"Wow! By the Prophet, we're pussycats compared to her. You think she'd dare do that in front of her husband?"

"Why shouldn't she? Strong is strong no matter where you are! But it's like you say, Umm Badawi, we don't have that in us! If I'm a minute late with the tea for Zaghloul, he'll make my life miserable. One time that goon—and you know he looks like a jackass!—threw the gas burner at me. See where the scar is on my shoulder?"

As the woman began to pull back her clothing to show her friend the wounded shoulder, I turned quickly back to the assembly.

The headmistress had finished her inspection and was standing in the middle of the school yard for the rest of the ceremonies.

To one side stood a group of schoolteachers, all women, all about the size of my auntie Umm Hassan, and all, apparently, went to the same dressmaker who fashioned her clothes: the same styles, and even the same cut. Not one curve nor one flare, nary a hint of a dart or a gusset, nor even so much as a button. One hook at the neckline and down the dress would go all the way to the ankle like a veritable sack.

I kept watching them. There were about seven or eight of them all told, all sour-faced as though every door of hope had been slammed shut in their faces and all that remained of the world was dark and dreary.

Only two of them were different: they stood off to the side together, whispering and looking at the headmistress, their eyes running over her from the tips of her Italian shoes to her Farah Diba hairstyle.

The girls, I swear, were every bit as naughty as the boys at my school. They winked and chattered to one another and hid their laughter. One of them gave her friend a pinch, which was repaid with a poke in the backside; a smooth, practiced hand pulling off a hair ribbon and getting an elbow in the side from her friend—but then the flag salute began: "Long live Egypt! Long live Egypt! Long live Egypt!"

My heart lifted to hear the feminine voices ringing out, and life was suddenly charming and beautiful. Down, I thought, with Leithi, Fouad, Darwish, Khairi, and the rest of them, down with their harsh tones, cracked from smoking water pipes!

The girls went into class; I went into the café facing the square. It had just opened its doors, the waiters still setting out the tables and dusting them off with the ubiquitous orange towels, hosing off the café floors and making everything clean and sparkling, although a faint musty odor still emanated from the interior.

When I made to go inside, a man wiping the sweat off his brow gestured to me to two chairs, one upside down on top of the other, to let me know they weren't quite ready to receive customers yet.

Meanwhile, I had been joined by a group of elderly men, who stood next to me, chattering, each of them with a newspaper under his arm or in his hand. Another three or four paced back and forth.

When a café worker untangled the two chairs, everyone headed quietly and purposefully inside. Each of them made a beeline for his usual table, and they began to take their seats. More elderly gentlemen began to trickle in from outside.

It appeared that the morning crowd was mainly pensioners. The waiters knew them by name, bringing them their usual without being told: tea with milk for one, ginger tea for another, and as for the gentleman in the corner, he had just lit his cigarette and had to be provided instantly with his black coffee.

Time passed. All I could hear was the scraping of chairs and the rustling of newspapers. The waiters were accommodating and polite, making no noise and arguing with no one, and the customary loud calls of café boys were absent. They were veritable angels of the café. Clearly, they had been carefully selected—or were perhaps under strict orders to remain quiet and be gentle with this type of customer.

I didn't stay long. Bored, I got up to walk the streets of Abbasiya. When school let out, though, I was right at the door of the school, a thousand eyes in my head. I caught sight of Nadia leaving school.

My eyes automatically went to the hem of her skirt. It was Chanel-length, as per the headmistress' instructions, and the few inches of ankle showing were so well-turned as to turn my head. Anyone seeing such an ankle could only sigh from the depths of his soul and say, "Thank you, God, for creating such beauty!" Her skin was pale, but the sun, insisting on making its presence known, had covered it with a light tan. Her head was held high. Her feet struck the ground with the confident, firm tread of a wild mare that no horseman had tamed.

I was overcome by the feeling that what I was looking at was mine—mine alone. Nadia was part of me, of my family, and I was part of hers. I could not stand the thought of anyone in the world caring for her but me, or seeing her, unless it was in passing, or just to say hello.

She crossed the street, and I followed. She got on the tram, and so did I. At the Cinema Misr tram stop, she stopped for a moment after alighting, looking around her, and our eyes met. She appeared unconcerned, but her eyes said differently. Well before al-Khalig al-Masri Street, I had hurried forward to walk alongside her.

She stole a glance at me and slowed her pace. "Go away. Someone might see us."

I didn't speak. I was too flustered.

"I said go away. Go away, Galal! Have you lost your mind?"

I said beseechingly, "I've been standing outside your school all day, just to see you for this one minute."

"I know. I know. I saw you a while ago. But go away now!"

"I've been looking for you for a month! I want to see you! I've been waiting at the tram stop every day."

"I've been ill. Didn't your mother tell you? She came to visit me twice. I thought, 'When he finds out I'm sick, he'll find some way to see me.'"

"Oh, my helpful mother! She tells me everything but what's important. If I'd known, I'd have come to see you in a white coat with a stethoscope over my shoulder, making like a doctor."

"Oh yeah?"

"You, lying on the bed, your hair on the pillow. You'd open your eyes and see me standing there, and then you'd say, like Leila Murad in the film, 'Doctor of the heart, darling of my heart!'"

"Quit that, now, Galal!"

We never did go across al-Khalig Street. We turned round as one and went back to al-Geish Street. We were silent for a while. I reached for her hand, but she withdrew it, looking at me shyly. The second time, her palm nestled docilely into mine, and I rubbed it and squeezed her hand gently. It was warm. Her fingers began to interlace with mine, one after the other.

"Just think! Me waiting for you at the tram stop, you waiting for me at the window!"

"Who said I was waiting for you at the window? I was bored, so I looked out the window and happened to see you."

"Is that so?"

"Yes, it's so."

"Look me in the eye and say it, then."

"There."

Overcome with love, we didn't even see Amm Idris coming, leaning on his stick. We saw him at the same instant, and I think he saw us too. Nadia gripped my arms, fear in her eyes, and I froze too. I stood there, paralyzed with shock.

"Did he see us?"

"No, he didn't. He's an old chatterbox. If he'd seen us, he'd have stopped to talk."

"I'm shaking all over. My mother would kill me!" And she tried to run off, but I gripped her hand.

"No, I'm going," she said. "I'm going to cross the street and go straight home. And you, you stay here! Don't you dare follow!"

"When will I see you again?"

"Later." She hurried off. "Later." I followed her with my eyes until the street took her away.

That night I went to bed with a secret in my heart.

28

WE MET AGAIN, AND AGAIN. We had a standing date for me to meet her at the tram stop every Tuesday at one o'clock. "If I'm late," she said, "wait till two. If you're late, though, I won't wait for you, not a single minute."

I agreed, my hand twining around hers.

I would always come from school early. I sat on a cement bench in the central portion of the stop, my eyes eagerly seeking the next tram from Abbasiya. When I saw the foremost car in the distance, I wished I could fly and meet it halfway.

If I was ever late, I expected her to do as she had said. But I would find her there, waiting for me, her bag at her feet and a magazine in her hands, usually *al-Kawakeb*. She would look up to see me crossing the street, and motion to me to calm my frenzied rush and slow down. Ashamed of myself, I would say, panting, "I'm sorry! I'm sorry. I ran all the way here."

"You're only ten minutes late. Just catch your breath. It's all right." And with that, she would lay her hand over mine, or use her handkerchief to wipe the sweat from my brow. I would look at her, my heart loving her more.

"How are you doing with your studying?"

Her question took me by surprise. "Great. Since I started seeing you regularly, I'm a new man. I devour my books. I want to score high, 80 percent or higher. If I could only get into medical school!"

"Have you thought about military school, or perhaps the police academy?"

"You know that people like me aren't allowed into the military, nor even the police. The people whose mothers . . . ." I trailed off.

Her eyes filled with compassion as I went on heatedly, "I don't know what I did wrong. I'm no worse than any other guy. I'm as much an Egyptian as you, as any other fellow in the street. Maybe more."

I was so worked up that it seems my voice had gotten louder, for two men near us broke off their conversation to stare. An old lady got up from her seat and came over to sit by us, saying, "What's the matter, kids? Having a fight?"

"Nothing's the matter, madam," Nadia said coldly. "Nothing."

She took me by the hand and led me away from the tram stop, the old lady still following us, remonstrating, "Really now! I was just asking! Nothing wrong with asking, is there? That's the trouble with girls these days: they're so impatient. Why, in my day . . . ."

She turned to a woman holding a baby, another child clutching the hem of her skirt, to tell her what things were like in her day, the woman rolling her eyes and looking in the other direction.

After a short silence, I said, "Did you know that my father died in the war?"

"I know. Everyone on our street knows."

"And my father's family back in the village—I wish there could be a time when you could come and meet them. They're salt of the earth, the real Egypt. They till the soil and grow everything we eat and drink." I added, hotly, "And my grandfather! My mother's father—If you could have seen his face as he was leaving!"

"I believe you, Galal, I'm sure of it. He must have been so upset to be leaving his home."

"Upset? Upset isn't the word. He was dying, being torn apart, as he was leaving."

"But," she asked, her question in her eyes, "why did he leave Egypt and emigrate, then, if he didn't want to?"

"They made him, my grandmother and my uncle. He couldn't refuse. God will punish them for their cruelty! The whole family ganged up on him!"

"Well, I'm just thankful they didn't take you along with them."

"If my grandmother could have, she would have. I was under my uncle's legal guardianship—my father's brother, I mean—and I still am. He wouldn't let me leave the country, nor even allow them to have a passport made out for me. And you know what?" I smiled, and her smile grew wider as she looked at me. "My mother told me once that my uncle was so afraid they'd take me with them that he had the apartment watched for a whole year. He sent some men from his village to our street. They'd walk back and forth, or stand outside Muallim Habib's juice store, for hours, and they sat so long on Amm Idris's bench, you'd have thought they'd never leave. And they would talk to him, trying to get him to spill secrets about me. Or there were times when they'd come knocking at our door, pretending they had the wrong apartment!

"Why, there was this one prize idiot who came to our door twice in the same day. The first time he said, 'Is Mr. Zanati in?' and my mother said no and sent him packing. She knew what he was about, of course. The second time he said, 'Is this Mr. Auf's house?'

"My mother said, 'For shame, and you a great big man with a mustache as big as a slipper! Lying and disturbing people in their very homes! You want Mr. Auf? He's in.' And then she started calling, 'Mr. Auf—I mean Galal! Galal!' Then she led me out by the hand and said, 'Here's Mr. Auf. What do you want with him?' And my mother laughed so much, she told me the man was so flustered he didn't know what to do or say. And finally he said, 'I don't mean this Auf. The Auf I want is married with children.' And he ran off down the stairs while my mom stood on the landing calling out, 'Don't you show your face again here, you incompetent oaf! And tell the man who sent you: shame on you!'"

I was laughing as I told Nadia all this, and she laughed, too. "That's it, Dr. Galal! Have a good laugh!"

I stared at her.

"That's right. I want you to be a doctor, an important man. You'll have a clinic in al-Geish Street, and another opposite where my school is." She went on, "They'll call me—" she cupped her hand over the side of her mouth, leaning shyly toward me.

I finished for her, devouring her with my eyes. "—Dr. Galal's wife."

She gave my hand a little pinch. "Hush! For shame! Amm Idris might hear us."

"Nope; it was pretty clear last time that his eyes aren't what they used to be. He can hardly see. And I bet he's half-deaf, too."

We took to talking about Amm Idris, of what a kind-hearted fellow he was and of his fun stories that had no end; of Said, Hagg Mahmoud's firstborn, who had bought an old Fiat from a friend of his who lived over on Ahmed Said Street, flaunting it with great pride outside our building, but finding out a week later that he had been duped: the car turned out to be stolen.

"Uncle Hagg Mahmoud was half-mad, he was so disappointed, and he went out of his shop with the ladle in his hand, adamant that he would crack his son Said on the head with it! And what's more, my mother says that Aunt Umm Hassan yelled in his face and threw a mug of water she'd been holding right in his face, as soon as he set foot in the apartment."

Nadia looked at me in a way that told me she wanted to go home. I stopped her.

"Nadia. Do you think your mother would say yes, if I asked for your hand?"

She stared at me. "Ask for my hand? Now? Wait till you're in university, at least."

Annoyed by the response, I said, "No, but what I'm asking is, would she say yes?"

"Well, I'm not sure."

"I'm serious," I said, even more annoyed.

She took my hand. "Of course she'll say yes! I'm her only daughter. I'm all she's got. She'll never stand in the way of my happiness." She smiled slyly. "What's your rush, anyway?"

After that, we didn't meet for several weeks. I would go to the tram stop every Tuesday, but she wasn't there. 'She might be ill,' I would say to myself, 'or maybe something else is keeping her,' but I didn't know what to do, if anything. I thought of asking my mother indirectly, or going up to her house myself, or using Amm Idris as a messenger, but I carried out none of these plans.

One day I saw her by chance on the stairs. She was on her way up as I was going out into the street. She looked around her, frightened and unhappy. "What's the matter, Nadia?" I asked. "You had me worried."

"Go now, Galal."

I moved closer; she stepped back, until she was flush against the wall of the stairwell.

"Go, I said," she entreated. "Go, if you love me."

"Nadia, what's going on?"

"I don't know why, but there's something different about my mother. She watches my every move, times me when I go out, and yells at me for every little thing."

"Do you think she's noticed anything?"

"I'm not sure. And what's got me more worried is that my uncle, Sheikh Mohamed, went to school and asked about me there. He's never done that before!"

199

"It might be nothing."

"Do you really think so? I wish it were."

And then she was in my arms, and I was pressing passionate kisses to her cheeks and lips, and she was half-heartedly pushing me away. "That's enough! You're mad! Stop it; someone might see!"

We came to ourselves at the sound of Amm Idris' deep voice. "Psst! Psst! You naughty kitties!"

He was directly facing us, and there was no question that he had seen us. Nadia's heart sank, and she didn't know what to do. She clung to me for support, then, with a final, fleeting glance at me, went away upstairs, leaving me alone to deal with that old viper, who pretended to see nothing, but knew everything.

I don't know where he sprang up from, whether from above or below, or whether he had just dropped out of the sky. He was bareheaded: his curly salt-and-pepper hair was relieved by a single patch on the side of his head, the size of a date, that was completely bald, not a single hair. His white gallabiya hung down a little distance below his knees, and in his hand he held a stick. His cunning eyes roved over my bloodless face. "A cat, Master Galal! A cursed cat, driving me mad! Black, its tail cut off, and every day it comes creeping round and over-turning the garbage cans the people leave out." I couldn't say a word. "Did you see it, Master Galal? I don't know what to do about the naughty kitty. It needs a whack on the head with my stick, to teach it not to do it again. What else? It only get what it deserve!"

"No, Amm Idris. I haven't seen any cat, nor even a mouse. You just saw me going downstairs minding my own business on my way to the shops. And why are you barefoot? You should be careful. You might step on something, and it might cut your foot. It could be quite serious at your age."

"What else? I took my shoes off so as to creep up the stairs all quiet-like, to catch that shameless, naughty cat!"

Walking up to my apartment, I left him there. 'Better cut it short with this fellow, Galal,' I said to myself. 'Likely as not he won't rest till he's caused a scandal.'

But he called after me, "Why going home, Master Galal? Didn't you say you was going to the shops? What a strange thing!"

I turned back to him. "Let me alone, Amm Idris." I went into my apartment as he went upstairs, my heart pounding. 'Please let it be all right,' I thought. 'If that old monkey goes and blabs to Madame Subki, we're done for.'

29

I DIDN'T GO TO SCHOOL the next day. First, I went to see Amm Idris. I wanted to ask him about it, talk about it, do anything to set my mind at rest. His wife, Sitt Shouq, was sitting in his place on the bench with a tray of rice in front of her, picking it over. She said, her fingers never ceasing their movement over the rice, "He's inside asleep, Master Galal."

"Still asleep? Till this hour?"

"Yes," she looked up at me, flicking away a grain of rice that had gotten stuck between her fingers, "and he'll stay that way till noon prayer, and maybe longer, too. You see, when Amm Idris falls asleep, nobody knows when he'll wake up again—not me, not the kids. Is it important? I could call out for him, and you might get lucky."

I waved off her offer. On the bench beside her, I placed my schoolbag, my sandwiches, and a rolled-up sheet of cardboard, secured with elastic, on which I had drawn a picture representing the October War for a governorate-wide contest sponsored by the Ministry of Education. Leaving these things in her trust, I went away.

My half-formed plan was to stand on a street corner close by the house, in hopes of seeing Nadia and finding out what, if anything, had happened after she left. I was panicky, and my heart was in my feet. Whenever I saw someone I knew coming toward me, I would hide away in a side street. I had no energy to talk to anyone, nor even to lift my arm to shake someone's hand. I couldn't stop asking myself what had happened yesterday. I had been going downstairs in the normal course of events, nothing premeditated. What had occurred had been outside my control, and hers.

Why did I say 'hers'? Why was I dragging her into something I alone was to blame for? I was the one who had started it. It was all my fault, from start to finish. I was the one who had exposed her before the gaze of Amm Idris, and I was the one who would have made her the subject of everyone's gossip if anyone else had seen us. Seeing her in my mind's eye, I hurt worse and felt even more pity for her.

My wait lengthened till it was past time for her to go out, so I kept walking. I couldn't stop remembering the moment when she had clung to me, when we had been surprised by Amm Crap. She had trembled with fear; I had felt her hands pressing my shoulders and upper arms, seeking protection. She had looked at me afterward, as she stepped backwards, clutching the balustrade, while I stood there like an idiot, not knowing what to do. I will never forget her face, contorted in fear, or her eyes, half-glazed over, nor the look she gave me after going a few steps up the stairs. Unable to bear that look, I had dropped my gaze.

It had never occurred to me—and I only realized it a long time afterward, after momentous events in both our lives—that that had been the last time I would ever see her.

I walked through the streets until the call to noon prayer sounded. I had never gone into a mosque before, nor had I ever prostrated myself in prayer except on special occasions, or when I had had a fight with my mother and wanted to rub it in that I was still a Muslim. It popped into my head that I could go into a mosque and pray. I crossed the street to the zawya from which the call came. It was only a small zawya, the muezzin standing at the door, turning to the left and right, hand up to the side of his face to amplify the sound, calling to me at the top of his voice to approach, to come, to bend my knees, take off my shoes, and enter. I made no answer: my feet made no change in their steady pace. After walking through the streets of Daher all the way to Ramsis Street, I went home once more.

My mother was not in her room, nor was she in the kitchen. I lay down on the bed and fell into an exhausted doze. I jolted awake at the screech of the door to our apartment. It was her. I went to her, but she spoke before me, surprise on her face: "What's this I hear? How could you do such a thing, on the stairs?"

Flustered, I said, "You found out?"

"Yes, I found out, smarty-pants! The news is all over the building! But even worse, the concerned party knows!"

I clapped a hand to my forehead and went back to bed. "Who? Madame Subki? Ah, Amm Garbage, you old troublemaker. I knew from the start that you were going to ruin everything."

"Garbage who?" my mother said, surprised. "And did he see you, too? Oh, misery!"

". . . I thought it was him who told on us."

"No, smarty-pants. The maid who works at Abul Saad Effendi's saw you through the window in the door, and she took it straight to Madame Subki." She looked at me absently, tapping her thumbnail against her lips. "Hide, silly boy! For heaven's sake, don't you know enough to hide? Go any old where, and do whatever you want! Not right here in your own home, you dumb bunny, letting people see and raise a ruckus!"

"Hide? Hide what? You've got it wrong, Mom."

"You don't say! Got it wrong, have I?"

"What are you saying? What kind of a girl do you think she is? This is Nadia we're talking about, Mom. Nadia's a respectable girl; she's not like that!"

My mother sailed out of the room, ignoring me. In a little while, she came back and sat on the bed, setting her tea on a nearby table. We sat in silence for a few minutes. She said softly, "I know the girl's pretty. Now I'm asking you calmly: are you just having fun—I mean, you know, a kiss, a date, that kind of thing—or are you serious, maybe thinking of marrying her?"

"Not again, Mom!" I slammed a hand against the headboard. "Not again!"

I stood and made to leave, but she caught my arm.

"Before I sit down, I'll have you know I'm in love with her. I love her. I love her." Wiping away a drop of sweat behind my ear, I added, "And what happened between us, I want to make it right. I'm ashamed of myself. I don't know how I'm going to look anyone in the face: Aunt Umm Hassan, or Amm Hagg Mahmoud and the others. And Madame Subki, above all; how can I even explain myself to her? And Nadia . . . ." I bit my lip.

My mother waved a hand, cutting me off. "Let's just take it step by step. Do you know who she's related to?"

"I know she has an uncle by the name of Sheikh Mohamed."

"That's right! A sheikh with an Azharite turban and a long coat. He comes to visit his sister every month, and the minute he sets foot inside this building, he sets to saying, 'Heaven protect us, heaven preserve us!' And he won't take his eyes off the floor all the time he's climbing the stairs. And her other uncle is Sheikh Mustafa: he's the Imam of Shaarani Mosque, right near here. And they say he's even worse. He won't let the women of his household show their faces to men, nor women either. Her mother, well, you can see for yourself: wearing a head scarf day and night, and all she's got to say is 'According to God and the Prophet this, according to God and the Prophet that.' Do you think the likes of them would let you marry her? A man whose mother is Jewish? And not only that, but whose grandfather and grandmother and aunts and uncles are all Jewish. Do you think they'll let you?"

"Grandfather and Grandmother? What have they to do with me? They're living so far away now, they might as well be in another world."

"For shame, Galal! They're the ones who raised you!"

"I know, Mom, believe me I know, but what I'm saying is that they've gone away and left us."

"And what am I, then, and what's your Grandfather Zaki? Did you forget them, Galal?" She added in a choked voice, "Son, I was just at Madame Subki's apartment. I don't want to repeat what she said. She said things that shouldn't be said, things no woman with a shred of dignity would take. I don't know how those people can even be Muslims, let alone sheikhs! And they have the nerve to prate on about People of the Book! 'Book' my foot!" She sighed. "Anyway, my boy, the woman says she wants to hush it up; she won't have her daughter's name bandied about nor her reputation damaged. But she says if you so much as come near her again, then on your own head be it. She'll tell her brothers, and they'll know what to do with you."

I sat there in silence. She watched my face. Finally, she said, "She says, too, that when the girl's finished school, they're moving out."

"Moving?"

I stared into space as she went on, in a low voice that moved me: "You're young. It's the same all over, Galal. She's a fine girl; there isn't anything wrong with her. But why a Muslim girl? Why, it was like the mother was mocking me for something shameful about me!"

I remained silent.

"My advice to you, my boy, is to stay away from her. I've got no one to stand by me, and I'm not strong enough to stand up to this kind of trouble, nor to people who'll humiliate me for what I am and what I believe. I've got enough to deal with already, son."

I felt my blood boil, surging like a fountain to my head. "Who dares humiliate you, Mom? I'll show Madame

Subki and Sheikh Mohamed later! I'll marry Nadia whether they like it or not! Just wait 'till I graduate from university!"

"Graduate? You don't think I'm staying in this country forever, do you?"

"Then where are you going?" I thought of Grandfather. "To my grandfather?"

"Yes, and as soon as possible."

Grieved, I said, "And leave me?"

"Leave you? Who said? I'm taking you with me. Just you buck up and get your thanawiya amma, and we're off to Paris!"

My eyes shone. "Paris?"

"Yes, Paris. Everything's arranged. And you've a job waiting for you, too. You'll be working with your uncle Shamoun." She gazed at me. "Quite a surprise, isn't it?"

I pulled the pillow into my lap and stared at her as she kept talking.

"And what's more, Susu, Mr. Sholah's son . . . ." My face tightened, and I leaned slightly forward. "Oh, he's a relative of ours; you don't know him. What was I saying? Ah. Susu was here on a visit a couple of months ago, and he said that Rachel's grown up into the prettiest young lady, and she's got money to burn! Do you know what she does?"

I listened more intently.

"She works with tourists from the Gulf! You know they can't speak French. She picks them up at the airports, takes them sightseeing and shopping, and accompanies them until they get back on the plane. And she earns seven or eight thousand francs a month! Minimum!"

"And if I went, what would I do? Go into business with Rachel, or perhaps be a porter like my uncle?"

"You just set your mind to it, and whatever you want will come to pass."

"No, Mother dear, not for me! I'm quite happy here."

Angrily she snapped, "Do you think you'll ever get to touch that Nadia as long as you live? You're dreaming! Think of your prospects, and come with us."

Miserably, I said, "It's not just Nadia; I like it here: our street, Amm Idris, the juice shop, school, the university I'm going to go to, and al-Geish Street . . . . Why would I leave all this and go to a country where I'm a stranger? No friends, no acquaintances, and if I should find work, I'd be a porter at best, or perhaps a garbage collector or a street sweeper!"

My mother looked upset, and I said, more urgently, "Mom, I can't live there. Go for a visit, sure: a month, two or three months even, but then we have to come back. Live there for always? Never."

"Speak for yourself, because I am going to stop there for always. I've done my duty by you. I've remained a widow and never remarried because of you; I've parted from my family for your sake."

"But, Mom . . . ."

"No buts. Do you know, your grandmother nagged me for ages to leave you with your father's family in the village and emigrate with them. I was the one who said no. I wouldn't. 'I won't leave my son all alone,' I said. 'I'm going to raise him, if it means I have to find work as a maid or go begging.' And your grandfather, too: many's the time he had words with your grandmother because of what she suggested."

"I know."

"And do you know, too, that your grandfather left you a thousand pounds in your savings account? Half his life savings. He did it behind your grandmother's back, left the money to help raise you. Do you owe him no loyalty, either?"

I was looking at her lips as she spoke, but my mind was fuzzy, and I didn't know what to do or say.

30

THEY SAID SHEIKH KHALAF HAD died. I was sitting in the hall studying; I had just finished a sample exam in math and was comparing it with the model answer in the study guide *al-Murshid*, finding that I had earned full marks. Leaping up in joy, I went to the balcony, saying to myself, "Medical school, here I come! You'll get Nadia, Galal, in spite of Sheikh Mohamed and all the sheikhs in the world!"

I looked down at the street from above: there seemed to be an unusual disturbance. Amm Hagg Mahmoud paced a few steps away from his store, then turned back, snapping at his shop boys to bring him his shawl and cigarettes from his desk, and fumbling at his pocket for his wallet and not finding it. He waved an impatient hand at the floor and yelled at someone in the shop to look for that, too, in one of the drawers or perhaps underneath the counter. He hurried to the door of our building, meeting Abul Saad Effendi and Captain Farid, our new neighbor, who were waiting for him.

Hassan ran out the door of the building, then whispered in his father's ear. Looking up, he saw me and gestured to me to come downstairs, then ran back inside. On the sidewalk opposite, two or three of our neighbors in the building were standing alongside the bean-store proprietor, the apron still round his neck completely taken over by oil and bean stains, not an inch remaining to give a hint of its original color. They waited an instant for Muallim Habib, who joined them, then walked off, met by Muallim Zenhom the butcher, coming from the opposite direction in the company of Hagg Shalabi, who owned the coffee store.

Abul Saad Effendi asked Sitt Shouq for Amm Idris. She told him that he had heard the news after dawn prayers, and she hadn't seen him since. Sharply, he said, wringing his hands, "Where is he now, then?"

"Huh? Where else should he be, anyway, but at the zawya. He's been there since then along with everyone else!"

"Why didn't you say that from the start?" He turned to the bystanders. "I called the office and got the day off when Duha, the little girl, told me on the way back from buying bread."

"May he rest in peace," sighed Hagg Mahmoud. "Years and years, we and the kids lived by his prayer calls. We always said he brought good luck, and we liked to pray when he was leading the prayer. I remember the evening prayer; the zawya was packed, especially in Ramadan. And dawn prayer with Sheikh Khalaf was something else! And the tahaggud prayer! People would sob out loud and cry real tears." He sighed. "Those were the good old days, when life was worth living, Captain Farid. And people came from so far off! Khalig Street, from over on our side, Daher, from Bab al-Shaariya, and all the way up from al-Geish Square. I swear, it's true!"

He caught his breath. "Why, there were so many people, it was impossible to seat them all. They'd get a mat from here and a mat from there, and Amm Zanati, who rents out chairs and tables and the like at the store in the block behind them, he'd send over a few carpets, and we'd set to saying, 'Set this one here; spread that one there,' until the whole street was blocked." He fixed his gaze on Captain Farid. "And meanwhile, you know the mosque behind us, the big one owned by the Ministry of Religious Endowments? Empty as they come: two or three rows behind the Imam, and thank you and good-bye. The only ones who went to pray there were the ones who were in a hurry. He was a blessed man for sure, a real saint of a fellow, not like that boor Abu Gamous!"

"Oh, that's right! Whatever became of him? He hasn't been seen mooching about on the streets lately."

"Rotting in jail for public indecency, if you please! One of the women hawking vegetables on the sidewalk—a more unfortunate creature you never saw!—thinking him a decent human being like you and me, hoped he would reconcile her daughter with her husband. So she went to him, the poor little fool, and the worst of it, she had only one eye and was old and, begging your pardon, ugly as sin. But what can you do with a man with a filthy tail? And to cap it all, he took her into the vacant lot behind the zawya, and people saw, and they were all shouting, 'Catch him, catch him, catch him!' They set upon him with old slippers and shoes! Enough of that; let's not speak of these things! He's been on prison fare for two months now, and that's the end of that."

He visibly reset himself to more appropriate concerns. "Let's go, let's go! It's time for noon prayer, and they'll soon be taking the man out for burial."

They started their procession. I heard a knock at the door to our apartment. It was Hassan. "Coming," I said. "Of course I'm coming. Just let me change."

When I told my mother, she was so upset to hear the news that I was astonished. "Who?" she said. "Sheikh Khalaf! May God forgive all his sins! He was a kindly man, with a great heart. I knew him well and saw him often. Do you know he attended my wedding reception when I married your father, here in this apartment? He was sitting right there, in that spot." She motioned to a chair. "Your grandfather Zaki used to sing his praises. 'Now *there's* a *real* Muslim!' That's what he would say. Do you know, I—" But I had to cut her off, indicating Hassan waiting outside. "All right, dear, of course you can go, but don't be late. It's exams in two weeks. Thanawiya amma, Galal!"

*

It seemed the news had spread throughout the entire Daher district. The zawya was swarming with people, as far as the eye could see, of all different ages. Children and adults, boys and girls: the crowds completely blocked the street. At the corners, and in the mouths of the narrower streets and alleyways, small trucks, an old bus, and taxis, some having arrived from the countryside, sat parked, along with two later-model private automobiles, one bearing an Aswan license plate. The drivers either stood waiting beside the vehicles or sat at the steering wheels, waiting to drive the mourners to the graveyard.

Hassan and I were at the top of the street when we happened to come to a stop next to a number of men with dark skin, thin builds, and bright white gallabiyas. We recognized them by the turbans on their heads: large, and twisted in the pattern of Amm Idris's. "They must be from Nubia like him," we thought. The strangest thing is that we didn't hear them speak a word, nor even whisper in one another's ears; they gave Death his due respect and observed the awful solemnity of the occasion. Their hands remained folded at their chests, and they remained silent.

Hassan and I did not venture any further forward, preferring to stand with these good people. If the tide of people carried one of us two steps forward or backward, the other would catch him and pull him back, lest we lose each other in the crowd.

A sudden hush fell over the assembled hordes as the body was carried out of the zawya. I was drawn to the foremost pallbearer: it was as though I knew him. Dear God! It was Amm Idris. My eyes had deceived me at first sight of him, for it was as though he was suddenly old, aged to eighty in an instant: perhaps through lack of sleep or fatigue, or perhaps it was the effects of grief and pallor upon dark skin. I had heard that he and the sheikh had been inseparable, and that even when the man had become housebound, Idris had visited him

214

without fail. It came over me then, the awe that had overcome me and Hassan when we used to see Sheikh Khalaf readying himself to call out for prayer.

The silence only lasted a moment: then an ululation burst forth from one of the assembly, followed by another and another, until the whole place was ringing with them. Small paperback Qur'ans were held aloft, high into the sky, the owners of the hands calling out, "There is no god but God, and Mohamed is the Prophet of God! There is no god but God, and Sheikh Khalaf is beloved by God!"

Hassan stood watching, enthralled, every second elbowing me to draw my attention to this or that, or show me what one or another person was doing. But I hardly noticed him. His words came to me muzzily, as though from a great distance, from another world separate from the one I inhabited. The sight of the crowd faded from my sight: the people became like shadows, and all I could hear of the voices was "There is no god but God." It was as though my feet were weightless, and I was soaring through the air. All at once I was overcome by a paroxysm of weeping and sobbing as I called out, "There is no god but God, and Mohamed is the Prophet of God!" Hassan, alarmed at my actions, put his arms round me, begging me to calm down, all the while looking around him in alarm.

Hagg Mahmoud appeared out of nowhere: he took me in his arms and recited the Fatiha and short verses of the Qur'an over me, as well as some prayers. I would calm for a moment in his embrace, but then I would start to gasp again and break into fresh weeping.

He and Hassan took me home. I remember that I slept till midnight, and when I heard the dawn prayer, I went downstairs to the mosque to pray with the others.

31

Dear Galal,

I write to you the morning of the day we leave the house. Since last night, I haven't been able to imagine what the morning sun will look like, nor how I shall leave this world where I was born and raised: my room, where I have gone to bed every single day of my life that I can remember, the only street I know.

I've been tossing and turning all night, hurting at leaving you, afraid of the new life I am heading for. I felt sorry for myself and started crying.

My darling, know that from now on you shall always be safe. I shall keep you safe inside my heart, in the deepest place inside it, and lock it up, and no one but me shall know the place: not my mother, not yours, not anybody else. They may see me sitting and reading or lying in bed getting ready to go to sleep, or somewhere or other, but if they had hearts, they would know that I'm not alone, but with you, talking to you as you talk to me, looking down shyly as you pat my shoulder or run your fingers through my hair.

You may not believe me when I tell you that I don't know my new address. My mother, God forgive her, was careful not to tell it to anyone, so that nobody in our building finds out: she hid it even from me and from her closest friend, Abul Saad Effendi's wife.

Galal. My father is dead, as you know. My mother's family raised me and provides for me, as you know. They have the final say in anything to do with me. My mother seems to have run to them and told them about us, and I'm paying the price. What's worse, she said to me two days ago that my uncle Sheikh Mostafa spoke to her about getting me engaged to his eldest son, who's a military officer. And before I could say a word, she said that if I argued, they wouldn't just make us move away, they would make me quit school and stay at home and be a housewife just like her.

What I want you to know, too, is that Aunt Camellia wasn't too upset at what happened to us; it fit in with her plans. I beg of you, for God's sake, don't cling to a hope that is doomed from the start. And here is why: if you try and do anything, even if it is just to try and find out my new address, you'll end up hurting me. My mother still has her spies in the building, and the news will reach her.

Nadia

June 5, 1974

On my way back from noon prayer, I had found Sitt Shouq waiting for me at the door to our building. She looked around and then said she had something for me. Seeing me surprised, she added, "Yes, something for you! A letter from Miss Nadia."

I looked up toward her balcony.

"What are you looking up for, son? There's no one there. They're gone. They moved out at midday yesterday."

"Moved out? Gone? You mean—for good?"

"Bless the child: still looking up! What are you looking for? For heaven's sake, look down. Look here; I'm over here!" And with that, she pulled the letter out of her bodice and gave it to me. "Don't let it fall into anyone's hands, Master Galal, for pity's sake, or lives will be ruined! And especially, don't let your mother see it."

"What did you say?"

"Yes, your mother. That's what Nadia said. And she said that she wanted to tell you that in the letter, too, but didn't have the courage."

When I got upstairs, I found my mother sitting on the floor in her room, two wooden trunks next to her, the kind with metal bands. In the middle of each, at the top, was a hasp like a door lock, secured with a padlock weighing more than a quarter of a kilogram. The trunks had been beneath my grandfather's bed, and I could not remember them moving an inch in all the years I had lived in the house.

The wardrobe stood wide open, its contents strewn everywhere: blouses, dresses, hangers, old bedspreads and coats, dressing gowns and nightgowns, empty or virtually empty perfume bottles, and slippers, house slippers and going-out slippers, some overturned. She looked up at me, smiling, eyes shining. "Where have you been, Galal?" she asked. "Shouldn't you be with me, trying on the things we're taking with us? Where were you? Why are you late? Didn't you say you would only be a minute?"

"I was at the mosque."

"Ah." She scratched at her jaw. "Well, why couldn't you have gone into your room and shut the door? Is it really necessary to go pray at the mosque?"

I didn't answer, still looking round at the clothing and other things strewn about the room.

"You know, Galal, not one of these old things is going to do. I'll look like a country bumpkin. Maybe these three frocks, and these pairs of shoes, and these underthings, but that's all." And she gestured to a pile of clothing and some shoe boxes piled up next to the bed. "Yes. The rest I can give away. But to whom? Who . . . who . . . wait a minute; what am I saying, giving them away! Galal, does Amm Younis, the rag-and-bone man, does he still come by? I'll sell them to him."

219

She looked up at me. "What about your grandfather's tarboosh? What am I to do with it? It's all dirty and oily and not worth a penny! It won't do you any good over there, Zaki, nor even here! It's not worth selling, or buying!" She glared balefully at it, then turned the same look upon me. "For heaven's sake, boy! Why are you just standing there pulling a long face?" She went back to turning the tarboosh over in her hands, talking to it. "And you, Amm Zaki, just one short month or so, and I'll be there! Do tell: what are you wearing on your head these days? You're probably wearing a hat, and you're a foreigner now! And you, Mother dear, I wonder how you're getting on . . . ."

I didn't stay for the rest of the soliloquy. I left her and went back to my room.

32

IT WAS A WONDER, TO be sure, worthy of the *Guinness Book of World Records*: a student in 3J scoring 87 percent on the thanawiya amma exam; indeed, it was worthy of alerting the newspapers, as Mr. Murqus, the administrative director, said. The man held the table of grades in his hand as he scrutinized me from the parting in my hair down to my shoelaces, then stared back at the table, then looked at me again over his reading glasses, eyes widening in astonishment, as though hearing a voice that told him he was in a dream. By God, though, he had every right! I was as flabbergasted as he and had not yet taken in the news any more than he had.

He pushed back his chair noisily and came round his desk, holding out his hand to shake mine. "Galal, I don't believe it! What've you gone and done? First place? First place in the entire educational district? I've been working in this blighted school for thirty years, and I haven't seen the like of it. First place in the district going to a boy from our school—that in itself is a miracle. But from 3J as well—if that doesn't beat all. 3J!" He looked over at Mr. Somaa, sitting next to him on a seat overlooking the school yard. "What do you say, Mr. Somaa? Isn't this a tale to tell the little ones, a bedtime story like the tales of Shater Hassan and Zeir Salem and Abu Rigl Maslukha?"

Looking me up and down, Mr. Somaa appeared to be searching for the owner of this face in his file of undesirable memories. I turned to Mr. Murqus, asking, "How did the others do, sir?"

"Others? There are no others left, son! All in the streets. All of them—all! Not a single one passed, of course."

"Leithi too?"

"Leithi? What are you talking about? That stinker, a man of education? Of all things, he came early in the morning to see how he did. You know what he came wearing? That useless lump, coming in a peasant gallabiya, a shawl over his shoulder like a tradesman, with a cane in his hand! Does he take us for a vegetable stall or a fish market? You know what he scored?"

I looked at him.

"He scored—wait for it—he scored *9 percent* overall. I swear to Almighty God. Listen to this, too: chemistry, mathematics, biology: zero, zero, and zero, respectively. I said to him, 'Seven years, Leithi, in thanawiya amma? Go find yourself another place, somewhere far away. You're not cut out for education or schooling. You don't even look the part any more, and you're not of school age. Why, even the math teacher appointed by the Ministry of Employment last year is your age: you and he were born in the same year.'"

The headmaster himself called me into his office. He shook me warmly by the hand and said that I had done him proud, and brought honor to him and the whole school, and just when he had given up on 3J after all attempts had failed. Mr. Busrati embraced me and turned to the headmaster. "It was a ghastly class, Headmaster, sir. All that remained was for a teacher to take out a weapons license and sling an automatic rifle over his shoulder as he came into the class, and fire one or two shots into the air by way of warning before starting to teach. But this boy," he gestured to me, "is of good stock, good family, and I have always foreseen a brilliant future for him! Why, it may well be that we are in the company of a future Dr. Ali Musharrafa, the nuclear physicist, or Dr. Anwar al-Mufti, physician to the president himself! As for his manners, well, he's polite, well-mannered, and obedient! What a joy to teach!"

Seeing the headmaster nod his head in evident approval, Busrati went on. "He's the product of my childrearing methods. I've been like a godfather to him. 'Buck up, Galal!' I would say to him, and he would say, 'Yes, sir.' I would say, 'I want you to do our headmaster proud in the exams, Galal!' and he'd say, 'Yes, sir.' That's how it would go. Yes, sir; yes sir." He turned to me. "Isn't that so, Galal?"

"Of course, of course, General Monitor, sir," I answered, caught between embarrassment and amusement. "May you always be an asset to the school!"

When I got home, Umm Hassan came out onto the stairs to welcome me with ululations and came up to our apartment bearing a dozen portions of sweet syrup and three conefuls of sugar, while Muallim Habib sent two crates of Spathis and Coca-Cola. Hagg Mahmoud, Abul Saad Effendi, and Captain Farid came, followed by the rest of our neighbors in the building, with their wives and children.

Sitt Shouq went round the guests bearing a tray of sweet syrup, and whenever she drew breath and raised a hand to her head to let out an ululation, those around her hastened to protect their heads, for fear of the tray that rattled and shook, balanced on her other hand. Her attempts at making a joyous noise, poor lady, failed utterly: the ululation usually stuck in her throat, or else came out sounding like the feeble meowing of an aged feline with some horrible disease of the throat.

At nightfall, Hassan took me to Cinema Misr. We watched *The Longest Day in History*, then *Sins*. I watched Abd al-Halim Hafez all through the movie as he wandered, lost, and Nadia Lutfi, his leading lady, seemed to me to be my own Nadia.

When I lay down in my bed at the end of the day, the specter of my paternal grandfather came to me, keeping me from sleep. I had not thought of him for months, maybe an entire year. I tried to get away from his shadow, but it haunted me. I would think of something else, put a pillow over my head, but to no avail. I woke suddenly to the sound of the call for dawn prayers. Apparently I had fallen asleep for a short while, and I could have sworn he came to me in a dream. The same turban, the same stick he used to lean on, the same face, only younger.

33

"LISTEN TO ME, GALAL. THIS far and no further. I've done my duty by you. I bore you and raised you, and I've put up with a lot for your sake. Now I want you to do as I ask."

This was the first thing my mother said to me as we sat at breakfast the next day. My heartbeat speeded up. 'She's definitely going to bring up the emigration business again. Heaven help us.' I pushed my teacup aside, looking at her surreptitiously. Her eyes were on me, her face somewhat tense: this told me that she had gathered all her energies, and that a battle was on the horizon if I didn't go along with her. By way of evasion, I gave her a false smile, but she ignored it, her face seeming to expect an immediate answer from me.

"Good morning, Mother!" I finally said. "What do you say we go out today to celebrate my passing my exams? Let's go to the pyramids. No; what am I saying. It's far too hot! What about the zoo?"

"Boy! I'm not in the mood for this. I'm serious!"

"We could look at the zebra, play with the monkeys. We could even ride the elephant!"

"Quit it this instant and listen to me!" she yelled in my face. "I've decided to emigrate. I'm going to go and live with my mama and papa. I want to have some time with them before . . . in case something happens; I'll regret it for the rest of my life."

"Let's just talk about it later."

"Not later, and not sooner either. I'm going and that's final."

"Mom . . . ."

"Don't 'Mom' me nor 'Pop' me neither. You're grown now, so show me how you're going to deal with it."

My own ire rose. "What exactly do you want of me?"

"We have to liquidate our assets in this country. We ought to find someone to sublet the apartment to, or else have the owners of the building pay us a sum of money to vacate. And tomorrow morning, off you go to your uncle in the village. Plead with him, fight with him, coax him, do what you must to find out what your share of the inheritance is and get it."

"You listen to *me*, Mom. In plain language, I can't leave here. I can't live there. I'd die. Suffocate."

"Suffocate?" she replied, aggrieved. A long time passed, during which each of us avoided the other's eyes. The only sound was the sound of my mother taking a sip or two of her tea, and the fluttering of a few pages of the wall calendar in a sudden breeze that had sprung up.

It was quiet in the street outside for a change, noiseless. "At least come and try it," she said. "Come say goodbye to your mama. Come and say hello to your grandfather. Or is that too much for us to ask of you, Galal? Too much for your poor mother, who never had a day's happiness because of you? Or too much for your poor old grandfather, who only wants to see you?"

"Mom!"

"Oh, never mind." She said it in a voice that broke my heart.

I spoke again, softly, words forced from me. "It's just that . . . to sell everything . . . it's just . . . how can we give up our apartment here? Where will I stay, when I come back? And I'm still a minor, and I can't claim my inheritance and my land legally from my uncle yet. It's still two, three long years at least."

"So you're coming with me?"

"I'll come, but at the end of the summer I have to come back."

"Agreed."

"Will you come back with me?"

"What?" she snapped. "Back? Back where? I've been counting the years, every year, and the days, hour by hour, and you say 'come back'? Back to whom? To Sitt Shouq or Umm Hassan or the women in the building? I can't sleep. My nights are long and my days are longer and—Oh, shut up."

"What's wrong with Umm Hassan, Mother?"

"Umm Hassan? What are you talking about? I want to live with my family. My people. I want to live with them and be with my own kind."

"Mom, it's not like that. You don't understand."

"I don't? Fine. Keep your understanding, Galal." I remained silent as she kept speaking. "You go to your uncle, and do your accounts. Find out your due, and get whatever you can get out of him."

"Yes, Mom."

"Go within a day or two at most."

"Yes, Mom."

"By week's end I want you back here with the money in your hand."

34

THE VILLAGE APPEARED FROM AFAR when the bus turned left and crossed the stream: the Eucalyptus trees, the smokestack of the mill, newer one- and two-story houses built at the borders of the fields with red brick walls and reinforced concrete pillars springing up amid the crops, with unfinished lengths of rebar protruding and corroded by rust and scraps of burlap tied to the ends and fluttering in the breeze. One man had beaten everybody to the punch and opened up a grocery store in the wide open field. A barrel of oil with black stains around its mouth stood by its door, with a larger barrel for gas with a small tap in it and a tub atop it bearing measuring jugs of different sizes.

All through the agricultural road, I had seen donkeys, burdened with bales of corn but snorting happily every so often, raising their heads and looking contentedly at the barns and sheds they passed, looking forward to resting their weary backs after such a long journey, and having a drink of water and a lie-down in the shade like the rest of creation.

Through the bus window, I observed the farmers in the fields. They were in work clothes: long-sleeved undershirts and baggy pants. I could hear the noise they made as they called to each other. I glimpsed some of them sitting in circles around a large teakettle wedged in among burning coals and others lying in the shade of trees or among the reeds, their weary bodies resting in a deep sleep, and the girls with the front of their dresses filled with ears of corn, emptying them out into piles, their laughter ringing out into the clear sky.

It was the start of harvest season. Joy had just been born, and its scent was everywhere.

When the bus began to slow down, the conductor approached me. Leaning on the edge of my seat with one hand, he said, "I take it the gentleman's going to Mansouriya?" I nodded, so he told me to get ready.

I alighted and looked round slowly, affecting confidence so as not to appear like a stranger or attract any curious attention, although, in truth, I was so taken by what I saw that a thrill went through me. How different was this time from the last! Last time, I had been leaping about, distracted by everything I saw. Now, things were different, and I was grateful that there had been an intermediary between myself and my uncle Ibrahim and that we had only interacted at a distance. I wondered, would he recognize me now that I was as tall as my grandfather, with a man's stubble on my chin? And how did my uncle look now?

I stood there, looking around until I espied a café a few yards off the road. I went to it. It was not like the cafés of our street: it was a mere hut, surrounded by a low fence of braided reeds. Part of it was roofed in with two sheets of balsa wood, the rest with burlap and palm fronds. The whole roof rested on four palm-tree trunks, not all equal in height: the ones in front were shorter, making the roof list forward, as though on the verge of collapse.

The wooden chairs were of a unique design. There was no way that these had been made in any workshop or by the hand of any carpenter, not even a novice. No, these had to have been made by the proprietor, the plump man slumped over the counter at the front of the café, as ten flies, at the very least, sported around the fringe of his turban's shawl. I ask you in all honesty, what was this? One chair with five legs, another with three, one with a single armrest. Furthermore, they were raised off the ground to a height hitherto unknown in the field of carpentry: anyone rash enough to sit on one of these without taking all the appropriate and necessary precautions would be, I venture to say, at fault, and on his own head be the consequences.

The tables were low—befitting a clientele of short stature, and more comfortable still if they happened to be midgets—and took to juddering and creaking if one touched them, however gingerly. This was in addition to the nails whose heads poked out everywhere, and if one's eyes were not sharp and quick and very thorough, one's clothing would immediately be the victim of an L-shaped rip which we call 'the lock and key.'

I preferred not to sit in the front, in order to avoid the dust that rose from the wheels of the tractors and the feet of passing animals in the street. I headed for the right-hand side, alongside the mill. I chose a seat where I could amuse myself by watching the people coming in and going out. A gentle breeze sprang up, raising a cloud of a different kind, making it hard to breathe. The smell of flour pervaded the air, its minute specks floating in the rays of sunlight that crept in through the reed stalks. I watched them swirling and eddying downward, settling on my pant legs, particularly at the knees.

I remembered the feed scale that had stood at the gate, although I had not seen it this time: they must have moved it to a location behind the mill, for I had seen the women with the sacks of grain heading around to the western side of the mill, then coming round the other side and going through the door, each holding the paper recording the weight and the sum paid. The donkeys laden with grain, though, had another, more winding route, ultimately leading around to the scale at the back of the mill.

My gaze strayed to the smokestack. It was no longer high, surrounded as it was by two three-story houses being built. The entire steam mill had been painted a bright, gaudy blue, giving it the appearance of an elderly crone yelling, "I am young and

231

pretty!" and being ignored by all and sundry. The wide open space where the donkeys used to be tied up was wide and open no longer, now home to a few stalls facing the road.

The mill had lost the awe-inspiring power it had held when I was young. Although I looked long at it this time, whenever I thought about it later in life, I only remembered it as I had seen it that first time, as a very little boy.

I didn't spend too long in the café. I left it and set off on foot toward my grandfather's house. Memory led me through the streets. I was nervous, of course, and apprehensive of my uncle's welcome. Little by little, things broke upon my memory that I had not thought were still there, and they began to set my heart at ease, its beats calming. The houses seemed to be welcoming me back. The man coming from the other direction looked as though he might be one of my grandfather's long-ago pair of guests who had come to him and sat chatting with him on the mat when I was there. The old woman sitting at her doorstep in the skinny strip of shadow cast by the wall had a face that was the spitting image of my grandmother. And these shops, and here . . . and there . . . .

Right at the corner of the road, I had seen a man in a waistcoat and a shirt of cotton batting, his folded gallabiya over his shoulder. He had seen me and my mother and run to us, shooing the children away from us with a stick of firewood he had picked up in the street as they jumped up and down before him. This house was where the woman with the unkempt hair and the gingham belt around her waist lived. Her stare had frightened me, and I had clutched onto my mother for protection, and she had clutched me right back with more fear in her eyes than was in mine.

I had not imagined that all this was still etched into my mind; I had not imagined that this would be anything but a business trip, a settling of accounts. Upon reaching a point in the road that branched out into several alleyways, I asked for directions. They told me that the old house was no longer standing; it had been pulled down after my grandfather Abd al-Hamid had died. They directed me to a red brick building that had been erected in its place.

I found a number of older children playing outside its gates, which were reinforced with black wrought-iron bars, each ending in a point like that of a spear. One of the children was fiddling with the steel doorknob, formed like a lion with a flowing mane and bared canines. I stood close to them, a pounding coming over my chest, my heart lost in the old gate, the wooden gate through which I had entered behind my grandfather on the very first day I had come, the western wall, the path, the storage room my mother and I had slept in . . . . Even the two mulberry trees weren't there any more. The owners of the new house had uprooted them, planting two ornamental bushes with blooms of a fiery red whose color was less than pleasing to my eye.

I hung back a moment to get my emotions under control, then walked up to the children, who had been staring at me in frank amazement and whispering.

I told them who I was.

They made no reaction whatsoever, neither positive nor negative. They greeted me very neutrally, as one would a passerby. One led me to a large room, showed me to a seat, and left. He didn't close the door properly, so it remained ajar.

The room was long and narrow, probably a place to receive guests rather than for everyday use. It had several couches in it, the traditional type without arms, upholstered in stupid colors that did not match at all. In one corner were three gilded chairs facing a table that bore ledgers and papers. Facing me were three large windows that gave onto the street.

I noticed that the boys I had met at the door had taken up positions from which they could have a good view of me, and that their numbers were increasing: there were ten of them now, although there had only been four when I came in.

Just to tease them, I moved to the opposite side and sat with my back to the wall, my head and arms as well as most of the rest of me hidden by the shutters of the large adjacent windows. I shrank into myself, depriving them of any angle to see me—unless, of course, they came upon a new method. I had to hand it to them: they were masters of this, and I had no doubt they would succeed.

The surprise, to me, was seeing my grandfather's picture on the wall facing me: I hadn't noticed it, perhaps out of nervousness when I first came in. His mouth was closed, a frown on his face, but his features, for all that, were gentle and kind.

The news spread through the house. I began to notice movement and murmurings, and eyes at the crack of the door: boys and girls jostling to see, their antics, of course, opening it wider. But a hand would soon shoot out and return the door to its previous position to keep the correct distance between us, meaning that they should be able to see me without my seeing them. After a while, I heard a feminine voice shooing the crowd away, and the door opened.

A girl came in, her hair tied back in a white kerchief with black stripes. She gave me a large mug of tea. I asked after the small glasses and the strong-flavored tea my grandfather had favored, and she said nothing. I held out my hand to shake hers, and she shook mine without covering her hand with the sleeve of her gallabiya as is the wont of peasant women when shaking hands with a man to whom they are not related. When I asked her name, she said, "Leila," and hurried out, stumbling as she went. I think she was my half sister, the girl in her mother's lap that day we had come when I was still a child.

Imam came. He hurried in, face shining with a broad grin. "Master Galal! Welcome, welcome, welcome!" And he took me in an enthusiastic embrace.

I had not seen him in long years. His face had dried up and shriveled. I was even more surprised to see the long beard he had cultivated, merging with his mustache, and that the hair that poked out from around the edges of his cap was white, curly, and not unlike the cotton used to stuff mattresses. He was emaciated: I could tell when I embraced him. He was frail in my arms, as though I could have picked him up and carried him.

I asked after my grandmother. He said she had died a year or more ago and was shocked that I didn't know: he said that he had come to my mother the third day after my grandmother's death, in secret, without my uncle Ibrahim knowing, and asked her to tell me and requested our presence at the funeral; it was bad enough she hadn't come to my grandfather's. He had asked her to come more than once, and she had replied that she was ill and unable to travel at present, 'and my son is busy with his studying, and after he sits for his exams, we'll come to pay our respects.'

He pushed his cap back, exposing his sweaty forehead. He mopped it with a handkerchief that lay in his lap, and said in shocked disapproval, "Do you mean to say she didn't tell you?"

I was silent. He patted my hand. "If it comes up when you're talking to your uncle, don't tell him you know, or that I told you."

Uncle Ibrahim threw the door open, a black look in his eyes. He was far taller and more muscular than I, his left eye a little crossed; I must not have noticed that when I was young. He had only increased in awe-inspiring stature after replacing his cap with a turban. He took me in for a moment in satisfaction. "Well, well, well, how you've grown, Galal!" He frowned, adjusting the neck of his gallabiya. "Really, Galal, I expected you to come to the Hagga's funeral. She's your grandmother after all. When your grandfather died, you were but a child; no blame could attach to you." He remained silent for a while, then added with displeasure, "But now, what am I to think? That you are ungrateful, and thankless?"

I was dumb. Imam stepped in, saying hurriedly, "How was he to know, Master Ibrahim? The fault is mine. I should have gone and told him myself."

He shook his head in derision. Silence settled upon us, broken only by mutual coughs and sips of tea.

Everything in the room stared back at us: the couches, the chairs, and the walls. The silence itself was like speech: it had a sound, and a heavy ring upon the ear. After a long, tedious silence, I said, "I have resolved to go abroad with my mother, and I need your permission, sir."

"My permission? Permission for what? My permission to emigrate, to leave the country, or my official permission for a passport as the government requires?"

The question took me aback. I looked at him in bewilderment. He added, eyes boring into me: "Aren't you still under age, and you need my permission for the passport people? Is that what you want? Or are you coming to say goodbye, and ask my permission to go? Aren't I in the position of your late father?"

Imam made to intervene, but my uncle silenced him with a gesture.

I stammered, "That was what I meant."

"Which of the two did you mean?"

I grew even more flustered. "Is there a difference, Uncle?"

"Yes, there is, and each of them has a different valuation, and a different price."

It came to me that he must be prevaricating and wished to take advantage of the position I was in. I looked at him sidelong. "I don't understand, Uncle. What do you mean by valuation and price?"

He looked at me for a while. "Listen, my boy. If you want my permission to take out a passport, you must waive your rights to your inheritance. Not for free—we'll buy you out— and then, goodbye. Whether you come back from foreign parts or you don't, it's no concern of ours, and then we shall go our separate ways for as long as we are still living. If, on the other hand, you want to visit your father's grave, or your grandparents' graves, pay your respects, visit with us for a day or two, and meet your aunt and your sister Leila and spend time with us all together, instead of just the two of us like this—and at the end of the visit, ask my permission to leave the country and stay away, on condition that you will come back again and not be fooled into staying abroad—in that case, I'll tell you, your land is held in trust, and not only that, but your name, too, will be held in our hearts. And all the money you want for the journey—for yourself and your mother too—is at your disposal, ready money."

Imam leapt up, yelling, "Bravo, Master Ibrahim!"

"You're right, Uncle." I burst into tears.

I couldn't help thinking, though, about what Uncle Ibrahim had said, nor did I know the source of my suspicion that he was playing me false and would prefer for me to leave with my mother and never return. Was it the suspicion and hatred for my father's family that my mother had planted in me? Or was it that I felt small and powerless, causing me to be careful and unconfident in the face of people who, compared to myself, were all-powerful, and to me, represented the unknown?

It was my sister Leila who won over my heart. I still remember her saying that she had been counting the days until she could see me, and that my image would be the one she saw whenever she thought of my father.

35

OUR FLIGHT LANDED AT ORLY Airport, and our feet trod upon the long tube leading to the French soil of the airport.

The passengers were happily chatting, laughing, and making fun of the flight attendants and of the airline meal we had been served a little while ago. Singled out for special attention was a short attendant with a Hitler-style mustache. He was a veritable wonder in form and function, a goof-off who had failed to fulfill a single passenger's request. Someone had asked him for tea; a lady had asked him for a pain-killer; and a third passenger, ever hopeful in the goodness of human nature, had asked him for a copy of that day's *Al-Ahram*. "Yes, sir; yes, ma'am; yes sir," he had said to all and sundry, then promptly disappeared.

When the wait had drawn out, someone got up to investigate. He found the man stretched out on a row of seats at the rear of the plane, fast asleep, a small pillow over his face against the noise of the airplane or any pesky passengers. When the passenger woke him, remonstrating, he leaped up and rolled up his sleeves, preparing for a fight. The passenger, for his part, was a big fellow, of the head-butting type, and but for the grace of God and the interventions of some good-hearted passengers, things might have gotten out of hand: we might have needed an ambulance waiting on the exit ramp.

My mother and I walked at the rear of the group of passengers, extremely afraid of what might happen if no one was waiting for us at the airport, our hearts beating in awestruck trepidation of this new world we were heading into.

Suddenly, we stopped at the end of the tube. I knew not why; perhaps because the man walking ahead of us had stepped to the side to light a cigarette, so we had followed suit. The funny thing is that he went on ahead, but we stood still, until the aircraft doors had closed and the flight attendants had started to leave, headed up by the man with the mustache. When we had stood there for a long time, and began to be joined by passengers from another flight, my mother and I began to look at one another, not knowing what to do. I felt her hand cold in mine, curling around my wrist. I gave her a reassuring pat, thinking, "I'm the man; I have to do something."

I happened to glimpse a group of our fellow passengers some distance away, standing before a billboard on the wall of a passageway. I took my mother by the hand and led her quickly toward them, still thinking to myself, "There's nothing for it but to stick with them. They're fellow Egyptians, after all; they won't let us lose our way."

There were three men, constantly guffawing and gesturing as they talked, an old lady, and a young woman carrying a small child who muttered and shifted against her chest. She looked as bewildered as us, staring at the billboards around her, bearing bright advertisements for Kent, Gauloises, Gitanes, and different brands of perfumes and alcoholic beverages, and at blond girls walking away from us, chattering rapidly with their own rhythm and intonation. "Ah," I thought, "so this is what French really sounds like!"

I grinned at the comical language, supposedly French, that Mr. Tadros had taught us in school. Around us walked tall gendarmes in dark blue uniforms and tall hats, the kind I had seen long ago in *Irma La Douce*, starring Hollywood leading lady Shirley MacLaine, and in *Gamila Abu Hreid*, starring our own leading lady, Magda.

We enjoyed this one-sided companionship, and I motioned to my mother to keep following in the wake of these Egyptians, who clearly appeared experienced travelers, not quaking in their boots like us. Wherever they went, so did we; when they stopped and turned back, we did, too. However, if they stopped to buy something or help the young woman when the infant squirmed and squalled, we would stand off to the side, close enough to keep our eyes on them until they finished their business and walked on, with us in tow.

After a long and thoroughly enjoyable walk, we found ourselves face-to-face with the passport control officer, followed by the moving belt at baggage claim, where we retrieved our bags. Truth be told, our bags, conspicuous among the others, must have looked to our fellow passengers like the height of style from the mid-1940s.

We had been so busy with the suitcases and their retrieval that we found we had lost sight of the company of the Egyptians we had been following. I was confused and lost, turning this way and that in search of them, hoping to follow them as we had done before. But it was no use; we had lost them for good. They had disappeared into thin air, I thought bitterly, as though I had been cheated somehow, or as though they really ought to have waited for us.

The tide of people carried us along, though, and we found ourselves heading in their company to the glass doors of the airport. Then my mother and I found ourselves outside.

A slight chill whipped up around us, although it was only late summer. We stood looking at one another, completely helpless and relying only on the Good Lord for guidance. Suddenly, it was as though the earth had split open and produced a beautiful young woman, with luxuriant hair, in jeans and a see-through blouse. She gave us a long look, a broad smile on her face. "Auntie! Auntie Camellia! Don't you recognize me? It's me, Rachel!"

"Why, Rachel!" My mother flung herself into Rachel's arms, and they embraced, kissing and hugging and crying, babbling about how they had missed each other. "You can still speak Arabic! I thought you must have forgotten it!"

"How could I, Auntie? We all talk to one another in Arabic." She turned to me. "Galal!" She hugged me, kissing me on both cheeks. I wasted no time in availing myself of the opportunity to do the same, as this appeared to be the custom in Paris.

She took us to a sporty Renault, which we learned was her own. She also told us that she lived in a large studio with a kitchen, bathroom, and private entrance on Rue St-Michel in the Latin Quarter, having had enough of living with her parents in Belleville, which was a district full of immigrants and poorer people.

We asked after my grandparents. They were older, she said, but still active, able to come and go and do their own shopping and errands, and lived in Barbès, a low-income district also mainly populated by immigrants, especially Africans and Moroccans.

"Is my father still working?"

"Really, Auntie, at his age? He retired two years ago."

"How does he live, then?"

"Oh, don't worry about him on that score. I give him a thousand francs a month, and he gets another two thousand in unemployment benefits, plus the money transfers from my uncle Isaac."

"Isaac!" My mother spoke my uncle's name with longing, and her eyes shone. "How is he now? How is he doing? Do you see him sometimes?"

"Of course we do. He comes to visit every year. He's doing really well, too. Now he's opened a supermarket in Haifa."

My mother pulled out a small handkerchief to dry a tear that had slipped from her eye, sniffling, "How could you, Isaac! Years and years and years without a word from you. I never would have thought you capable of it!"

Keeping her left hand on the steering wheel, Rachel placed her right on my mother's shoulder comfortingly. "We miss you too, Aunt. We have been counting the days until you come, and until this little monkey gets his thanawiya amma!" She looked back laughingly at me in the backseat. I could see the mischief in her eyes through her thick hair, flying in the breeze that blew in the window.

My mother smiled in satisfaction, though tears still threatened. "I wish I could see him again, Rachel."

"What a pity! He just went home to Israel a week ago. He stayed at your parents' for a whole month, with his wife, Hanna, and his daughter, Esther." My mother shook her head, visibly upset. "There, there, Auntie; he'll come again, and you'll see him, not once, but ten times. If you miss him too much to wait, I can arrange a visit for you and Galal to Israel."

I looked out the window, staring at the broad streets we rode through and the plump buildings that lined them, their walls punctuated with small statues and reliefs and short, slender decorative columns flanking the windows. They reminded me of the old buildings in Sherif and Adli and Abd al-Khaleq Tharwat Streets in downtown Cairo, and at the intersection of Fouad and Ramsis Streets, buildings I had only glimpsed and had not imagined could still be etched into my memory.

My mother, apparently sensing my discomfort, changed the subject, asking what had become of my Uncle Shamoun. Rachel said that he had no luck, and couldn't keep a job more than a year. "Where is he living now?" my mother asked. "Next to your grandfather, or elsewhere?"

"He lives in the Twentieth Arrondissement. It's a dangerous suburb, full of gangs and unemployed people. It's full of organized crime, drug dealers, and pretty much any other kind of shady business."

"Isn't Shamoun afraid to live there?"

Rachel laughed out loud. "It's not like he has anything they could steal! They wouldn't even look at him! Besides, everyone on his street knows he's a street sweeper and doesn't have a penny to his name."

"A street sweeper?" my mother gasped, although she did know from my grandfather's letters that he had been a mere porter. I wondered why she was so shocked; a porter wasn't that great a step up from a street sweeper, after all.

"Yes. If I didn't help him out financially, he'd starve. Auntie, he just couldn't cut it at any job out here. He worked at a kiosk run by an Algerian, but he messed things up so bad the owner fired him. Then he tried being a porter, but that didn't work out either. Whenever he put a bag on his shoulder, he'd drop it and smash everything inside. Then he sat around for a year maybe. Then the local authority put out an ad for street sweepers, and he got the job. He's been in the position for a while now, and there haven't been any problems. But it's only a matter of time before he messes something up and gets fired again. Do you know, Auntie," she said, disgruntled, "sometimes when I go by the Rue de l'Opéra or Boulevard Haussmann, I see him standing there with his broom. I wave to him, and he sees me, looks me in the eye, but he won't say hello back. It happened again and again till I thought, 'Fine. I won't wave to him again.'"

"Shamoun? Good old Shamoun? Why, he was always so nice, always had a good head on his shoulders. What's changed him so?"

"It's not that, exactly," Rachel said. "He's just pining for Egypt. If it was up to him, he says, he'd have gone back there long ago."

"He wants to go back?" my mother said, astonished.

They never stopped talking for a moment, until the car came to a halt outside a modest building in a narrow alley. It was not that different from our building on Daher Street: in a neighboring building was a butcher's shop with a sign above it in large Arabic lettering: 'Sheikh Munji's Halal Meats.' I was drawn in by the sight of two men standing outside it talking, French words mixed in with their Arabic.

The moment we stepped into the building, I heard my grandfather's voice calling out to us, "Galal! Camellia! You're here!" and he leaned over the balustrade.

I stood there, looking up at him. Despite the distance that separated us, I immediately noticed the changes in him. When Rachel nudged me up the stairs, I took off running as I had done on the stairs of our building, my heart calling out to him.

36

OUR APARTMENT IN DAHER WAS a veritable paradise, compared to the apartment where my grandfather now lived. Two bedrooms: the smaller, which they had designated our room, held a bed, a wardrobe barely big enough for one person's clothes, and a coat rack that hung on the wall. The room also held two couches, each as old as my grandfather, each convertible to a bed. But how? This was the issue. My grandfather tried to conduct the experiment on one of them in our presence, and failed. I bent to help him, following my grandmother's instructions as she stood over us, the toes of her shoes nudging my leg. A loud squeak sounded, then a large cloud of dust, smelling strongly of wood shavings, washed over us. My grandfather took to coughing. This was our cue to pause and open the door to clear the air by means of the cross-draft coming in through the kitchen window. The room, you see, had no windows, merely a small casement that opened onto a service stairwell with still air that brought no breeze.

We set to trying again to unfold the couch, but again, always at the last minute, the couch would dig its heels in, refusing to complete its cycle. We would return it to its original state, cursing the couch and the carpenter who had made it.

The more we tried, the more convoluted it became. On perhaps the tenth try, the couch slipped smoothly and easily into the desired position at first—then it ground to a halt, refusing to budge forward, or even backward. We could find nothing for it. It was certainly not a bed, nor had it returned to its original function as a couch. At the end of his patience, my grandfather gave it a mighty kick, then went off to the bathroom to mop the sweat off his brow. My grandmother, taking it all in stride, said in English, "No problem! In a while I'll call in the concierge, and he'll know what to do about it."

I was not surprised by the foreign airs of my grandmother; if she hadn't done that, she would not have been Madame Yvonne, Old Beaky as they called her back home.

The larger room was my grandparents' bedroom. The first thing we noticed when we came in was that it was damp, and so dark that you could not see a thing in the room at midday with twenty-twenty eyesight unless you pressed the switch and turned on the three electric light bulbs suspended from the ceiling.

The furniture was a marvel: at first glance, it appeared to have belonged to Marie Antoinette, but it was filled with holes, woodworm, and scratches. I doubt that anyone, no matter how acrobatic, could have balanced on the stool at the dressing table. If he did, he would then be unable to rise without assistance from the logistics department. The mirror did not discriminate: it was suitable for both sighted and sightless persons alike. As for the bed and wardrobe, well, the less said about them, the better.

My grandmother said that she had bought all this junk for 300 francs from a market she called the Market for Fleas, or some such. This was where secondhand things were sold, like in our secondhand markets.

The entire apartment appeared to have sworn eternal enmity to the light of day. All of its windows gave onto a service stairwell inhabited by a number of cats no less bold and presumptuous than the ones Amm Idris used to chase with his stick.

When I asked about them, my grandmother snarled, "What can we do about it? It's all that filthy butcher downstairs' fault. Some cat steals a piece of meat and comes running in here, and fifty of his friends come chasing after it, and they have their fight in here!"

Telling day from night was quite a job in that apartment. You had to go outdoors or stand on tiptoe and look through the iron bars of the kitchen window, for this was the only window with any kind of view.

But the kitchen, to give that room its due, was large, big enough for a midsize dining table. This was just as well, because there was no hall as such: just a long corridor, a little broader than usual, in which a number of chairs stood facing one another as though in the traditional arrangement at a funeral. At the end of the passageway was a space set aside for the gas pipes connected to the wall, emanating the warmth used to heat the apartment.

For two whole days, I did not set foot outside that awful apartment.

My mother and grandmother spent most of their time in the kitchen, talking all the time, dropping their voices to a whisper whenever they divined that someone was approaching the kitchen. My grandfather and I sat together on two of the chairs in the hall.

He was unshaven, his face not only gaunt and pale with advancing age, but positively ill, as though he had been overtaken with some disease. He would look intently at me, and I would imagine that he was about to speak, but he would not. Occasionally he would raise his eyebrows slightly, but they would soon droop again, and he would nod off, head slumped forward. The doze would not last long, a couple of minutes; then he opened his eyes and smiled at me, wiping imaginary drool from his lips. Most of the time, nothing came out of his mouth when he slept, but he had gotten into the habit.

Then, he would leave his chair and go get his pack of cigarettes. It was hard for him to walk, for his legs were infested with varicose veins; his head bowed forward on his spindly neck. My mother, noticing, asked my grandmother about my grandfather's health. "It's because he can't stop looking for things to be unhappy about! He wakes up unhappy and goes to bed unhappy. 'Go out,' I tell him. 'Breathe some fresh air and get a change of scene.' Many's the time our son Isaac has begged us to visit him. It's just a four-hour plane ride, and we'd be in his house, and make the boy so happy! But it's no use, my dear."

I'm not sure what made me imagine that my grandfather's eyesight was failing, too, and that he had become hard of hearing. I gazed at the door to the room he had gone into, still ajar. I could see no movement coming from inside and half-feared hearing a cry and a thud of something hitting the floor, and that we would run to my grandfather and find him in a coma. But he would suddenly emerge, knotting the belt of the brown dressing gown he had just put on around his waist. It lent him a certain stature as he stood at the kitchen door, calling out to my grandmother, "Why all this talk of depression, Yvonne? Didn't you hear the doctor say that all that's wrong with me is some varicose veins and some roughening of the joints in my neck? Is there no end to your made-up stories and lies? And what you want me to do I never will, not if the sky falls."

The voices in the kitchen would hush, almost certainly whispering about the thing my grandmother wanted and that my grandfather was refusing to do. I noticed that my grandmother was more patient now and did not enter into quarrels with him as she once had. I overheard her telling my mother once that he never ceased to rebuke and blame her over nothing, sometimes in front of strangers, and that she was putting up with him because it was the decent thing to do. "How long has he been like this?" my mother asked, patting my grandmother's knee.

"The past two or three years." My mother fell silent. "And get this, he says he would have liked to spend the last two or three years of his life in Egypt, and be buried there. Talk about senility!"

"Poor Father."

My grandfather would come back and sit by me, pulling a Gauloise out of his pack. The filterless cigarette was short and squat; he lit it, puffing in my face. This was something he had never done back home. He had always smoked either in the bathroom or on the balcony, and when my grandmother had called out to him, he had told her that he couldn't come in for fear of the smoke hurting me.

The cigarette smoke was thick, the smell of it more like cigar smoke. My grandfather was fiddling with his front teeth with the tip of his little finger. At my attempts to lighten his mood, he would nod and smile. I would remind him of the old days in Daher, and he would lean back, stretching out his legs before him. "How's Muallim Habib?"

"He's fine. He sends his regards, Grandfather."

"And Hagg Mahmoud, Abu Hassan?"

I paused. "Oh, Grandfather. He misses you to no end, and he sends you a thousand greetings!"

My grandfather had no notion that we had followed his example and slipped away in the dead of night without telling a soul, and that all these greetings came from me. I wanted to curse my mother! She had made me leave without letting me say goodbye to those who were dearest to me, and we had crept out of our apartment like thieves in the night or fugitives.

"And Labib, the shoe repairman?"

I told him that his store had been closed for years, and we had no news of him; he was surprised. "That's not right, Galal. Shouldn't you have asked after him, found out what was keeping him from opening the store? What about Sheikh Khalaf?"

"He died, may he rest in peace." I added the traditional condolence: "Long life to you, Grandfather."

"Dead? Do you say he died? God rest his soul." He sighed. "Your mother didn't tell me in her last letter. She really should have. All her letters are idle talk, and she never tells me the important things." He turned toward the kitchen, calling on my mother, annoyed. She didn't hear him, though, so he turned back to me. "I suppose you don't go down to Azhar Street, either."

"Oh no, Grandfather; I've been there several times."

"Did you have a look at Hagg Desouki's store?" I stared. "Hagg Desouki, the fabric tradesman whose mother's funeral I took you to." I made a motion of my head as though remembering. "For heaven's sake, son, Hagg Desouki, where you kicked up a fuss listening to Sheikh Abd al-Baset reciting the Qur'an."

I tried to go along. "Ah yes! I remember, Grandfather."

"Tell me; is my old watch store still there, opposite his?" I didn't speak, whereupon he went on, "And is Abbas, my old apprentice, still standing there?"

I looked at the wall. I saw a recent picture of my grandparents hanging there in a large frame. Tucked into the bottom of the frame on one side were two old, small photographs of myself and Rachel. On the other side were two recent photographs of children I didn't know, perhaps the offspring of Uncle Isaac or Uncle Shamoun.

"He's a solid boy, good at his work. When your watch breaks down, Galal, go get it repaired there. Tell him who you are. Say, 'I'm Muallim Zaki's son,' and he'll take care of the watch like it was his own, and he won't charge you a thing."

I turned my attention back to him, nodding. He fell silent, his gaze wavering, and he pulled his robe tighter about him, to cover his knees. "Do you think I could go back home?"

I looked at him without a word. My grandmother emerged from the kitchen, heading for her room, and he fell silent. When she had closed the door behind her, he said, "You know she wanted us to go live there, with Isaac?"

I felt the blood rush to my face, and made no answer. "Israel isn't my home. It might be home to Isaac, or young Rachel, or even Shamoun. But me . . . ." He looked at me, then dropped his gaze. "God forgive them, they made me do it."

I fell silent and looked down, too. With a final glance at me, he fell asleep again.

37

Rachel came to visit a week later. She wore light gray linen capris with a tie at the calf and a see-through blouse that barely came down to her waistband. It seemed she was bra-less, or else her bra was so thin that her bust moved freely, her breasts bouncing with her every movement.

For the first time, I understood the true importance of the word 'perfume.' My nose had been living in the gutter, understanding nothing of scent except for the one-pound and one-pound-fifty cologne bottles I bought from Amm Zuzu. Strangely enough, when I asked him for a twenty-five piaster discount on a bottle, he would look down his nose at me, saying, "My prices are fixed, and my stock is perfex!" Noticing my stare, he would say, "That means it's gen-u-wyne, young Galal. Gen-u-wyne! It comes direct from the factory, and no haggling."

I'd always argue on, asking for a discount, and he would get mad. "Look, sonny, I sell guaranteed name-brand stock. If you like the price, you're welcome to buy; if you don't, well, you can find yourself an onion, and take a sniff of that."

"Amm Zuzu . . . ."

"Zuzu indeed! Go on; push off! What would you do, then, if I let you have a sniff of the essence of roses or jasmine that costs four pounds? What would you say then?"

"Let's see it."

"It's not for you, sonny; I'm keeping it for the high-end customers."

Oh, to see you now, Amm Zuzu! Where were you, with your loose-fitting jersey and the threadbare beret that hid your bald pate! I swear, if I had listened to you my nose would now be lost beyond redemption! If you were with me now, and took one sniff of the perfume worn by Rachel, you would understand, nod once, turn tail, get on the first plane to Egypt, and quietly set fire to your stall and all your stock. Believe me, Amm Zuzu!

This was the first time I had realized that the sense of smell had a power all its own, capable of making one's blood heat and quicken.

I must have smiled, or something must have showed in my face, for I saw my mother smiling at me, a question on her face. Rachel came toward me, perching on one arm of my armchair, playfully flicking a finger against my nose, her midsection and one hip pressed against my shoulder. My eyes, against my will, flitted to my mother: she was watching us contentedly.

Rachel dropped her handbag onto the floor, balling up the light cream sweater in her hand and dropping it in my lap, followed by the wine-red scarf around her neck. I felt it: definitely silk, with a brand name on the edge: Mademoiselle Coco Chanel. Meanwhile, Rachel apologized for her absence. "I was busy with a visitor from Abu Dhabi who arrived suddenly with his family, and he wanted to see all of Paris from top to bottom as quickly as possible before he left for London."

My grandmother said to her, stealing a look at my grandfather, "So you've got money, then."

"He was very generous, Grandmother; he paid very well, and if I had asked for more, he wouldn't have said no."

"Hand over two thousand francs, then, and tomorrow we'll go buy the ring I told you about."

My grandfather looked at her disapprovingly. "For shame, Yvonne. What will the girl think?"

"Grandfather!" Rachel said with reproof, half-rising. "Don't carry on so."

"I will, 'so' and more. I've told her a hundred times not to take the children's money. We have enough. Ring, indeed! She's got twenty rings in the closet in there!"

"So it's come to this, Zaki," choked my grandmother, pulling out a small handkerchief from her bodice to dab at her eyes. "Talking to me so, in front of the children! Teaching me right from wrong, at my age? This girl I'm talking to, who I have faith won't disappoint me, why, she's my little girl! I raised her, and I've got rights."

And so began the conflagration. None of us managed to contain my grandfather, who burst out yelling, and, not content with rebuking my mother, turned on Rachel, calling down curses on her and her father and mother and the world and everything. They all left him alone and went into my grandmother's room, leaving me alone with him.

It took him a whole hour, plus three or four cigarettes, to calm down. He asked me then, yawning, "Didn't you bring any newspapers or magazines with you, or anything to read?"

"Newspapers?"

"Yes, newspapers."

"Well, Grandfather . . . ."

"You didn't," he cut me off. "Right, then." And he rose, lifting up the cushion of the chair he had been sitting on, and pulled out a copy of an old magazine called *al-Geel*, or 'The Generation,' that used to be published in Egypt in the 1960s. Then he drew up his legs onto the seat and began to read.

Not two minutes passed before he put it back, looking from the walls to the ceiling to the chairs, one after the other. His face was like a blank page, no life in it. When the voices of the people in my grandparents' room rose, he would lean forward, listening intently. When their voices subsided, he would turn to me. 'Now,' I said to myself, 'now he'll speak,' and I looked at him encouragingly. Only he didn't, ignoring me and going back to staring at the room.

255

The next time he turned to me, I said, "How do you pass the time, Grandfather?"

"As you can see," he answered in a lukewarm tone, "either in this chair, or lying on the bed."

"Why not go out a bit, Grandfather?"

"Go out?"

"Yes. Walk around, amuse yourself, do something."

"Do something? Right. Yes, well." And he broke into loud yawning that went on for quite a while. When he was done, he stretched his legs out before him and slumped.

There was a small insect, a little larger than an ant, on the edge of his seat. I had noticed it standing there for quite a while. It was probably one of the inhabitants of the holes and scratches in my grandfather's bed, lost in the apartment, waiting for him to take the bus, so to speak, home.

The provoking thing suddenly took an inexplicable fancy to his ear. It had made its way persistently up the sleeve of his pajamas, then took the straight path of the seam until it reached his collar. One hop, and it was at the base of his neck. I never lost sight of it in this hairy region but followed it until it blazed its confident trail and made its way into his earhole, unnoticed by him.

He drew his legs in again, a sad smile on his face. "You want me to go out, Galal, sonny-boy? Where to, I'd like to know? There's no Muallim Habib's store here, nor Clot Bey Street, nor Ataba Square. What would I do if I went out into the streets of this city? Look at the Beatle boys, or the naked women?"

And with that, he trudged off to the bathroom. One of his pajama pant legs was rolled up twice, the other straight. He was swimming in the jacket, skinny arms poking out of its too-short sleeves. My gaze followed him until he disappeared behind the bathroom door.

38

As I MADE TO SIT in the front seat of her car, Rachel said, "I hope you don't mind; we've got to make a quick stop at the Champs-Élysées. I've got a work appointment, and then we can go on." When I nodded, she added, "The Champs-Élysées is on our sightseeing list, anyway, so we can start there."

As she drove through the streets, I looked at everything all around, feeling as though I were in a spaceship following the events taking place on another planet: the people hurrying by; the hats; the umbrellas against a sudden squall of rain; the dogs walking along with their owners, as though it was not only their right but a duty; the redness on people's cheeks; the long tendrils of hair creeping out from beneath people's woolen headgear; the cats being carried in baskets, ribbons of every color round their necks; Citroen 5CV's, with their strange appearance.

I was like a country bumpkin just arrived by parachute and left to his own devices, trying and failing to read the signs or billboards, goggling at a couple kissing in public with neither shame nor any prick of conscience.

My eyes were drawn to a set of steps descending into the bowels of the earth, men going down them and emerging from them, and I was astonished, for I had only heard of underground trains in the media before, and had certainly never seen one. I was so taken that I didn't hear Rachel calling my name. She had to poke me in the shoulder before I finally turned to her.

"Hey, kid! Where did you go?" She was so coy when she said it, the sparkle in her eye so mischievous, that she turned my head, heating my blood.

I pulled myself together and said, trembling, "Oh. Right. Paris really is like they say."

"You haven't seen anything yet! What'll you say, kid, when I take you round the places worth seeing, and out to the Lido! And after that to the Bois de Boulogne, and I'll show you what goes on there. We are going to go wild."

I leaned back against the headrest, enjoying the moment. She looked at me with joy, long fingers pushing back her cascades of hair.

"You know," I said, "I really feel bad for my grandfather. Why's he keeping himself locked up in that burrow? It's so nice out here; he should get out more."

"Your grandfather?" She laughed loudly, turning to me. A small golden cross slipped free of the décolletage of her blouse, together with a scrap of gold chain. I looked at it oddly, and she clasped it, flushing. She whipped her blouse open and stuffed it into her bra, revealing a large part of her breast. It wasn't olive-skinned, like I had expected, but very white, with a faint pink flush. Higher up, on the side nearest her armpit, I espied something like a mole, with a few yellow hairs around it.

"It's for work. Don't go getting any strange ideas." I listened attentively. "You know I'm a tour guide, and I'm self-employed. I don't have a company or anything like that; I work alone. And all my clients are Gulf Arabs. And as you know, they've got this thing about Jews." She fell silent a moment. "There was this bastard who started this rumor at the Café des Pauquettes, where I work, that I was Jewish. I kept on denying it till I was blue in the face, and now whenever I go there, I keep this ready, and before I go in the café, I take it out."

I smiled. "Why not wear a gold Qur'an, like some women?"

"It's not like I wouldn't! You know, I did think of it. But I thought it was a bit too much, and it was a cover that might be blown too easily. You know, my reputation is my greatest asset." I turned my eyes back to the road, the remains of my smile still on my face. "Don't you believe me?"

"Does my grandfather know?"

"Your grandfather, you say? Your grandfather doesn't belong in this world we live in, and he'd do better to find a grave to crawl into."

"My grandfather?"

"Yes, man, your grandfather! He is a period piece, a fossil. I wish we'd left him behind in Egypt. He could have stayed in that neighborhood of his; what's it called."

"You mean Daher?" I said through gritted teeth.

"That's right. Daher. So, what do you plan to do here?"

"What plans?" I answered, looking at her nose. I hadn't realized before how curved it was. "What are you talking about? I'm going back to Egypt in a month or so."

"Egypt?"

"Yes, Egypt."

"But Auntie said . . . ." She trailed off. I asked her what she meant, but to my annoyance, she wouldn't give me a straight answer. Finally, she said, "Sorry, Galal. I hope you're not offended. The thing is, Auntie Camellia led me to understand you would be staying for a while, so I figured I'd find you something to do to with your time. I thought you could start with harvesting grapes. There's still a while left in the harvest season, and I could find you a place there."

"Grapes? What are you talking about?"

"I just meant something temporary."

We parked the car close to the Place de l'Opéra.

We walked to Boulevard Haussmann, where she took me through a number of streets to a clothing store called the Galeries Lafayette, and then to another store no less magnificent, where she bought a number of men's shirts, two pairs of pants, a pair of running shoes, and a raincoat with a hood. She even bought a dozen pairs of underpants and a dozen undershirts, all in my size. Seeing the surprise on my face, she said, "These are for Andre, my boyfriend. He's exactly your size."

We tossed our shopping bags, seven or perhaps more, into the backseat and headed for the Champs-Élysées.

This was no ordinary street but a seductress, beckoning to you with her willowy form and come-hither eyes. Once seduced into her clutches, one was lost forever: straight lines of chestnut trees, glittering and broad stores that you would never get tired of looking at if you spent half the day there. Restaurants, boutiques, the Lido nightclub with a great sign above it announcing that evening's entertainment, and Espace Cardin, filled with painters, sculptors, and the stars of music and song.

There was the Arc de Triomphe, its solid form imposing in the distance, and the obelisk standing like a stranger in the Place de la Concorde. There were cafés with wrought-iron awnings covered with heavy fabric of orange or dark blue filled with customers enjoying the music, reading books and newspapers, or chatting quietly, unless they were Arabs, in which case the chatting was at the top of their voices, accompanied by gesticulations in every direction. Suddenly, though, and rather strangely, the clamor of their voices would subside, their heads drawn together, and their speech would take on a serious tone, their faces betraying that the discussion had turned to some momentous matter. I fancied that this was the moment they had glimpsed a member of their country's intelligence services passing by, or perhaps a woman they were plotting to conquer.

I walked at Rachel's side to the middle of the Rue des Paquets. It was not midday yet, but most of the tables were occupied: Gulf Arabs, Arabs from the Levant, tourists from the land of Uncle Sam and from Japan, and a couple from Africa—him in a dark safari suit with dark headgear, a grim expression on his face, and darker than black coffee. The lady was very cheerful, radiant in her patterned national dress, her completely bare arms shining in the sunlight streaming in through the window with undertones like aubergines fresh from the field. The only French people in the place were two men and a woman, all three of them over seventy.

Rachel seated me at a table deep inside the café and ordered me an ice cream, then went to a table where two Gulf Arabs were sitting. One of them was short and fat, the too-big collar of his shirt revealing a wobbly double chin. He was clearly a man of the world. The other was thinner and younger, apparently still in training. They greeted her warmly, and she whispered something to them. They both threw me a quick, uninterested look. She had probably told them that I was her chauffeur, or a distant, poor relation.

She was wearing a short skirt, to mid-thigh, yet she crossed her legs as she sat. She was sexy, and her motions and the way she bent her upper half forward were enough to crush any resistance. The older man was more resistant: his eyes, beneath fleshy eyelids, stared emotionlessly, without revealing his intent. The problem was with the younger, for there was no power nor force of conscience, no medicine nor yet a tranquilizer made that could hold him back. He was positively vibrating in his seat, feet fidgeting up and down like a child about to pee his pants if not taken immediately to the toilet. Strangely, he made me a party to whatever it was, looking at me resentfully every few moments, as if to say, 'Get lost. What are you doing hanging around, you bastard!'

My ire rose in turn: my blood boiled with the desire to walk up to her, say a few well-chosen words of reproof, and snatch her away from this corrupt whelp. When we left the café, and she said, "Now we're off to the Latin Quarter and Notre Dame Cathedral," I excused myself, saying I had a headache and needed to go home to bed.

39

"Not again, Galal! Not again! This takes me back to Egypt, when I'd have to drum on the headboard to wake you up!" My mother's voice was not a little irritated, as though coming from a great distance, and Nadia and I were in another world.

She and I were in my grandparents' old room in Daher, steps away from his old armoire with the ancient mirror that distorted everything. My attention was caught by a large sliding aluminum window, closed with a rusty padlock. The window in my grandfather's room had never been that big, and its two wooden panes had always been wide open. The room in my dream had no door. The only other opening was a casement high up in the wall, through which a breeze nipped in, accompanied by the cries of hawkers in the street, and Nadia was in my arms. I gathered back her hair, finding a deep scar on the surface of her neck; it was unhealed, and looked painful. It occurred to me that it might have been made by a claw or something sharp. I made to ask her about it, but my tongue wouldn't obey my command and lay heavy in my mouth. When I spoke, it was so slurred that it sounded like the speech of the dumb, so I fell silent.

Finding her unmoving, I thought she had fallen asleep leaning against my chest and looked up at the mirror before me. The black hair cascading over her shoulders had a few white hairs mixed in, and the ends were split. The bottoms of her calves were flabby, with stretch marks; her feet, which had been sculptural in their beauty, were pitiful. I pulled her to my chest, feeling no warmth in her body. I shook her: not a pulse, not a movement, her color gone, her hands limp and weightless around my neck.

My eyes flew open. The world before me was foggy. My mother was standing by the bed, looking at me, just closing her mouth. She appeared to have been calling for me, and seemed to have stopped when I opened my eyes. I followed her movements through half-closed eyes as she walked toward the open window and unconsciously pulled the covers up over my chest for protection against the spike of cold air coming in through it. As she busied herself with closing the window, I remembered the beginning of the dream.

Mr. Fawzi, the P.E. teacher at our school, was there. Handsome, with straight hair and hazel eyes, he had always inspired my dislike, which he met with equal distaste.

In the dream, we had been about to come to blows over Nadia. He said she was his girlfriend and had had a child by him, a child as beautiful as the new moon, while I shrieked at him. He laughed at my cries, revealing unusually large, gold-capped front teeth. I was stunned, for I had never seen him this way before, and his teeth had always been healthy, with no cracks or decay.

My desire for a fight died, and I was afraid. He took a few bellicose steps toward me, and I lost control of my limbs, freezing in place. I could not move my feet to run away, and my gullet was producing gasps like a drowning man's.

I looked at my mother, and she said, "Come on; get up. Come on, come on. Rachel's here; she's waiting for you in the hall."

I woke fully and looked at her. She held a bag in her hand, one of the bags of clothes Rachel had bought when we were together the previous day. She took out a shirt and a pair of pants and asked me to put them on. The rest of the bags sat on a nearby chair. I turned to her. Satisfaction in her eyes, she said, "They're all for you. Rachel didn't want to tell you then; she thought it might be a nice surprise." She smiled. "There isn't a girl in the world like Rachel. Pretty, and kindhearted, and takes good care of her family."

She looked at me, evidently expecting me to join her in a duet. I looked away, a piercing pain suddenly striking me from wrist to elbow: countless needles, relentless along the path of the nerve, followed by a numbness in my suddenly useless hand. My silence lengthened as my mother added, "And Galal, my boy, what's more, she's a money-maker. Friends and acquaintances and contacts everywhere! A better businesswoman you never saw!"

With a glance, she indicated that she had said what she had to say, and the rest was for me to tell her. I felt nauseous. Something sticky and ugly was clotting my intestines, acidic fluid rising up in the back of my throat, burning and unpleasant. I pushed the bag away, telling my mother I was sick. I pulled the covers up over my head without hearing her response.

Everyone came in—my grandparents, Rachel—surrounding the bed, and my insistence that I was not feeling well grew ever louder. My grandfather was extremely anxious, and my mother looked worried. But there was something else on her face, something I did not detect until later.

Rachel laid a reassuring hand on my shoulder. Encouraging me to get up, she said, "Come on, Gel-gel; don't be lazy! I've a whole itinerary planned out for you today, and we won't get back till the small hours."

My eyes squinted up as she went on. "First, we'll take the *Bateau Mouche*, and I'll show you the Seine. Then we'll have lunch in a great Greek restaurant in the Latin Quarter. Stuffed vine leaves and kebabs and everything your heart desires." I opened my eyes. "And I've two tickets to the Moulin Rouge. There's a fabulous show on there, and I can show you Pigalle, the red-light district."

I saw Mr. Fawzi. That rat had never been on my itinerary

on any day of my life; I had only ever spoken to him once or twice at school. He didn't even know Nadia, nor had he ever heard of her; and here he was, with me, in a dream! And with Nadia!

"Come on; get up! If you don't come with me today, you'll have missed half your life, as they say!"

I didn't answer.

Finding me a killjoy, Rachel left, and my grandmother grew tired of urging me and followed suit. My mother went off in search of an aspirin. My grandfather alone remained seated on the edge of the bed. I would have liked to tell him the truth, to tell him I was weary of the world, but I did not.

40

FOR FOUR WEEKS, I HAD gone to Friday prayers at the Grand Mosque of Paris. I went and showered as Muslims do in the morning, performed the morning prayers and the additional Sunna prayers, and concluded the prayer by sitting on the prayer mat reciting my rosary. Then, I would place the rosary in the pocket of my shirt, leaving its green tassel hanging out of my pocket, put my white cap on, and go out into the street. By this time, Amm al-Sheikh Munji al-Ayyari, a Tunisian living in France and owner of the neighboring butcher shop, would have closed up shop and would be waiting for me. We would then walk to the metro station together.

When I lived in Egypt, such rituals had not occupied much of my attention. Many times, I had heard the call to Friday prayers in the street; walked over to any old water tap, or asked Sitt Shouq, the doorman's wife, for a bucket of water; performed ablutions; and set off for the mosque, with neither rosary nor cap. I have no idea what made me cling to these rituals in Paris.

I was grateful that the family had grown used to it; my grandmother merely made a little sucking sound of her lips to show disapproval or shut herself up in her room until I had shoved off.

The first time, though, had not gone so smoothly. Apparently my grandmother had needed to pee badly that day, and she burst out of her room in a desperate dash for the bathroom, only wearing one slipper. Naturally, she couldn't help seeing me in a chair in the hall, reading the Qur'an from a small prayer book in my lap.

I was droning the words out loud, rocking back and forth and nodding my head, with half-shut eyes. When I heard the click of the bathroom door and saw her coming out, I stopped my recitation but remained bent over the Qur'an, surreptitiously stealing glances at her.

Her hair was wild, droplets of water running down behind her ears. She must have noticed what I had been doing. She took two steps on tiptoe, then stopped, seething with animosity. My heart started to pound.

Old Beaky simply could not restrain herself. The accursed woman simply lost it. She gave free rein to the viciousness and aggression in her blood that had been given this unmissable opportunity, and she burst into action immediately, full speed ahead.

She took me by surprise. That old harridan ambushed me! In the blink of an eye, the ashtray was flying through the air and striking the wall. When I moved, startled, she followed up with a cassette tape that had been on a nearby chair. She scored a direct hit with that on the tip of my nose, and it fell, tape partially unspooling out of it, at my feet.

Having fired her opening shot, the old crone stood with her hands on her hips, in blatant challenge, while I stared at her in disbelief. Yes, the set of her jaw said, she had done it, indeed, and if she had still had her health, she would have pounced on me like a cat and taken me by the throat as she had done when I was younger.

I leapt up, of course, my right hand clutching my nose, which was bleeding. We had a screaming match that brought out my grandfather, still half-asleep and yawning, followed by my mother.

My grandmother yelled at the top of her voice, "Look here, I'll have you know this isn't the Sayyida Zeinab Mosque, or al-Hussein!"

I retorted equally unpleasantly, driving her to plumb even greater depths of invective, while my mother tried to stanch the blood with her handkerchief and push my grandmother away at the same time. My grandfather, not knowing which of us to speak to, would speak first to one, then the other.

The matter was not settled until my grandmother said, "When you want to recite the Qur'an, go read it at Sheikh Munji's, the downstairs neighbor! He's a half-man, and filthy like you!"

My grandfather roared. It would have been all right even if she had insulted me worse, he said, for I was her grandson after all, and, he said, she didn't really mean anything she said to me. The issue was Sheikh Munji; the man had had a long history of fights with my grandmother, and when his name was mentioned, my grandfather, fearing a renewal of hostilities, ended the matter with a conclusive victory in my favor.

It was the first time she had ever patted me on the shoulder and apologized.

Sheikh Munji had been one of the first people to move into the apartment building. When my grandfather first came to live there, they had been neutral toward one another, neither friendly nor unfriendly; but with my grandmother, things were quite different. The pair had hated one another at first sight.

The man was a veritable wonder: a giant of a man, with a constitution of iron and a mighty beard. He would come and go with a belt at his waist bristling with knives. His principles in life were: "Your enemy is the enemy of your religion," and, "No compromise with those who injure you." Therefore, she kept a safe distance.

Her efforts were confined to his wife, Sitt Zahira Bu-Saf, the "mealy-mouthed holier-than-thou with spindly legs like a goat's," as my grandmother called her. There were low-level aggressions and insults: once, when my grandmother was climbing the stairs, they threw down a turnip, which landed on her head.

This had become a turning point in the conflicts between the two families, and the use of violence in its resolution. My grandmother had burst into their apartment and laid waste to all she saw, striking both the wife and the two children, one of which had not yet learned to walk. The matter ended up at the local constabulary and the damages were valued at the time at 200 francs.

Three years of fights, during which my grandmother had been brought up twice before a judge on charges of assault and battery, plus vandalism, had followed. The first time she had been fined; the second, sentenced to a month's imprisonment—the sentence was suspended—plus damages.

Sheikh Munji, too, had been subject to a fine, for breaking my grandfather's spectacles.

The clashes were now over, each of the two parties avoiding conflict with the other, indeed avoiding conversation altogether. My good-natured grandfather, though, had no objection to the friendship that had sprung up between myself and Sheikh Munji, perhaps saying to himself, "What's the harm? Might it not break the constant state of armed truce between our families?"

41

Sheikh Munji al-Ayyari and I would head for the Barbès-Rochechouart metro station. He would buy me an Arabic-language newspaper from the kiosk adjacent to the station, or a bar of chocolate.

I would make to pull out my wallet, or reciprocate by buying him something in turn, but he would hold back my hand heatedly. He viewed me as a younger brother, or maybe a son. I felt comfortable, and walked docilely and gratefully by his side.

He went into the station ahead of me, and we would take the escalators down to the platform, and thence the metro to Jussieu station. There was not much traffic at that time, perhaps a few tourists on their way back from visiting the Sacré-Cœur, or on the Butte de Montmartre, close to the station, on their way to their downtown hotels.

All along the sidewalk there were, of course, Frenchmen and Frenchwomen, but not many, and all elderly. In their hands they carried plastic bags and paperbacks. As was the norm here, they made no noise, and kept themselves to themselves.

The noise would begin when the clochards awoke. These were pitiful folk: men, women, young and old alike, who, vanquished by the world above ground, had abandoned it for the burrows. They had built settlements underground, on the platforms and in the corners of the metro stations of Chatelet, St-Denis, Pigalle, Barbès, St-Lazare, and others. Some were unemployed; some were mentally ill; some had the complexes of a fourth-rate politician on his tenth defeat in the local council, having received his final dismissal from the party he had represented; some had discovered that they had wasted their lives and decided to descend into the bowels of the earth, where the real world resided; some were veterans, upholders of noble principles, and artists who, once upon a time, had been the talk of the town.

Most of the time, the clochards lay in their foul-smelling rags, surrounded by bottles of cheap wine. They frequently awoke from deep sleep to take a swig from the bottle, hurl a few insults at passersby, then immediately fall asleep again, snoring. I would be stunned to see this, and if I had possessed a stopwatch I would have timed these moments of wakefulness to the second: a minute or less between the clochard's waking to do his business and his falling asleep again—and snoring at that. Yes, snoring! And not your common or garden low, polite snoring, but nerve-racking grunts that couldn't help but distract and irritate, no matter how far away one stood. 'How I wish,' I thought, 'I could find a professor of sleep to explain this mystery to me!'

Their sleep was a blessing, though, for no sooner did they wake up than they took to panhandling. A franc, a sandwich, a bag of potato chips, a carton of juice, a cigarette: anything at all they saw in your hand. Then they would take to swapping the filthiest insults imaginable, and loudly too, their faces red, veins popping out, gesticulating in each other's faces to make you think that a fight must now break out, and you must move away hastily for fear of getting hurt.

They inevitably defied expectations, though, their voices suddenly dying for no logical reason. They might content themselves with spitting in one another's faces or exchanging rude gestures with no concept of propriety or shame.

The fights were generally over territory. Each clochard had his own patch, a one-by-two-meter section of platform that was his kingdom. This was where he slept, received his visitors, and placed his possessions. No other clochard could approach without his permission and approval. The fight might also be over a female clochard, usually over seventy, or over a piece of bread that one of them had snatched out of the hand of another, or a gulp of wine filched by one of them from a sleeping platform-mate.

If you lingered a little on the platform, it was possible to see a sane and respectable clochard come out of his corner and form a peace initiative between the warring parties, feet never tiring of the shuttle diplomacy he undertook between one and the other; eventually, all would be forgiven, the warring parties reunited and peace restored, whereupon they returned to their guffawing and ill-bred talk.

But all this was nothing compared to the hullabaloo that sprang up when the local authorities descended upon the station to remove them by force and take them up to the surface of the earth in order to give them a hot bath at the mairie, or municipality headquarters. Oh, what a black day for everyone waiting for the train! The clochards were not in the habit of giving in without a fight. They acted like toddlers whose mothers insisted on giving them a bath: they scurried in all directions, pursued by the officers, and the station would become a circus, or perhaps a scene from some farce.

The leader of a group of mairie officers would yell to one of his men: "Jacques! Catch that old man hiding among the passengers!" Jacques would obediently dart off, whereupon the leader would shout, "No, stupid! Not that one! That's a Japanese tourist. Were you thinking of giving him a bath too? That one, the bald one, the old guy with a bottle of wine in his hand!" The leader's ire would rise. "Not that way! Are you blind? That way! There he is, hiding behind the fat lady!"

The fat lady would look behind her in alarm as another man from the municipality jogged up, huffing and puffing, clutching a pair of clochards by the back of the neck, like rabbits. Another clochard would be jumping from one platform to another, followed by two officers, cheered on by their leader, "Good job! Good job! Get the old fox; don't let him get away!"

Then he'd turn to another of his men. "And you, Maxime, are you going to just stand there? Get the old man running over there without any pants on! Quick, quick! The shameless old beggar just wedged himself into the crowd!"

Panic would reign as all the passengers looked around in search of the shameless clochard running naked among them, not caring to cover even his private parts. Cries would come up from the passengers, especially the women, and they would curse Jacques Chirac, then the mayor of Paris, for not putting a stop to these rascals.

Sheikh Munji and I would stay away from the clochards, so as not to pollute ourselves and thus ruin our ablutions, as he phrased it.

On Fridays, there were other Muslims on the platform on their way to prayer. I recognized them by their clothing: safari suits, tight around the armpits; a cap or rosary in hand; and shoes at least a year past their normal lifespan. They were poor, simple folk with kindly faces.

They recognized us as well, greeting us with a wave or a gesture. The sheikh's customers would come toward us and pump our hands warmly. Sometimes one of them would complain about the meat he had bought the last time, saying it was poor quality, filled with gristle and fat, whereupon the sheikh would quell him with a terrifying glare. If the customer was not cowed, the sheikh would tell him, "We are on our way to prayer; this is not a fit time for frivolities or talk of business."

When the train arrived, seats virtually empty, we would take seats facing one another by the window. Sheikh Munji knew my whole story and never tired of giving me advice in his Tunisian dialect. "Listen, my son. This city Paris is like an ogre: if you live here, it swallows you up. Why stay?"

I would not answer. Running a hand over his beard, he would say, with a mix of pity and contempt: "Why should you stay? What would you do? Be a shop boy for a butcher, or a shop boy at a grocery store, or sweep the streets? Is this what you want?"

I stared at him.

"You look confused. Ask your God for advice with an istikhara prayer. Do you know how to, or do you not?"

My face must have showed that not only did I not know how to perform the istikhara prayer, but I had never heard of it. He said: "You do not."

I nodded, and the sheikh began to teach me how to perform it, starting with the ablutions and the number of prostrations, and so on.

A Frenchman who had gotten on at the previous stop showed some displeasure at our loud voices. Munji noticed, but paid him no heed, continuing his conversation with me in tones that grew progressively louder, punctuated by earth-shattering coughs that rebounded off the roof of the metro, all the while looking at the man as if to say, 'Haven't you heard of Sheikh Munji before? Perhaps I should challenge you to a duel to show you who I am.'

Realizing that he had no chance with this bearded sheikh, the man withdrew, muttering dire French imprecations under his breath. I believe that they must have been very rude references to the sheikh, because he went visibly red in the face. He controlled himself, however, waving a hand. "Ignore him. He's a nobody. By God, if we weren't on our way to prayer and in a hurry, I would have broken every bone in his body."

The Frenchman had not gotten far yet. He could tell from the sheikh's tone that the man was insulting him in Arabic and turned to us, waving a hand in anger, while the sheikh, too, half-rose. "By God, if he doesn't get out of our face right now, I'll give him a thrashing he'll never forget!"

I grabbed the sheikh's hand to calm him down, while he said to the man, "Marche loin! Marche loin!" which means, in rather bad French, 'walk far away; walk far away.'

The Frenchman, realizing that the sheikh was not just bluffing but seriously meant to fight him, went to the door, clearly intending to step off the train at the next station, leaving it and its odd passengers behind.

After a while, the sheikh calmed down, saying, "Go home, my boy. Be a doctor or an engineer, and grow up in your own country. No matter how far you go in Paris, no matter what you achieve, it'll never amount to anything."

"But, then, how come you're living here, Sheikh?"

"I'll tell you this, my son: Here, we are living as though we were in Tunisia. Our food and drink are a hundred percent Tunisian. We know nothing of the land of the Franks but the passport." After a beat of silence, he went on. "Besides, you're not like me. I'm living among Tunisians, but you, who do you have over here?"

"I have my mother, Sheikh."

"Your mother, my boy, has decided to stay here because she is not estranged. Your mother is living among family: her father, her mother, her brothers and sisters, people who are Jewish like her. You do not even have the social circle that she has." I remained silent. "Other than your mother, who else do you have? Stay with your grandmother? Would anyone stand to live with that old harridan? She's a bitch, and her father was a dog!"

I was annoyed. Suddenly I discovered that, although I had no great love for my grandmother, hearing her insulted was not a thing I could tolerate.

The sheikh, however, didn't notice and sailed on. "And I ask you, I beg you on your mother's life, explain this to me: How can a well-mannered boy like you, good people, be living with such a grandmother? Answer me that! I swear, if I had not been born into this world a Muslim and a God-fearing man, I would have given her a drubbing, and gotten rid of her ruinous face!"

I grew more and more upset, but he was still speaking. "As for your grandfather, he is a gentle and easygoing man, but he's a lightweight, easily swayed, and no personality of his own at all."

We parted for a few moments, each placing his ticket in the station turnstile and passing through.

He jogged after me, speaking with his mouth, face, and hands, reaffirming his view of my grandmother. "Did you ever hear of a woman attacking a peaceable house and running amok, attacking children and adults and infants three months old? Even my poor little one didn't escape unharmed; she kicked him with her foot. She has given my wife Zahira a complex! Would you believe it, even now, she sees your grandmother in her nightmares, now holding a knife, now with a weapon in her belt, for all the world like she's going to the wars! May she never prosper, that she-devil!"

We emerged from the metro. Steps away stood the Grand Mosque of Paris, with its Islamic-style ornamentation and proud, tall minaret. Sheikh Munji fell silent, and I saw his eyes roving over the people standing outside the mosque. All of a sudden, he broke into smiles and turned to me, saying he had seen a friend or acquaintance. Craning his neck, he would call out joyfully, then follow up with a wave of the hand. "Zein al-Abidin, come over here!"

The man, Zein al-Abidin, waved an arm, making his way through the crowd toward us. In a Tunisian dialect we could hardly understand, he said, "Good to see you, good to see you!"

"Good to see you! This is my young friend Galal. I'll take him home after prayer and we can meet in the afternoon at my store. Actually, no; I tell you what: come to dinner. Your auntie Zahira's making a wonderful meal! Couscous with alwash, and grilled vegetables, and bureek with tuna."

The man left. The crowds of Muslims reached all the way round the corners of the mosque. There were Africans from Senegal and Djibouti in their loose, brightly colored traditional dress; Moroccans; Tunisians; and Algerians. The younger men were dressed like Frenchmen, while the middle-aged and elderly wore burnooses of white, beige, and dark brown, paired with mules. I could hear their loud chatter long before I got to the mosque, bursting out as sharp and quick as electric sparks, in their North African dialect full of French words.

Hawkers stood around selling incense, rosaries, and Eastern perfumes, their wares spread out on low tables or on the sidewalk. There were always one or two of them selling tapes of the greatest Qur'an reciters: Abd al-Baset, al-Husari, and Sheikh Mustafa Ismail; the sermons of Sheikh Kishk and Sheikh Badri; and the 'religious' books of the type that sought to strike fear into people's hearts, that spoke of the torments of Judgment Day, of the angels armed with staffs and iron bars to beat those who had neglected their prayers, or women who didn't listen to their husbands. There might even be a book tucked in that spoke of the correct way to practice marital relations, and the arts of courting. The local authorities wouldn't look too closely at them, it being Friday; close by was a police car to secure the area and keep order, officers in tall hats standing around it.

When I was done with prayer, I took the metro to the Latin Quarter. I would browse Gilbert's bookstore, and sometimes another in the alleyways further in. Both specialized in second-hand books, and their customers were numerous and varied: men of culture, frivolous readers, young, old, serious readers, and browsers. The shelves held everything your heart desired: books on geography, history, philosophy, law, and physics cheek by jowl with sex manuals and erotic or pornographic literature with explicit pictures. If you looked carefully, you might find a book by Simone de Beauvoir or Jean-Paul Sartre, or Cocteau, or an anthology of Balzac or a work by a great Orientalist such as Durkheim or Margoliouth. The price for these was all the same: twenty francs.

On an ancient table, pushed into a corner, I would find gigantic hardbacks, their pages yellow, pockmarked with holes and scratches. As I turned them carefully, I would find dead insects in the crevices and spines, clearly long expired. The titles, as I read them and translated them to myself, were *Das Kapital* by Marx, *The Wealth of Nations* by Adam Smith, Victor Hugo's *Les Miserables*, Dickens's *A Tale of Two Cities*, Mikhail Sholokhov's *The Mother*, Albert Camus's *The Stranger*, and so on. These were discounted to ten francs each, but no one was buying—everyone stood clustered around modern works, illustrated books, and trivial publications.

Afterward, I would go wherever my feet took me, into old streets and alleyways. Frequently I would see a clown in colorful costume, nose red as blood, coming toward me, joking around with me and my fellow passersby. I looked away. There was usually a conjurer, displaying his sleight of hand, calling for customers to take part in the show. I watched for some minutes but usually tired of it and left. There were strange sweetmeats with unusual flavors, sold in stores where the proprietors were Tunisians and Moroccans, Greek and Turkish food, and souvenirs of the Eiffel Tower and the Arc de Triomphe.

From afar, I saw a circle of people. Approaching, I found them to be clustered around a man stripped to the waist, holding a stick whose tip was in flames. He would bring it up to his mouth and blow a cloud of some liquid that burst into flame when it touched the stick, as though the flames were coming from his mouth and the stick. I smiled, remembering the time my grandfather Zaki had taken us to the Darrasa Mountain and we had seen this performance at the Awlad Akef Circus.

I walked on, a stranger, lost—I stopped before an old musician with a fiddle, upon which he played traditional French tunes full of melancholy. I had been told they used to play these mournful melodies in the Middle Ages before saying goodbye to their sons, going off to plunder the treasures of the Orient in the name of the Cross.

I followed the busker through the streets, stopping close by whenever he did. I thought with fleeting longing of my grandfather who had died, and my paternal grandmother, and Nadia, swallowed up by the world, and the bitter bile rose in my throat, something pressing on my chest. I needed air. I left, going out into the broader expanses of St-Michel and St-Germain.

It was October, and the clouds were thick, the tall trees that lined these streets bare, their yellow leaves strewn on the ground. My depression would deepen. Umm Kalthoum's voice would fill my head with its smooth, gentle mourning as she said,

Take me to the place where my beloved is,
I burn with longing and ache for bliss,
If you're going to the Nile so fair, know that my sweetheart
    is there,
Take me to the place where my beloved is.

42

My feet took me to Notre Dame Cathedral. I had visited it twice before, but I had only now noticed the wooden confessionals. I stood close to one of them.

Inside were priests, and the men and women awaiting confession sat silent and somber on wooden seats. None of them looked up at the other, and if their eyes happened to meet, they nodded then went back to their solitude. With a heavy tread they walked toward the priest who was about to receive their confession, but from whom they were separated by a wooden panel with a small opening that allowed them to hear each other.

I watched them as they emerged, looking relieved, as though they had let go of a heavy burden. Strangely, some of them, including young men, would weep inside, and come out with pain still written clearly across their faces. I felt sorry for them, and wondered at the kindly man inside, who sat there listening to people's torments and pains, but what did he do with it all?

This time, too, I first saw the famous bell tower. I had never imagined that the bells were so immense. I remembered *The Hunchback of Notre Dame*, which I had bought at a secondhand bookstall at the used-book market in Ezbekiya Gardens. I had been in junior high back then and formed my own image of Quasimodo, the hero: a man bowed under his hunched back, but strong and powerful, the locks of his dirty blond hair peeking out from beneath a worn old cap. His feet, I fancied, struck the floor powerfully, his shoes gaping and full of holes. The poor man came to my mind as he dangled on the bell ropes in ecstasy when his Esmeralda had looked upon him with kindness.

I went outside, walking on the basalt cobblestones in front of the church, mourning the hunchback who had been chained to a post especially erected for the purpose, upon learning that he had a heart that loved like other people's hearts.

The clouds were at their thickest that day. Tiny drops of rain fell, accompanied by flakes of sleet the size of butterflies, and me without an umbrella. I didn't mind, though, nor think of going home. I left myself to the whims of the metro, and it took me to the Place de l'Opéra.

When I went upstairs, the rain was heavier, mixing with snow in large, cottony tufts. A sudden hush fell, and I felt a shy ray of sunlight shining in the sky. After a moment, I looked up, seeing the disk of the sun, fully there and proud, shining in the sky, parting the clouds. It only lasted a moment, for the clouds quickly came together again to cast a gray pall over everything. Nobody seemed to mind, going about their business, umbrellas and waterproof coats in evidence, doing their job admirably, knowing that this was their season.

I hurried into the shelter of the arches over the sidewalks, and walked until I found myself on the path leading into the courtyard of a building. I stood there for a moment, contemplating a gaggle of schoolchildren hurrying by wearing woolen clothing and jackets with sturdy hoods, their schoolbags secured to their backs with shoulder straps as they laughed and played. One of them jokingly half-shoved a schoolmate toward a speeding, oncoming car, another pushed soft snow into one's face or sneaked up behind another friend, yanked up his clothing, and pushed a fistful of snow onto his bare back.

I stood there watching them in my humble, Eastern-style clothes: the shirt I had bought for three pounds from Omar Effendi, the homemade pants, and the V-necked woolen jersey. I thought of my route to school every day, of the tram, the conductor who chased us schoolboys from car to car.

I said to myself, "If I live here my whole life, what can I do with these blond people with their fair, fair skin, in their boots and hats?"

Two schoolgirls passed, and all my heart longed for was the Daher neighborhood and Abbas Street.

43

NOT A WEEK LATER, I woke my mother one morning. She blinked in disbelief as I stood before her, fully dressed, air ticket and passport in hand.

Our argument was more of a fight. My grandfather burst in through the door. They all tried to dissuade me from leaving. Even my grandmother appeared upset, and tried to snatch the passport out of my hand. But nothing would sway me: not my mother's tears, not my grandfather's pleading eyes.

My mother plopped down on the edge of the bed, complaining loudly to the world about the life she had wasted raising me, the husband who had died, and the son who was as good as lost.

The cloud of depression hunkered over the taxi that was taking us to the airport. "You'll be back soon, right, Galal?" my grandfather said hopefully.

I looked at him without speaking.

"Say something, son!"

"If God wills it, Grandfather. I just have to be secure in my future career first."

"Your career?" my mother snapped. "Is there no future for you but there?"

I pressed her wrist. "Don't worry, Mom. I'll write."

"Write? The best you can do is write, Galal? I can't believe you could bring yourself to abandon me! How will you get any sleep in the house all alone?"

"Don't press him now, Camellia," said my grandfather. "Galal is our boy, and we're the only family he's got. He'll be back." Then, to me, "Isn't that so, Galal?"

I whispered, "It's so."

After a moment of silence, he went on, "How are you fixed for money, my boy?"

"I'm fine; don't worry."

He pulled an envelope out of his jacket pocket. "This is all I had in the house: two thousand francs. All our money's in the bank, my boy, and you're leaving so suddenly—" He turned to my mother. "Camellia, take off that gold chain you're wearing. And you, Yvonne, take off your rings."

They did, and he gave these things to me. When I demurred, he pushed them by force into my shirt pocket.

We parted at the airport gates. I checked in with my ticket and placed my suitcase on the baggage scales. Then I sat down on a nearby seat.

In an hour, it was all over. They closed the counter, the baggage handlers left, and they began to call upon the passengers for boarding. When they realized I had not boarded, they began to call my name: once, twice, ten times. I just sat there. I couldn't respond. I didn't know what to do. I did not rise, move, nor even think what to do. I did nothing. I was helpless, my mind blank. I saw myself, defeated.

After a pause, they called my name a final time. They said it was the last call.

I did not answer. They were calling on a man who was already dead.

Notes

abaya: Long, collarless, sleeveless, cape-like jacket worn over a gallabiya by men of wealth, power, and position.

Abu Rigl Maslukha: Literally, 'the one with the skinned leg'—a monster to frighten children with, sometimes said to be a folk representation of the devil.

alwash: A topping of butter or oil that has acquired a reddish color as a result of being cooked with tomato puree.

Amm: Literally, 'Uncle,' but 'Amm' is often used to address older men, whether or not they are relations, as a title of respect coupled with some familiarity.

Amm al-Hagg: The informal 'uncle' and 'hagg' may be combined by working-class people as familiarity combined with respect.

al-Ataba al-Khadra: An area of Cairo now simply called 'Ataba.'

Bashans: The ninth month in the Coptic calendar.

cats' eyes: In Egyptian folklore, cats in dreams signify false friends or traitors.

a confirmed Sunna: A saying or a practice attributed to the Prophet Mohamed that can safely be confirmed to be non-apocryphal.

dervish: In Egypt, the mentally ill, especially low- to medium-functioning individuals like the so-called 'village idiot,' are thought to be closer to God and are euphemistically called dervishes, implying that God has selected them to serve Him.

effendi: Old-fashioned title for a white-collar worker.

Farah Diba: The exiled empress of Iran. She started her exile in Egypt and became a fashion idol with women of the era.

287

fard: Obligatory religious practice.

fesikh: Ancient Egyptian delicacy that survives to this day: mullet, carefully rotted in the sun.

"food prepared by the hands of my mother": A quasi-superstitious aversion to eating in the home of a Christian or a Jew persists among many conservative Egyptian Muslims.

gallabiya: Unisex long, flowing, one-piece garment, common among lower-class Egyptians.

Ghazal al-Banat: This movie title means 'cotton candy,' which translates literally as 'girls' spinning,' a pun since the movie is about the plans spun by a young girl.

gibbah: Long, collarless gallabiya traditionally worn by Islamic clerics who are graduates of al-Azhar University.

Hagg: Title of a man who has performed the Mecca pilgrimage.

iftar: The evening meal that breaks the daylong fast during the month of Ramadan.

istikhara prayer: 'Consultation': an extra prayer to God to help with momentous decisions.

al-Kawakeb: Literally 'the planets' or 'the stars'—a celebrity magazine of the time.

Khawaga: Literally 'foreigner,' the word was a title applied to Egyptian Christians and Jews.

kushari: Egyptian dish made of a combination of rice, pasta, lentils, chick-peas, fried onions and tomato sauce (Cairo), or rice and peeled lentils (other areas of Egypt).

"Long Tail Woman": In Arabic, 'Umm Deil,' meaning 'possessor of a tail' or 'woman with a tail.'

ma'zoun: Religious official specializing in Islamic marriage licenses.

military school, police academy: At the time, these were the most prestigious schools in the country.

millieme: Defunct coin, one-tenth of an Egyptian penny (piaster).

Muallim: Literally 'teacher,' but used in traditional milieu as a title of respect for a business owner.

mulukhiya: Egyptian national dish. Green soup made with minced leaves of the plant *Corchorus olitorius.*

Murqus: Coptic Christian name, the equivalent of 'Mark.'

Orango, Sinalco, or Spathis: Now-defunct local brands of soft drinks.

Salamoni Abu Gamous: Loosely translatable as 'Buffalo Man.'

Sayyidna: Literally 'our master,' most often said of prophets or important saints, but also used for religious instructors.

shaf' and witr: Shaf' is a prayer with an even number of prostrations, witr a prayer with an odd number. These are extra prayers that a devout Muslim can elect to perform at an unspecified time after the final evening prayer.

Shater Hassan and Zeir Salem: Two folk heroes.

Sheikh Abd al-Baset Abd al-Samad (1927–88): One of the most famous Qur'an reciters of all time. His recordings are still best sellers today.

Sheikh Kishk and Sheikh Badri: Proto-extremist preachers.

Shenouda: A Coptic Christian name.

Sitt: Title for a lower-class woman, literally 'woman' but corresponding in usage to 'Mrs.'

Speaking Newspaper: Name of an Egyptian newsreel on film about ten minutes long, broadcast in movie theaters before the main movie until the late 1970s.

taamiya: The Egyptian name for falafel.

tahaggud: Extra prayer performed after the evening prayers, with no set number of prostrations. It may last all night, although in practice it usually does not.

thanawiya amma: General secondary-school certificate. Traditionally a big deal in Egypt since the highest-scoring students have their pick of the universities.

umda: Village elder whose word is law, especially in remote villages where the government apparatus has no reach.

Umm Hassan: Literally 'Mother of Hassan.' Often, Egyptians will call a person by the name of his or her firstborn. 'Abu' is the male equivalent.

"yellowed like a lemon": In Egypt, because of the predominant skin pigmentation, people say "You look yellow" for "You look pale." The "yellow" here probably means that Galal's grandfather was livid with rage.

SELECTED HOOPOE TITLES

The Televangelist
by Ibrahim Essa, translated by Jonathan Wright

A Rare Blue Bird Flies with Me
by Youssef Fadel, translated by Jonathan Smolin

Time of White Horses
by Ibrahim Nasrallah, translated by Nancy Roberts

*

hoopoe is an imprint for engaged, open-minded readers hungry for outstanding fiction that challenges headlines, re-imagines histories, and celebrates original storytelling. Through elegant paperback and digital editions, **hoopoe** champions bold, contemporary writers from across the Middle East alongside some of the finest, ground-breaking authors of earlier generations.

At hoopoefiction.com, curious and adventurous readers from around the world will find new writing, interviews, and criticism from our authors, translators, and editors.